Recipes for an Unexpected Afterlife

"A grizzled baker finds himself on the biggest quest yet . . . adopting a kiddo! Munden's stunning debut is filled with incredible heart, delectable treats, and hilarious mishaps. It's a recipe for comfort with a dash of adventure!"

—Rebecca Thorne, *USA Today* bestselling author of *Can't Spell Treason Without Tea*

"*Recipes for an Unexpected Afterlife* is like a perfect winter stew. Cozy and heartwarming, it's filled with memorable characters that feel like a warm hug. Munden has brewed one of the most creative and intriguing fantasy worlds I've ever read, worth experiencing alongside a hot mug of your favorite drink. Tales like this are needed."

—Stephen Warren (@quincystavern), creator of Quincy's Tavern

"An evolution of the cozy genre that somehow manages to feel both nostalgic and brand new at the same time. Within this wonderful world of undeath is a story brimming with good food, great characters, and a reminder to live your life (or afterlife) to its very fullest. I loved every single word of it!"

—Jaysen Headley (@ezeekat), global top-five BookTok influencer

"*Recipes for an Unexpected Afterlife* is as satisfying as a hearty orken meal and twice as comforting. With a heap of found family and a pinch of spooky, Rottgor's quest to build a loving afterlife felt just as restorative for me as it was for him. *Recipes* is perfect for fans of cozy, healing journeys and, of course, classic fantasy food."

—R.K. Ashwick, author of *A Rival Most Vial* and the Lutesong series

"Lush with delicious prose, *Recipes for an Unexpected Afterlife* is a warm tale that makes you yearn for a world that does not exist."

—Kay Synclaire, author of *House of Frank*

Recipes
FOR AN
Unexpected Afterlife

Recipes for an Unexpected Afterlife

DESTON J. MUNDEN

Published by Cozy Quill, an imprint of Bindery Books, Inc., San Francisco
www.binderybooks.com

Copyright © 2025, Deston J. Munden
All rights reserved. Thank you for purchasing an authorized copy of this book and for complying with copyright laws. No part of this book may be reproduced, or stored in a retrieval system, or transmitted in any form or by any means, except in the case of brief quotations embodied in articles and reviews, without express written permission of the publisher.

NO AI TRAINING: Any use of this publication to "train" generative artificial intelligence (AI) technologies to generate text is expressly prohibited. The author reserves all rights to license uses of this work for generative AI training and development of machine learning language models.

Acquired by Meg Hood
Edited and designed by Girl Friday Productions
www.girlfridayproductions.com

Cover: Charlotte Strick
Cover illustration, hand lettering, and inside cover illustration: Ellie White
Image credits: Tartila/Shutterstock (branch fleuron)

ISBN (paperback): 978-1-964721-65-1
ISBN (ebook): 978-1-964721-64-4

Library of Congress Cataloging-in-Publication data has been applied for.

Printed in China

First edition
10 9 8 7 6 5 4 3 2 1

This is a work of fiction. Names, characters, places, and incidents are either the product of the author's imagination or are used fictitiously and not to be construed as real. Any resemblance to actual persons, living or dead, organizations, events, or locales is entirely coincidental.

To Uncle William, I wish you were here to see this. I love you.

To my family and friends, who supported me through this grueling process.

And to you, the reader.

PROLOGUE

Around a Fire

Razgaif watched, slacked-jawed and eyes wide, as his father performed his magic over a crackling flame. Not the magic of runes engrained into the world and all its people, one much simpler, one that brought his family together. His heart raced, yearning for the secrets of such spells.

He scooted closer, the fire's warmth brushing his bare chest and the soles of his feet. His father's cane pushed him gently back once more. His father was a large orc, skin of coal and hair of ash, his wide shoulders and thick stomach filling the space around him.

"Patience," his father said again, his voice low and melodic, like the rushing river carrying a run of jumping salmon. He must've said it a thousand times by now, never losing his cool. Razgaif kicked his feet, watching the contents of the cauldron bubble and pop. His heart raced with pleasure every time he witnessed his father's greatest form of magic.

A few steps outside their den, his brothers and sister were playing at swords and axes, night coming down upon them. There were times he joined them and practiced his skills of war.

His mother, Chief of the Onyx-Ax, said that he had a talent for it. *Meant to be a Champion, defender of your people,* she'd said. He didn't want that. If they needed him, sure, but this . . . this magic was what he craved.

Razgaif the Older looked over his shoulder, and the large, bushy beard that covered his mouth twitched, as though he was smiling softly underneath. He read the thoughts written across his son's face. "I suppose this is why you share my name," he said quietly, rubbing his son's head. "You'd rather learn how to fill a stomach than split one. I suppose that's a relief for me. No children of mine will go hungry when I'm gone." He laughed. His father's laugh was always one that made little Razgaif smile back. "Come. If you're going to watch like always, I'm going to put those small hands to work."

Razgaif squealed. This was his favorite part. His father put down his large wooden spoon and took his son to the cutting area. An array of vegetables and herbs, as well as a manageable fillet of roc, stretched across the long stone slab. The Older put a knife in the Younger's hand, guiding how his son held the blade. It was a smaller obsidian knife made by the blacksmith of the clan. The Younger's knife. His first. Razgaif looked at it and grinned, pride surging in his chest.

"Ah, that look," his father said. "You're my son, all right. Here, cut these up. Finer pieces. Take your time. There's no rush. Do you think you can do it?"

"I can," Razgaif told his father. But his hand shook.

"Believe in yourself, son," his father said without turning, returning to the pot and stirring its contents. "Even pieces."

Those words gave him the courage he needed. Razgaif the Younger worked the blade methodically, starting by cutting what he knew best: the carrots. The shape of the orange, brown, and purple cave carrots was easy for him to cut now, as it was the first responsibility his father had given him when he'd seen the curiosity in his son's eyes. Razgaif pushed the strips of vegetables aside and moved on to the potatoes and celeries. Each chop challenged him, but he slowly made his way through what felt like a mountain of ingredients.

Sweat trickled down his temples as his hand shook over the slab of roc before him. Poultry wasn't easy for him, with sinew and fat hiding in unexpected places. The little orc swallowed his fear and began. The knife found its first challenge.

"Remember to cut away from yourself," his father urged, not turning around. "Careful with your fingers. You don't want to end up like Pa."

"I'm being careful," Razgaif said, his voice shaky. He heard his pa's smile more than he saw it. Strength returning, he continued his task. The meat fell away at his blade as he worked it into smaller and smaller chunks. A few close calls and a lot of time later, the roc was in roughly even pieces. He seasoned it the best he could, tossing the vegetables and meat in a mixture of herbs until they were coated. Excitement buzzed in his chest once more. "I did it," he said aloud, eyes brimming with tears.

"Wash your hands before you start crying."

Razgaif nodded and washed his hands in the basin. "I did it," he repeated to himself.

"You're going to make a fine *siefu* one day," his father, the current war cook, said.

His father took the plate of chopped, minced, and diced food and slid it into the stone oven. "One day, I'm not going to be here. I expect you to keep your sister's and brothers' stomachs full. Perhaps you'll have children of your own, and you'll get to see the look in their eyes that I see right now." He ran his fingers through

Razgaif's thick hair. "Now get your mom and your siblings. It's almost time for dinner."

Razgaif nodded, marching toward the entrance of the cave. He took a deep breath. "Dinner's almost ready," he shouted. He heard his brothers and sister groaning, the valor of battle stolen by their grumbling stomachs. His mother's voice urged them on. They would change their tune once they entered the cave—they always did.

The smells of the meal wafted through the air. Sage, redseed, and thyme rose from the roasted roc, the scent blended with the earthy vegetables. The accompanying stew brought a burst of spice to the air, with freshly hunted bison falling apart within the thick soup. The Older carried out a basket of fruit he had foraged that morning: persimmons, apples, pears, and small orange-like fruits named frostbiters. The pudding came out last. Razgaif the Older never made desserts unless the feeling struck him. He wasn't much of a sweets orc, the only stark difference between father and son. Razgaif the Younger bounced, happily taking the pudding from its cold-enchanted box. The pudding was made of a rare bean, brown and flavorful, and topped with cream and a crumble his father made.

"I wasn't going to serve this today," the Older told his son, "but you've been brave and patient. Good job, kid."

The rest of the family soon came in from the day of training, tossing their weapons and their tools to the corner of the cave. Together, they placed wooden plates, clay cups, and metal utensils on the mammoth-bone table. After half an hour of chatting, the meal was served. The *siefu* served the meal as always, filling the plates of his wife, sons, and daughter before himself. Once the plates were full, Razgaif's father bowed.

"I give thanks to the gods for the strength to serve this meal to my family once more. May the food be nourishment and the company eternal."

Razgaif the Younger watched his family take their first bites. They had shared hundreds of meals, but it never got old. His father's deliberate chewing, his mother's focused bites, his siblings' rowdiness for one piece of the meal or another—the sounds came as a warm comfort. *I want to hear these sounds forever.* One day, he'd be a *siefu*, a battle chef. Maybe the Champion, too. *I'll protect smiles and fill stomachs.* He liked the sound of that.

ONE

One Small Push

Nothing Rottgor did in his life was worth a grain of salt, and that trend continued well into his afterlife. He was starting to believe he had wasted his second chance.

Lord Commander Rottgor Onyx-Ax of the Famine Blade blankly stared at his weapon hanging over the unholy green fire burning within his stone hearth. Plenty would deny his claim of mediocracy. Evidence of his achievements surrounded him in his quarters, amassed over thousands of years since the reign of Halik Aseimon, the Worm King, the first and thankfully last of his name—the man that had raised Rottgor from death to undeath. During the first centuries of his afterlife, he unwillingly served that king—then he had willingly betrayed that king, and became one of the founding members of the undead city under a different necromancer Lord many years later. He had experienced war season after season, era after era, all while having his poisoned Deathblade—Malferioel—at his side. It was a sword he wished to break every time the sun rose over Necropolis.

Today, as always, his cowardice steered him away from breaking himself from its hold. The blade would remain unbroken.

His bony bare feet led him to his bed. Death Knights needed no sleep, yet each one of them found comfort in the sheer make-believe. He sat on the covers, tracing his finger down his withered charcoal-black body. Shame struck him as it always did when he was confronted with his body. Once a massive and strong orc, he had been reduced to thinness and protruding bones by endless years of rot. Patches of gray and green cropped up time and time again, but the mold and the rot were kept at bay by the warlocks of the academies surrounding the area, a simple thanks for the knight's protection and guidance. Those kindhearted kids had none of the cruelty of the necromancers of the past, instead guided on a path of goodness by proper instruction and direction. If not for them, he wouldn't have a hair on his head, an upright body, or the glowing green eyes that let him see. They never asked for anything aside from his unwavering protection.

Rottgor pressed his thumb against his palm, the cold sliminess of his flesh familiar. *What can I do for the city beyond holding a sword? What more can I do than hold a sword?* Malferioel, the Contagion, hummed with corpse flies from across the room, vying for his attention. Even from his bed, he could smell the blade's putrid stench: rotten flesh, festering wounds, durian fruit, and corpse lilies. It called to him, the only relic left from his time under the thrall of the Worm King years ago. He had learned to use it for goodness and righteousness, bending its will against the will of the broken shambles of his soul. But the blade whispered, always wanting another's flesh to poison, another plague to spread. *Is this all I am? Will I only ever be known for death and plagues? History may remember a warrior, a hero. I see only a weapon.*

He shook off the thought. The men expected their Lord

Commander soon. The Duke Council, the Languished, and the Unwreathed still needed his protection. Rottgor donned his obsidian-black armor. It covered his body from head to toe, leaving none of his undead body showing, aside from his glowing green eyes, which pierced the darkness. The armor gave him back a bit of the bulk he'd had in life and in the beginning of his undeath, always making him feel a bit stronger in his body's current hollowness. The spikes on the shoulders, the hard angles, and the ebony darkness of the midnight metal brought a reminder that this was armor meant for use. He pulled the helm a bit tighter over his head. *One more day,* he told himself, not for the first time. One more day, and then he would figure out something else to do with his droning afterlife. Rottgor groaned. One more day, and then he would become a lot more.

He brought his ax today, refusing the call of the sword.

Lord Commander Rottgor left his barely furnished room and headed through the corridor toward the main hall of the Voidborn Citadel and the Blackspear Château. Necropolis lived up to its reputation. A training and teaching ground for the more . . . undesirable runes such as necromancy, plagues, blood magic, shadow tethering, and otherworldly summoning, its nature came through in the architecture. The entire castle and its connected home were made of the same black stone, the magical ore, of which his armor was made, once it had been tempered and transmuted enough. The walls and ceiling were in the third era's style, harsh pointed corners and an unforgiving verticality stretching to darkness. Rottgor kept to the purple rug, watching his step amid the lightless shadows and lavender torchlight. The only sound around him was the constant clank of his armor as he descended the corridor, heading toward the throne room. In the quietness, he was caught off guard by the familiar, ever-mischievous smile of a woman suddenly at his side. It belonged to the Duke's granddaughter, Lady Cleo Crowsilk, the heir apparent of the Voidborn Citadel.

"Lord Commander Rottgor, your timing is always so precise. I was just thinking about how lonely I was, walking to this meeting all by myself."

"Your Grace . . ."

"I will hear none of that nonsense today, ser," Lady Cleo said, raising her hand. "I will enjoy your company, and you will enjoy mine. That's all I have to say on the matter." She suppressed an emerging smirk.

Lady Cleo Crowsilk, one of the few heirs left of the Crow Father's long lineage, was a beautiful magiian woman with dark skin and fierce eyes the color of blood oranges. Her full lips usually formed a bit of a frown, though she never seemed upset. Rather, her expression held a certain commanding sturdiness built from years speaking among liches, summoning demons, and negotiating with different types of undead. *Perhaps she's always just slightly disappointed,* Rottgor thought. All those immortal, undead creatures, and none of them tickled her wit. Today, she wore her house's colors, purple and gold, in a simple sleeveless dress and a massive multilayered choker spread across her collarbone like a web. She ran her hand over her shaven head, passing the slightly tipped ears she inherited from her high-elvish grandmother. She tightened her hand around her leather-bound tome. An accomplished mage in her own right, she was never without it, even when she *was* without guards.

"Where are your men?" Rottgor asked. "Or at least your handmaids?"

"Both bored me, so I left them," Lady Cleo said. "Is that a crime?"

Rottgor snorted. "Ask that of your grandfather."

"And what exactly is he going to do? I'll kick his phylactery down a drinking well."

"You really shouldn't say stuff like that."

She rolled her eyes. "I know where it is. It would be a half-day trip *at best*. Never mind that, ser. Now you *have* to walk with me. By your own words, I'm in danger walking alone."

Rottgor shook his head, groaning. "Fine."

"Great." Lady Cleo hooked her arm in his and led the way. "Have you thought any more about my offer, Razgaif?" Razgaif. His living name, not his dead one. She alone used it and only around close company. "You've served your time as a Death Knight long enough, and your magic can sustain you for many more years. Do you honestly wish to spend the rest of your time on the planet standing around my family until *I* take the Carnation Throne? If it comes down to it, I will discharge you myself when that time comes, as I would rather not rip that fine black cape off your back and strangle you with it."

"Lady Cleo."

"What did I say," she said, putting her hand up once more. "I will not have you making any more excuses. I've given you *enough* time. You keep saying"—she coughed, taking on his deep, raspy voice—"'Well, fighting is all I know. If I don't have a weapon in my hand, what am I?'" She continued, "I'm saying this as a friend. I'm saying it as Galelin's friend. There are plenty of other Death Knights. Thankfully, not as plentiful as before, but we can manage to lose a few. You are one of the only ones left from the age of the Worm King. You deserve *better* than staying in this castle, no different from a living statue waiting to be animated for another war. I will personally fund any endeavor for you as long as you pick something *you* want to do. You deserve free will after it has been stripped from you so many times."

Rottgor's throat tightened. The Worm King's voice whispered to him. *Serve. Bend. Break. Your will is mine.* The words had scarred him worse than any weapon that ran across his skin. *Serve. Bend. Break. Your will is mine.* That day he'd first woken up, the day he'd opened his eyes as a servant of the undead horde, his ideas of free will broke. His choices after that, both good and bad, seemed more a course of destiny, of things he *had* to do rather than what he wanted to. He swore he heard his unholy blade buzzing once more in his ear.

"I've been thinking about it," he admitted. "I've been thinking about it for centuries." The moment on the cliff, standing beside Galelin, lived forever distilled within his memory. His mind drifted to that moment—that last day of darkness, as he and his five comrades—the Six Shadows—founded this city and vowed its protection.

Lady Cleo tilted her head. "Go on."

"I . . . I'm not quite sure what I want to do. I can't tell you that I'm sure of what I wish to do, but I've been yearning for something different. Something new. Something . . ."

"Exciting?"

"The opposite?"

"Oh." Lady Cleo smiled for a second time—a rare occasion indeed. "Have you considered something you wanted to do before you became such a prestigious warrior, a fearsome Death Knight, and Commander of the—"

"All right, I get it."

"You have a lot of titles, my friend, much like I do." She laughed. "But truthfully, can you even remember that far back? It's been hundreds of years since you've been living. How long can a dream live without nourishment? How long has it been since you've thought about you—you underneath all that bloody history? Who was Razgaif?"

Who was Razgaif? The question cut deep. He knew of the man from his memories, almost a far-off acquaintance he had met once—a long time ago. Rottgor considered this question as they walked through the haunted hallways of Necropolis, a quietness overtaking their conversation. The Lady of Silk and Talons kept her friends close, and it was an honor to be among them. *Her harshness means she cares.* Rottgor bit down on his shredded lower lip. *She's right, of course, I'm wasting my . . . death away.* He growled a thick *orken* curse to himself, realizing soon after that he hadn't spoken *orken* in a long time. Lady Cleo pretended blissful ignorance.

They made it to the Voidborn Citadel's throne room, a massive hall leading to the Carnation Throne. Warlocks and necromancers lined the hall. They came from around the world through Necropolis to learn, and many of them went into service for the Three Whispers, the councils of the three major political forces of the city. Lady Cleo greeted them all with grace, though some wanted her removed. The room stretched upward and outward seemingly endlessly, gaping darkness huddled in corners. Stained glass windows of reds, purples, and blacks filtered what little light came through to the land of the dead. A long carpet led up several black marbled stairs, each section holding chairs for the council members and divided by long curtains featuring each of their political sigils.

Lady Cleo led them through dark curtain after dark curtain, carved skulls of the Worm King, his wife, and his generals on display, now nothing more than necromantic night-lights for the children of better people. A satisfying end for the Worm

King—transformed into a soulless piece of furniture still wearing the broken teeth Rottgor had given him upon his death. *He's dead, and I'm alive... in a way.* The thought always hit him, but today struck differently. *What if I did walk away from what he made me for? Serve. Bend. Break.* The desperate words of a dead man haunted him still. *Your will is mine.* No more. He wondered if Cleo had brought him this way for a reason, to hammer her point and force him to face his past after so many years of avoiding any sight of it. *I'm free.* The skulls at their backs, they finally made it to the stairs' summit.

The Carnation Throne—on which Lady Cleo's grandfather slumbered—stood as a grim warning to all who sought evil within their ranks. The Worm King's bones, blackened from the renowned necromancers, had been burned by holy fire and salt, and stripped of soul and power. They had peeled what remained of the Worm King's flesh from his body and dried it into dyed red leather. Everliving Carnations grew from the Worm King's broken elbows, crimson and mulberry-purple petals coating the ground. Lady Cleo walked around the side of the throne and tapped a sapphire soul gem at the back, awakening her grandfather.

The Duke of Liches arose from his slumber, swirling up toward the ceiling and back down again. He was a large ghostly man, all bones underneath his shell of pale-red soul fire. His large golden skull face, massive clothes, and tattered magic were wrapped in chains and old armor that made him look the part of the dangerous warlock. In truth, he was one of the more benevolent rulers Rottgor had ever spoken to, agreeing to sit on the throne only until Lady Cleo came of age and declared herself ready for the job. He had done this with each of his children, all of whom declined a place on the throne. No matter how long it took, he would rule until he found someone who wished for its seat. Luckily, he had found that in his granddaughter, Lady Cleo. Duke Jamis Crowsilk, the Lich of Red Asters, floated back to his throne, Cleo at his side. Rottgor fell to one knee.

"Lord Commander Rottgor," Duke Jamis began. His voice sounded as though it bounced from all the corners of the throne room at once, warm and filling as a hearty soup fresh from a campfire. "Thank you for escorting Cleo. It appears she abandoned her guards once more. Do you want new guards, Cleo? Is that the point you're trying to make, my dear?"

"No. They deserve their jobs, but perhaps they should show a personality." Lady Cleo laughed. Jamis joined in.

"Fine, I understand that," Duke Jamis said. Lady Cleo then turned to him, and he bent down as she whispered in his ear. Rottgor arched an eyebrow, grateful for the darkening shroud of his helmet. The Duke laughed once more. Not a laugh of someone who had heard a joke—one of overwhelming joy. "That's a fine piece of news. About time. About time. I'll announce it once this meeting is complete. How about that?"

"That's a wonderful idea, Grandfather."

Duke Jamis flicked his hand, dragging over a slightly smaller chair for his granddaughter. She sat, dismissing Rottgor to the rest of the men of his dark order.

Rottgor stepped to the side, in front of the rest of the black-armored men. His order of Death Knights, the Ruinous Guard, stood in a practiced straight line on either side of the Duke and next-to-be Duchess of Death. From a distance, they appeared to be sentient black suits of armor, eyes glowing greens, reds, blues, oranges, and purples through their dark helms. Quite a few wore their Deathblades, their runes on silver and gold weapons. Much like Malferioel, each blade carried a scent and sound. Rottgor knew them all.

Lord Danzo Blightsun and his polearm, False Life, stood by his side. Danzo was one of the older Death Knights, though still younger than Rottgor by several decades. Once a Lord of the Sunlands, he possessed the slender build of his people, lithe and light. His armor was the opposite. The traditional Sunland black-and-red warlord armor made him appear thick-shouldered, wide-chested, and longer-legged, and ended at his bone-exposed feet, which constantly glowed with fire. The most interesting part of his armor was that it lived, a part of his soul attached to it. The gaping ogre face at the belly of his armor twitched a faint smile, while Danzo's actual head faced forward at attention. "Lord Commander," he said, "how goes it?"

"Another day," Rottgor told him. The words slipped from his mouth. He hadn't shown such an obvious crack in his will before, though he knew Danzo always saw the cracks, no matter how thin. He inspected people on the same level as he did pottery. The eyes of his armor squinted into two glowing slits.

Luckily, he didn't have to answer for himself.

The members of the Duke Council, the living and secular members as well as the vampire covens, and the rest of the political parties came in. The Languished, the main ruling body of the undead, came first, led by Deathspeaker Azael. The liches, wights, ghouls, and revenants came in file behind them. As the Deathspeaker passed, his corporeal form—a dozen-eyed ghost—nodded in their direction, his misty body freezing the world around them. Soon after came the leader of the Unwreathed—the summoned folk, such as the fae, demons, and other planar beings of Necropolis. Their leader was the colossus beast of the Burnt Rooms, Brother Vuldul the Warwalker, fourth son of the Baron of Pain and brother to the current Baroness of the Burnt Rooms. His massive wings, thunder-pounding hooves, and dark-red skin contrasted with his calm and peaceful nature. He, too, nodded toward the Ruinous Guard before stopping and folding his arms through the sleeves of his sunset-colored silk robe printed with cranes and sticks of bamboo. The council members took their seats across from one another, settling into the flow of the meeting.

Years of practice had honed Rottgor's abilities as a hardened guard, always watching and not listening. The political landscape of Necropolis—the living, the undead, and the summoned—teetered often. The living, of course, held the most political power, given their shorter lifespans and general squishy mortality. The other two groups, however, needed representatives, as well as laws in place to protect them. Servitude without a choice was slavery, and everyone in Necropolis knew the cost of that. Thus, this council was created to be a governing body of voice for the living, the undead, and the beyond. Rottgor's duty now was to protect the keepers of this peace, nothing more. A simple life, a quiet and simple duty. Nothing complicated.

Serve, protect—believe in what's right. He repeated the words in his head, looping them like a music box. His eyes flicked from side to side, searching the crowds. Only a few times had he been forced from his autonomous station into action. The most recent of such was years ago, when the former Deathspeaker before Azael had tried to stoke a rebellion off a perceived slight. The misunderstanding ended in no deaths, just hurt feelings and a scar from the Famine Blade that lingered deep. From that point on, Rottgor knew never to lower his guard, never to break his vigilance.

Time slipped past him. Discussions flew by, bits and pieces coming through to Rottgor at times. The conversation spun toward its usual direction—the living, the summoned, and the undead struggling over their places within the city. Some of the living, despite holding the majority, still voiced loud concerns over the expanding rights of the summoned and the undead. Rottgor kept his focus still, watching the sunlight trickle in from the stained glass and spill across the floors. By the time the major discussion came to a close, the throne room no longer needed the glowing skulls' necromantic lights. Familiar rumblings suggested a coming recess: the clanking of Brother Vuldul's teacup; the slight, anxious movements of the Deathspeaker's cloak; and the off-topic ramblings of the Duke. Rottgor prepared himself, his stiff and motionless body cracking back to life. The sounds came in, the countless discussions and whispers striking his ears.

"One more thing," Duke Jamis said. "I would like to announce the Seclusion of one of our best and most heroic members of the Ruinous Guard."

Your Grace! he shouted in his head. Lady Cleo looked at him, a mischievous smile again on her lips.

"Lord Commander of the Ruinous Guard, Rottgor Onyx-Ax of the Famine Blade, will be taking his Seclusion from his duties among the guard and its soldiers." The room gave a collective gasp, though more than half didn't need air.

The Seclusion was little more than an undead retirement, releasing individuals from all their active duties to experience the life they missed. Very few got to this point, most having to be put to rest long before then, whether through sorcery or battle. Rottgor had never entertained the thought that Lady Cleo would push it upon him, and certainly not today. *I wore her patience too thin, it seems.* Rottgor shifted his feet, no longer the merciless knight forged for blood but a boy unsure of what to do or how to stand. Eruptions of praises and congratulations swarmed over him. The Ruinous Guard, to his surprise, were the loudest among them.

Danzo, soon to be Lord Commander Danzo, gave him a strong pat on his back. "I knew something glorious was happening today. Congratulations, my dear friend."

Rottgor lost all the words he had ever known. He trembled. The members of the Ruinous Guard shuffled him off to prepare for his Seclusion. Rottgor looked over his shoulder to Lady Cleo. That mischievous smile hadn't disappeared, only it was hidden by small, measured bites of the figs she plucked from a plate by her throne. *Good luck,* she mouthed, waving him away. He gritted his teeth. *I should've known she would do this.* Rottgor had been idle about his path for too long, and she pushed him into the great unknown of his future.

TWO

The Shaping and the Seclusion

The Warlocks of the Eyeless Order knew how to make an old Death Knight feel special.

Despite their ominous name and eye-covered robes, the members of the Eyeless Order exuded a peaceful gentleness and greeted him as he entered the temple and lay on a long stone table. Well taught through the colleges in Necropolis, the Order cared for the undead of the city, especially those of high station, like Rottgor. Algarus Darkenmoon, their leader within the Bonemaker Temple, personally took the job for Rottgor's Seclusion.

Algarus's thin body was shrouded in layers of rune-printed cloth, making him appear more of a ghoul than a living man. An oversize hood hung over his head. His eyes were bound by magical bandages, glowing with the blackest of magic. Glimpses of his face revealed him as a levia, one of the dragon people, with thin, pale scales and a beard so gray it betrayed his age. He walked over to Rottgor and leaned over him on the stone table, which sat on one of the altars that surrounded a massive skull-shaped fountain spewing fresh spring water. Rottgor raised his head slightly at Algarus's approach.

Algarus touched the ring of skulls around his neck. "My friend, Rottgor, I would've never guessed it was you I'd be releasing today. I swore the acolytes were playing a joke on me."

"I wasn't aware it was happening so soon either," Rottgor said, letting out a frustrated snort. The back of his head hit the stone slab. "One minute, I was there on guard duty. The next, they were announcing my Seclusion." He growled under his breath. "I feel robbed of choice."

Algarus's head tilted up, revealing a bit of his face among the shadows. Rottgor prepared for the inevitable quip. "Robbed of choice, you say? Or robbed of never having to make one?"

Rottgor hated his friend's wit. "I suppose the latter," he said through gritted teeth. "I wasn't ready."

"Would you have ever been? It's been centuries for you, my friend. You have seen my grandfather, then my mother, and now me take the helm of the Eyeless Order. I feared that you would see my son in this robe. You've had all the time in the world, yet you chose to stay where you believed you were most needed but where, truly, you were most comfortable. It's easy to know what you'll do every day when it's all you've ever done. Or at least all you ever remember doing." Algarus paced around the temple, plucking various potions from the shelves. "You see, you have almost the life remaining of a normal orc, Rottgor. Fifty or sixty years, give or take. The magic that raised you is strong, but it's not eternal. This is no better time to begin living with what you have left."

Algarus sat the bottles at Rottgor's side. The contents were . . . unsettling. One narrow bottle held a small tentacle, thrashing back and forth. Another contained an eye, peering around from one side to the next. The substances in the bottles grew progressively viler, some containing materials that Rottgor had never seen. Dealing in undead magic and alchemy was not the cleanest of jobs. Algarus, however, took care of every bit. "You may not have chosen to be undead, but you've already had centuries stolen from you. Why not spend the last bits finding the happiness you craved?"

Rottgor chewed on that thought. "I suppose you're right."

"Now, I'm going to need you to relax." Easier said than done when the hooded man brandished a knife from his sleeve.

Rottgor rolled his shoulder back, forcing stillness. Wearing normal clothes didn't feel as good as he thought it would. He'd kept it simple with a fine black tunic, leather trousers, and soft black boots, but now he couldn't keep his eyes off the thinness of his own body. Without armor and a weapon, he was held together by flesh as thin as parchment, revealing yellow bones. His tusk was long since cracked, and his little hair was clinging to his scalp. *A rotting corpse held together by the whim of a Worm.* He bit his lower lip, focusing on the light fixture above. Algarus circled around the stone table.

"Has anyone told you what's going to happen next?" Algarus asked, his voice holding the same measured tone as that of his parents and grandparents.

"I don't like thinking about it," Rottgor admitted. Few in the Ruinous Guard had gone to Seclusion, and the few that had hadn't stayed in Necropolis.

"Well, typically, we do more of a final remake. Not the ones like after a battle or when you're rotting or falling apart. This one will be a bit more permanent. With the worry of battle behind you, we can reshape the flesh and bones at the cost of the battle prowess an undead body gives. You won't be able to march endlessly or live without substance like you have for centuries. It's very much a mock life . . . but I stress again that you won't be as strong as you are now. The speed, the power, the magic, the general ungodly amount of durability . . . all gone. You'll be a normal orc—perhaps even less than normal considering the strength of your people—but you'll have your body back for the most part. Is that something you are willing to live with?"

Rottgor gritted his teeth. A choice. The power of a Death Knight was a thing he'd learned to live with. *No. Not live with— depend on.* The rot rune, *Festrain*, had become his heart, its vile magic running through his silent veins. He scarcely remembered the rune of his birth, but he remembered this one. *Festrain*'s cruel, terrible power ripped away life, leaving marrow-eaten bones and poisoned meat. He had left entire towns to starve . . . if he had spared anyone. The gruesome strength, the undying body meant for killing, served that single purpose of destruction. He'd tricked himself into thinking otherwise. Once he'd broken free of the Worm King, his sword became justice and justice alone. But then why did this feeling of dread loom over him? Was the thought of being stripped of most of his power that terrifying? Power was a drug, for evil and good.

Rottgor exhaled and let go of his fear. "That seems fair, I guess." A part of him reached toward the unknown, the light at the end of the tunnel. The other part of him burned at its glow. *A chance for something more,* he reminded himself.

"Good, good. You're never going to be the same as you were when you were alive. I'm not going to promise that, but this is a well-deserved rest, Rottgor. Allow yourself peace after all this time." Algarus pulled out his last tool, a sizable hook imbued with blood magic. A shaper, the college-aged Warlocks of the Eyeless

Order called it. *Not my first time under the hook, but maybe the last.* Courage mingled with his nerves; he swore he felt a weak heartbeat from his chest. "Are you ready, friend?"

"I am," he said, nodding.

Rottgor forced his eyes shut and, struggling against his supine position, wordlessly removed his clothes to raw nakedness. The shaper slid across his skin. "Painful" wasn't quite the word he would use for the feelings of a knife against him. "Uncomfortable," if anything. The shaper moved his body as though it were clay, reconfiguring what was there. Nothing prepared him for the sensation of being opened up and carved, as if he were a pumpkin. Things that shouldn't move—at least not on a living subject—shifted and altered. Algarus reached Rottgor's stomach. The warlock poured the vials within him. Rottgor felt it soon after, the movement of organs for the first time since his undeath. The feeling somehow sickened him, the open air against his exposed innards. He tightened his eyelids. Living creatures swam through him. *What* exactly, he didn't care to find out. Bones cracked into place, and blood began pouring through dead veins. After a few hours on the table, Rottgor felt Algarus close him up. He worked on the outside of Rottgor's body a bit more, putting the finishing touches on his undead canvas.

Rottgor opened his eyes. The light from the hanging chandelier burned his vision. He blinked it away. *Odd.* Things like that never bothered him before.

"You'll take some time to recover. Undead bodies tend to heal back to where they were—more or less. But remember, you're *not* as you were. Things you found easier as a Death Knight may be difficult now. Soon you'll experience more familiar sensations. Don't be alarmed. You may not have felt them in a while, but the symbiotes within you need a normal living environment. By the way, I'm going to need you to inhale."

Rottgor coughed. Panic settled in. The breathing was new. He had gone centuries without a single breath. He even felt . . . a heartbeat. It wasn't fast, perhaps a messy three beats a minute. Rottgor touched his chest, mesmerized. The warlocks had come so far. The cost of his undead powers seemed minimal now. "I'm . . . ," he said.

"Don't speak. Experience life and its glory. It will come back to you in time." Algarus instructed Rottgor to sit up, then helped push the orc upward. "Drink this. Take it slow." He brought a wooden bowl to Rottgor's cracked, broken lips. *Did everything always feel so heavy?* The cool liquid tasted amazing—surely only basin water. *I can taste.* . . . He swore it was the sweetest liquid in the world, forged by a craftsman of the gods. He tasted the filtering rocks of the underground pool, a soft, cool earthiness at the back of his throat. The world itself opened up once more. He wiped the water dribbling down his chin. Weakness still ravaged his body. An unknown feeling. A warm one on its own. He found his feet soon after.

"How're you feeling?" Algarus asked. "You're welcome to lie down more if need be."

"Better," Rottgor said, donning his clothes. They, too, weighed on him, as though they were made from metal instead of soft cotton and leather. "A little . . . sleepy?" Such a strange word to use, one he hadn't uttered in centuries.

"Good, that means the shaping was a success. Like with everything, take all the time you need. The flesh remembers and soon you will, too. Godspeed, my friend."

Brother Algarus gave Rottgor a gentle pat on the back, wobbling his once immovable stance. Rottgor gave a slight nod, fiddling his thumbs. Algarus left him, bowing low as a sign of respect for the service of the great Death Knight. Rottgor heard his footsteps echoing along the stone floors, step after step, ascending toward his room at the top of the temple. The simple things became clearer: The chirping of birds came from outside the lancet windows, singing along with the rustle and bustle of Necropolis's dark and friendly people. Alive. Not quite. Just a little short. Rottgor listened, wished, and wanted. *What's next?* he thought, watching the members of the Eyeless Order file in. The young warlocks, necromancers, and alchemists greeted him, smiling, a few shouting their congratulations. Little did they know how much their words touched him. *What can I do for them without a sword in hand? What am I without it?*

Rottgor scurried out of the temple like a rat under the floorboards. The gray morning mist began burning away, leaving a soft haze in the city. The feast and his official retirement ceremony weren't until the evening, the delay meant to give the participant time to adjust to their new way of life. Gods, he needed it. His legs were as weak as water and his arms dangled at his sides. His eyes ached in the brightness, no longer as sharp as a trained hunter's. As great as sitting sounded, a walk was the thing he needed.

The tight streets of Necropolis stretched out in all directions. Sharp, pointed stone buildings rose toward the dim skies while twisting black-and-gray cobbled streets wound like snakes emerging from dens. Yew and cypress trees swung heavily in the wind, coating the land of the dead in endless leaf needles and plump red berries. He watched his step, mindful of the moss-covered memorial stones and cemeteries woven through the residences of the living. Rottgor had lived in this city for centuries, not once stopping to smell the flowers. He felt coolness against his clammy skin and the woody, spicy evergreen smells rushing up his chest. Finding a wooden bench under a tree, Rottgor took a seat.

Hours passed. The new sensations never stopped. Rottgor allowed himself to listen to his body, remembering what Algarus said. He did feel weaker. He reached out to his rune, feeling nothing. *Festrain*, the pit of slow death, had always been there before, eating his body and soul away as it had his foes. In his mind's eye, under the darkness of his lids, he envisioned it as thousands of insects ravenously tearing at the carrion underneath the dirt of his flesh. But now, nothing met him on the other side. *Festrain*—his weapon, his justice, his curse—had unraveled into odd sprawling lights outside his vision. Runes evolving and changing was hardly out of the ordinary, but this . . . He wondered and hoped.

"You seem a bit lonely," a voice said. "Care for some company?"

The speaker, who had taken a seat beside Rottgor, was a thin, well-set elvish man, short for his people. His skin was pale and smooth, brown hair short to the scalp. There were some dwarvish features in him, too, Rottgor noticed—the wider nose and those jewel-bright eyes, the color of stormy-blue opal, and a budding beard cut to the stubble. *A high elf-dwarf?* Not the most common, but possible given the new era. The thought of it made him smile. The young man—"young" being a rather open term for anyone with elvish blood—offered him a warm drink in a fine wooden mug. Rottgor took it, the heat pleasant in his hand. "A couple of my friends and I saw you over there just starin' into the abyss for *hours*. Had to come check. We got enough things dying on the street around this place." He laughed. "Name's Calfe Metcoat. Don't say it. Yes, like the baby cow, but throw an *e* at the end. A pleasure to meet you."

"Same here. Rottgor."

"As in, Lord Commander Rottgor from the castle?" Calfe said. He whistled. "Ooh wee! Out here meeting a famous soldier. What are ya doing way out here then?"

"Well . . . ," Rottgor said, chewing down a nervous stutter, "guess I hit my retirement age."

"Undead folks can retire? Really? I ain't gonna say that I know everything. Do I say congrats?" Calfe arched an eyebrow.

Rottgor rubbed the bridge of his nose. "Typically. But I don't feel very . . . congratulatory."

"Right. Gotcha. Congrats then. Have any plans? Must be right nice havin' all this time to yourself now." Rottgor gave an involuntary grunt at that. Calfe laughed. "Ahhh, one of those 'I don't know what to do with myself without work' types." Calfe straightened his leather jerkin, a stylish addition to his fine cotton shirt, black trousers, and supple leather work boots. A working man, and far from a poor one. The type of fellow who did what he had to do. Calfe wiped his hands on his trousers. "How 'bout this? You come join me at the Rattling Ribcage on Blood and Frost. Let's say tomorrow, around noon? We'll talk more. Enjoy your drink, pal. You've earned it."

Calfe sauntered back to his comrades, leaving Rottgor to his own devices.

The former Death Knight turned civilian nestled the warm drink in his hand. He forced his tense shoulders to relax, slumping against the park bench. A soft, whistling wind wrestled more tree needles from their bony branches. He brought the liquid to his lips. Coffee. Chocolate added, maybe? He hadn't had one in years, not one he could taste. Death Knights didn't need taste when sustenance was already a long-abandoned nuisance. The cream's sweetness rubbed against the soft bitterness of the dark-roasted beans, both warm and smooth in his mouth. He held the sip in his mouth before swallowing it, soft tears rolling down his face. Such a simple joy that swelled his slow-beating heart. He held the cup, a breeze hitting his face. He wanted more of this. *Why did I wait so long?*

The Seclusion ceremony wasn't planned to be a long affair, more his speed. Every Seclusion was unique, crafted for the participant and their specific service in their afterlife. Lady Cleo, soon-to-be Duchess and his personal friend, knew him well enough to know what he wanted: a feast, time with a few friends and fellow knights, and an escape at a proper time of night. *Direct and to the point. No doubt for herself as well.* Rottgor took the seat of honor at the middle of the table, ordinarily reserved for the Duke or Duchess of Necropolis. Despite his being slightly bigger than the seat, the chair made him feel small, as though he didn't belong in such a valued position. Rottgor fixed the collar of his acolyte's robe for the thousandth time, overlooking the crowd mingling below the raised platform. Orange and pink from the sunset's light poured through the opened windows, bouncing off the oak tables and the dozen gold goblets and silver cutlery. The dinner hall was crammed with those who respected or adored him, above and below, including the living, the undead, and those in between. Very few knew him outside his armor and without the blade.

He feared that was all he measured up to.

Lady Cleo picked at her plate, swishing a tender piece of steak through its garlic-butter sauce. Those blood-orange eyes caught the red sunlight, giving a sinister gleam to an already stern expression. She sipped at her wine. "You haven't touched your meal," she said calmly. "I know the shaping gives the undead an appetite, but you've been hesitant."

"Drinking was one thing. Eating . . . is somehow terrifying," Rottgor admitted. "And of course . . . the very idea of this ceremony hasn't truly given me any peace."

Lady Cleo took a longer drink from her strawberry wine, draining it to the bottom. One of her handmaids filled it once more. "Are you upset with me?" she asked. There wasn't an ounce of regret in her voice. She expected the worst.

"No, Your Grace."

"Second question. Would you lie to me?"

Rottgor laughed. "No, Your Grace."

"I thought I'd at least have the decency to ask. I knew you wouldn't be upset, but if you were, I knew it would pass. Someone had to make that decision, and it wouldn't be you. Some people retire on an injury, others for leisure. You would do neither and that was unacceptable."

Whether or not he was upset wouldn't faze her in the slightest. Decisions, to her, simply had to be made. Jumping from one idea to a "maybe" and back again wasted time she didn't have. She gathered the facts and consulted those who would fill the gaps in her knowledge. She made her own informed decisions and stuck to them. He knew that by now. That aside, he had answered her truly. He wasn't upset. Lost, but not upset. He had clung to the idea of being a Death Knight for so long that it became a rope in his hand. One that he never climbed but hung on to for fear of whatever was at the bottom. This was his first time looking up. "I've been wondering, thinking about what you said. There's bound to be something that I wish to have. Something that's meant for me. I—"

"But you don't have an answer." Lady Cleo sighed. "Surely

there's something you've always wanted. Perhaps craved. Think about it. Think about Razgaif, not Rottgor the Famine Blade."

"About that. I can't feel my rune anymore," Rottgor said.

"It being subdued is a normal part of the process," Lady Cleo said, then paused. "Excuse me, pardon? At all?"

"At all," Rottgor repeated.

She blinked, turned, and downed the rest of her second drink. "I'm going to need to hear that again. *What?*"

"Nothing. I feel nothing there. A blackness. Well, ribbons of lights, but nothing else." A rune was a person's birth connection to the magical energy—aether—around them. Everyone had a rune, with varying degrees of strength, as well as elements and uses. Rottgor reached out his pale gray-black hand, willing *Festrain* to his palm. No eruption of ethereal green flies and maggots. No horrid smell. Not an image of a wilting flower, falling dead petals against his fingertips. The magic that had withered armies, poisoned waters, spoiled earth . . . gone, vanished. His slow-beating heart shook at the thought of being free from such a power. His fingers, too, quivered at the heavy burdens falling from his tattered soul. "See, I'm trying. . . . Nothing."

Lady Cleo seized his hand. Magiians knew magic more than any race, besides perhaps the high elves. As a Crowsilk with a bit of elvish blood, Lady Cleo possessed a sense of magic that remained among the best. It took only a second and she unhanded him. "There's something there, but it's not *Festrain*. Whatever the shaping did, it broke what the Worm King rewrote when he raised you. You had to have guessed that *Festrain* wasn't yours. It was an unholy gift shoved within you, a weapon installed within a siege engine. Give it time. . . ." Her face became solemn, brows furrowed. "Eat your food. It'll grow cold," she said, like she was scolding a child.

He did as he was told, the silence between them sharp as the Lady of the Dead retreated into her thoughts. Alas, he didn't have time to savor the food or enjoy its taste as he would've wanted. His first meal was marred by the simple act of socializing. Quite a few came toward the table to give him congratulations, starting with the Ruinous Guard and continuing through the people he knew less and less. Toward the end, nobles and merchants tarried long for his favor, hoping to snag the blessing of his presence for a job. Rottgor declined. He'd had enough of that kind of service to last several lifetimes.

In breaks between the nobles fishing for favors and the idle talk, Rottgor observed a single group of orphans from the Living Vine, who had been invited by Lady Cleo herself. They scurried around the castle, eyes wide and full of joy, laughing and eating the way adults couldn't. Some recognized him. They pointed as though he was some hero. He supposed he was to them. Rottgor built this city and had streets and places named after him. A legend. A story. He smiled at them.

One smiled back.

The little girl who'd caught sight of him, her eyes the color of cut rubies or a maple leaf in fall, stared up toward him in wonder. Rottgor waved. A scent of roses wafted through his nose, though there were none in the hall. Goosebumps ran down his arms, an unfamiliar feeling given that he'd been dead a day ago. When he looked up again, the girl was gone, disappeared from the crowd. Rottgor leaned back in his chair, wondering if he'd actually seen her at all.

"Rottgor," a voice said, snapping him out of his trance.

The woman who spoke was a veiled levia woman. Thin and muscular, her preferred form's skin was the color of glossy bronze, her cheekbones high and full, eyes oval. She peered around the room as she walked toward him, regalness exuding from her steps. Her long, golden-draped dress, similar to those worn by the people of the far eastern land, beyond that of the Shroud and the Glimmer Glade, shone in the torchlights. Her wings were thinner than the usual dragon wings, closer to that of the Summersweet fairies than the dragons of the Red Archipelago. The leathery webs between the staker bones were rotted, covered in wilted lotus buds and locust-eaten wounds. The right side of her face was forever covered by black vines and a larger black lotus where her eye socket should've been. Rottgor shook his head, a weak laugh escaping his breath at seeing one of the last reminiscences of his past. Tytli, the last of the Six Shadows besides himself.

She slid further toward him, her steps silent as nightfall and just as graceful. She looked him over, fingers laced before her, one eye looking through a thin veil. Black lotus petals cascaded down one side of her face, disappearing against her cheeks. She gave a quick bow. "You're looking well, friend."

"You're . . . you haven't been in the city for years," he said. Rottgor smiled. "Tytli Bhihadra. To what do we owe the pleasure? And you don't have to lie to me. I know I look terrible, Lili."

"I was in the area. I thought I would give you a visit for your accomplishment."

"When are you going to join him?" Lady Cleo asked, sipping her wine. "Or do I have to force you as well?"

"I'm not under your *direct* service, Your Grace. Besides, you know that my mission is far from complete."

Lady Cleo pursed her lips. "A mission that happens to have no end."

"It has an end." Her light voice became sharpened at the edges, dark in its tone. "And I will not quit until my purpose is complete. You know that."

Lady Cleo turned away, an annoyed sigh rushing through her lips. "Do as you must."

Tytli turned her attention back to Rottgor. "What now?" she asked. "What does the great Famine Blade do now that he has time on his hands?"

"I don't know. I haven't figured that much out. I hope to get some peace."

"No, you don't."

"Yes . . . I do."

"Hm." Tytli frowned. "I thought maybe you would join me on my quest. I could always use another blade."

"That's behind me," Rottgor said.

"And what's in front of you?" she asked.

Rottgor tapped his fingers against the table. "I'm not sure. Not roaming around Dargath, though."

"It appears I may have misread you." She gave a soft laugh that had no humor in it. "I see. Well, please call me if you have any trouble within the city. I will be here. You are a dear friend to me, Rott. Do not forget that. But as you know, my mission will always go first."

"I know."

Tytli brought him in for a brief hug, wrapping her long arms around his neck. "Enjoy your Seclusion, friend." She gave one final bow and fell back into the crowd.

By the time the congratulations ended, there was only a faint taste of the dinner on his tongue, pleasant, meaty, and herby, but not enough. "That was a lot," he said, sighing. Exhaustion enveloped him so tightly he thought he might fall asleep where he sat.

"I apologize. In every ceremony, there are people out to get something they want, but I'm glad you enjoyed the little guests. You're a hero and a figure in many stories." Lady Cleo's face hadn't changed. Rottgor saw the gears grinding in her head, a puzzle snagging her attention away. *Perhaps I shouldn't have brought the rune up.* Nothing bothered her more than an unknown. "Are you having a good time?" she asked, instantly snapping back to reality.

"I think I am, but I don't think I will last much longer." The attention would surely pass. Perhaps only half an hour left if lucky—

Duke Jamis floated over from his chair on the other side of the hall. Rottgor slid down the back of his honored seat. He knew what was going to happen next. "We're here to honor one of our dearest and oldest friends, Rottgor. Here before even the first bricks of our Necropolis, our friend stood, raised by a terrible tyrant yet becoming a hero. One of the last remaining of the Worm King's generals turned heroes and founders, the Six Shadows, he fought alongside figures like Tytli Bhihadra and Galelin, the legends within the Worm King's army that threatened our lands, who then defied their tyrant and brought us peace. Knowingly or not, they changed the way the undead were viewed, even inspiring my grandfather Hrafon II, the Crow Father, to embrace his power, to use his power over death for goodness and justice. Without them, without him, this city may not even be here.

"After years of servitude under both the evil and the just, he takes his path. Surely he does not know what comes next for him." Duke Jamis Crowsilk stole a small glance at Rottgor, the glowing flames of his lich eyes piercing through the space between them. "But I know that he will do more than what he has been doing. He has a kind heart, kinder than he has any right to be, given what he has gone through, the things his body was forced to do under the Worm King's control. Even now, I wish I had dared to let such a marvelous person go sooner, but it took my granddaughter's words to sway this influential and powerful icon from our court. It's a new age, and he deserves to *live* his days in it, not serving it in the way of a sword but in the way of his heart."

Duke Jamis Crowsilk raised a goblet of Cold Souls. The drink—if one could call an ethereal magical substance made of pure aether for the nourishment of all-powerful, undead wizards a drink—chilled the air. Little soul-like wisps toppled down the sides of the silver cup, dripping against the lich's bony and ringed fingers.

"We raise our drinks to him, to our friend. The once feared, now adored. The once bloodied, now cleansed. The once serving, now served. Razgaif of the Onyx-Ax clan, known as Rottgor the Famine Blade, by the power of Duke Jamis Crowsilk II and his named heir, soon-to-be Duchess Cleotraeli Crowsilk, we release you from your duty as a Death Knight of the Realm to your Seclusion in the world that you helped build. Let us toast."

The crowd below erupted into cheers. No matter their walks of life, these people knew him. He felt a flush of embarrassment. Rottgor's past wasn't perfect. Forced to do terrible things, to hurt and kill the innocent without a will of his own, trapped within this decayed and cold body, he thought he would never be redeemed. Maybe he wouldn't be. He always told himself that this was his judgment—his gavel had long been struck, and he'd been made to wither away in service, like his brothers and sister, for his crimes. Yet here he was. Released. The chains gone. A sliver of guilt ran through his mind. *No. They wouldn't want me to return to dust, given this chance. They would want me to live.* It was his time to fade into the background. He hoped they understood. He hoped, and for the second time that day, he allowed himself tears.

THREE

The Climb

Malferioel haunted him, sheathed on his back alongside the rest of his meager belongings.

Undead citizens fell into two categories: undeniable hoarders and those who carried nothing at all. Rottgor fell firmly into the nothing-at-all camp. Everything he owned fit into a single leather satchel—just necessities, a few trinkets from a past he barely remembered, and, of course, Malferioel.

Wrapped in layers of leather, the Deathblade whispered faintly, its glow barely visible. He didn't know why he'd brought it. Lady Cleo had put the option before him. A Deathblade's materials, soul, metal, and magic could be reforged, made into a weapon for another righteous hand of the Ruinous Guard. But the blade had been baptized by the blood of the innocent, the bones of the guilty, and the heart of a tyrant. It was still his burden to bear.

Or perhaps what tempted him to bring it with him was that he had so little. The sword was his, despite its past. As he traveled along the beaten roads of Necropolis, he found a loneliness to it all.

He stepped carefully along Blood Street, named after his dear friend Galelin. It was the undead city's longest road. Blood Street was an ideal starting point for his journey, marked by the pale-red bricks, stoic gargoyles, and tall black lanterns lit with eternal flames. He took another breath, letting the autumn air fill his lungs with the taste of acorns and maple. The emptiness of the morning came as no surprise. The city was known for its late nights, not its early mornings. *Shame*, Rottgor thought, *it's a beautiful city.* He never appreciated what he had until he walked it himself, unburdened . . . for the most part.

The light fog of the morning burned away, dew drying off the blades of grass and countless flowers. His slow pace down Blood Street took him past Famine, Abomination, Hive, and Desolation, ending at his destination of Frost Street around noon. The sun now burned against the skin of his back through his thin light-green tunic. He didn't sweat, more so burned underneath his cotton layers, praising at least that the day held a little of its initial cool. He kept to the shade, walking down the lines of taverns, inns, and food carts. Frost Street was a place for rest on the edge of town, welcoming weary travelers. Rottgor never had much time to explore the establishments on these fringes. He slunk through the shadows, an unfamiliar rumbling quaking through his stomach. When Algarus had mentioned hunger, Rottgor hadn't expected this. At this rate, all his retirement coin might end up in the pit of his stomach.

He came upon the Rattling Ribcage, mind muddled by the rumbling in his stomach. The tavern was smaller than both the Lich's Brew and the Boundless Fae but shared the same welcoming appeal. Its red two-story wooden frame showed signs of age, worn more by love than neglect. Frosted windows concealed the interior, revealing only an ominous red glow flickering like small fireballs. Above the ragged door, clinging to its hinges, hung an old sign of two skeletons dancing arm in arm. A few younger college-aged warlocks and alchemists hung around the entrance, some Rottgor recognized as warlocks of the castle. They nodded in his direction, a few gawking as though he were made of solid gold. More than ever, Rottgor wished for a hood on his tunic.

He squeezed past them to the door. To his surprise, it opened before his fingers touched the knob. A skeleton soldier met him on the other side, ancient with yellowed bone, touched by moss and grave flowers, and shielded within golden armor from a lost civilization. Its right eye glowed yellow in its socket, while the left eye remained a void. The skeleton cocked its head back, a rattling sound rippling from the spot where its spine met the back of its skull. "You're new here," the skeleton said, with a thick northern accent from the land of the frozen berserkers. "You're the one that Calfe said he was meeting. Come along. Name's Hedeon Hudson."

Hedeon squared his large shoulders and gestured for Rottgor to follow. He must've been quite the giant in life, given that his skeleton alone towered over Rottgor. Hedeon strolled toward the counter, his clinking bones a constant sound in the tavern. The inside of the Rattling Ribcage told stories that the outside didn't. The ominous red lights he'd seen from outside the frosted windows were the soapstone lamps burning small pyres of will-o'-the-wisps at each of the glossy, buffed tables. Chairs of all shapes and sizes surrounded those circular tables, and more skeletons like Hedeon walked around, serving guests. All the skeletons seemed to come from the Seven Northern Lords, bearing golden and bronze armors, furs, drinking horns, and bearded axes. The aesthetic spilled into the decor, showing off the colors of Clan

Hudson—seafoam green, yellow, and white on a plaid tartan—and their dozen accomplishments. Massive hydra heads, pieces of earth elementals, and a legendary amber-preserved tentacle from a kraken were only some of the trophies they displayed. Rottgor slipped his way to the bar, his neck craned and his jaw slack. Hedeon's teeth chattered, a common sign among undead skeletons that they were pleased. "Glad you like the place. Not much of a tavern hopper, eh? Well, glad I made a statement."

"How'd you . . ." Rottgor searched for the words. *Find yourself?* "Get started?"

Hedeon's one eye flickered out, not unlike a candle having burned to the end of its wick. "I'll tell you one day, but not today."

"A story for a story?" Rottgor asked, arching an eyebrow.

"Sounds like a good payment to me."

The door opened behind them. Calfe strutted in, tossing his half cloak at a coat-hanging pin. It landed perfectly on one of the hooks. Calfe pumped his fist and twirled on his heels, continuing through the tavern. A few patrons who appeared to be regulars rolled their eyes; others cheered for the short man. Calfe took both reactions in stride. He caught Rottgor's glance from across the Rattling Ribcage and smiled. Calfe settled in beside Rottgor, his chest barely hitting the counter. "Hedeon, whatcha serving today?"

"Viking's Blood Mead, garlic roast chicken, roasted parsnips and greens, and fresh bread served with mammoth-bone consommé."

"I heard that garlic is bad for the undead," Calfe said.

"Not true," Rottgor said, "better for us than you think. There are vampires and blood mages who have *some* issues with it, but it's nothing more than a mild allergic reaction."

"Eh, really now." Calfe reclined back a bit, resting his

shoulders. "Then we'll have that. Double on the mead, if you please, good man."

"Right up." Hedeon gave a small nod and headed toward the back of the tavern.

"So," Calfe said, "what does a retired undead soldier do with his spare time?"

"It's surprisingly full of nothing," Rottgor admitted. "I'm kind of lost at the moment."

Calfe laced his fingers together. "Do you have a place to stay? I got a fella that needs to get rid of a property. He'll sell to you for cheap or I'll knock his teeth out."

"You'd do that?" Rottgor squinted.

"Nah, don't look at me like that. I know someone who needs help." Calfe readjusted himself. "Trust me. I've gotten good at knowing who I want to talk to."

"You weren't always good at it?" Rottgor said, stifling a laugh.

"Takes some bad decisions here and there, every once in a while. Right, Hedeon?"

"He ain't a bad guy," Hedeon shouted from the kitchens, "just a pain in the butt."

"You barely have a butt," Calfe snapped.

Hedeon laughed. "I'm a skeleton. What's your excuse?"

"Can't do anything around here without some criticism." Calfe waved his hand. "Don't worry. I'm not gonna let a former Death Knight wander the city without making a few friends."

Rottgor folded his arms. "Did you research me?"

"I don't know if you've noticed, but you have a street named after you, pal. And it's kind of hard to miss when you have a full-blown ceremony in your honor at the castle. You have made quite the name for yourself. When we met, I thought you might've just been one of the regular Death Knights, but not one of *the*

Death Knights. *The Six Shadows.*" Calfe rubbed the back of his neck. "Makes me sound like I'm trying to get close to you for your fame. It ain't like that."

Rottgor shrugged, tapping his fingers nervously against the bar. "I believe you. You didn't know who I was when we met, so you had no reason to be kind. Besides, I get it. A favor for a favor, and reaching out goes both ways. You see a business opportunity of some sort, and I'm willing to oblige."

"You ain't wrong." Calfe kept the rest of his thoughts hidden behind a wide smile. Rottgor had lived on the edges of royal courts long enough to know that nothing came for free. Some people kept their strings hidden; others laced them in gold for everyone to see. Calfe wasn't that type. Rottgor watched the struggle behind the man's eyes, reconciling what Rottgor was sure was another question lying in wait.

Before Calfe could gather his words, two server squirrels scurried from the kitchens, golden plates attached to small harnesses on their armored backs. The first one gave a bit of a bow, and Rottgor returned it graciously. Pleased, the squirrel flattened and clicked a small button on the side of its bronze-plated armor. The loaded dinner plate slid down its back, landing perfectly before Rottgor. The second squirrel served its dish to Calfe.

"Thanks, little guy." Rottgor scratched the creature underneath its chin. "Let me let you get back to work, champ." The rodent gave a salute and left its guest to his food.

Rottgor unpacked the silverware from its leather-and-jute cover—smaller than the castle's, made of metal, and showing wear here and there. Well used, well taken care of. He ran his fingers over the fork, tracing the grooves of the runestone patterns etched into its handle. His fingers quivered, holding the little utensil as though it were a weapon. The crispy roast chicken doused in oil and fresh seasoning, the pile of vinegared greens and honey-glazed parsnips, and the hunk of bread and cheese accompanied by a glistening red-brown broth—the sight of it all brought back sweeping memories Rottgor didn't know he still had. *Long ago . . . and much too far away.* A longing roamed through his chest. He took a cautious bite, a bit of chicken and a scoop of the greens and parsnips.

He chewed.

At the Seclusion ceremony, he hadn't given the food much thought. Too many drifting thoughts then. Here, he savored every bite. The chicken was perfectly herbed, with notes of pine and evergreen among the softly cooked white meat, which was tender and juicy. The bright, sharp greens cut through the sweetness and earthiness of the parsnips. He went for a bite of the bread before Calfe stopped him.

"Try dunking the bread in the broth, you'll enjoy it."

Rottgor did as instructed, took a bite, and felt a big smile spread across his face. The taste of the broth warmed his still-cold insides, rich and smooth through his body, complementing the soft sweetness of the potato bread. He cleaned the entire plate and soup bowl before the servers came back, carrying a tall glass of mead.

Relaxation coursed through Rottgor's half-alive body. The strength he got from the food was different than what he remembered from his living days, although his memories of that time were hazy. It came as a burst of life within him. He didn't want to think about how the undead machine of his body worked and cared not for the details. He closed his eyes, gathering himself. The lights of his rune danced in the darkness of his head.

"Don't fall asleep on me," Calfe said, laughing. "I know how good food can do that to a person."

Rottgor opened his eyes. He grunted, rubbing his belly. "That was nice."

"I'm glad you enjoyed it." Calfe was already sipping on his drink. "What do you say—after you finish your drink, wanna see the house I mentioned and see if it's up your alley? It's not that far of a walk, if you don't got anything to do."

"I wouldn't mind." Rottgor took a sip of his own mead. It tasted somehow of a candied flower, hibiscus surely, and perhaps a fruit of some kind, with bitter notes toward the end. "What's the fruit in this?"

"Snoberry. It's snoberry. The folks up north love the stuff." He laughed. "Good taste for a dead man." Calfe paused. Another unsaid thought flickered across the short man's face. "Have you ever thought—never mind. Finish your drink."

Rottgor pondered what Calfe refused to say. He seemed to have an idea. Brilliant, ambitious, and driven men often did, sometimes too many for their own good. Rottgor understood. A wanderlust roamed in his chest, too, the simple want of a place like this . . . a place to call home. Maybe something more. His sword hummed through its sheath, reminding him of all he had been up until this point: maggots and flies.

※

"Just round these couple of blocks," Calfe urged.

Of course, the building was on Famine Street. Rottgor rubbed his chin, a little annoyed at the irony of it all. The Six Shadows each had at least one city street named after them . . . and this one was his. Rottgor had refused to visit the place in all his days in the city. Yet here he was, standing on the off-green stone tiles and surrounded by an endless sea of squat wooden and stone buildings. Ironically, Famine served as a residential district and a market street, filled with black metal or dark duskwood carts. There were more trees than Rottgor expected—black apple, plum, and pomegranate—and mounds of mushrooms and berry bushes between them. Vegetables sprouted from plots sprinkled between the streets, owned by several farm families of the city. Rottgor bit his lower lip so hard that his old, broken tusk made him bleed. Such a beautiful place dedicated to an orc whose salted earth starved thousands and killed many more. It left a sour taste on Rottgor's tongue. But he followed.

To his relief, there weren't any statues of him, or of the other Six Shadows. They preferred it that way. When they'd founded the city, they had agreed that, first and foremost, the city should be dedicated to the Crow Father and his family line. Duke Jamis and Lady Cleo hated the idea of the Six Shadows receiving nothing after all they had gone through under the Worm King's thrall, but they respected the founders all the same.

Most of Necropolis's orcs—Duskgraves, Bladeborns, and what was left of Rottgor's dwindling tribe, the Onyx-Axes—had taken residence in that district, their homes mimicking those of their homeland. One such house was where Calfe led him, a two-story building made of sturdy, dark stone, multilayered thatch-and-tile roofs upon each jutting section, and boarded-up but well-maintained half-arched windows. Rottgor froze and shifted his feet, glancing at the meager belongings on his shoulder. It wasn't enough to fill a single room in this building. He bit his lip once more.

"How do you like it?" Calfe asked.

Rottgor fumbled for words. "It's . . . a lot."

Calfe laughed. "You'll see why in a few. Not all of it is meant for a home."

Rottgor folded his arms but followed the small dwarvish elf to a dwelling a few houses away. The building was much smaller than the first property, somehow matching its majesty all the same. Another dwarf opened the door. He was sturdier than Calfe, wider and muscled, eyes a dark shade of coal. None of that stopped his lips from quivering when he saw Calfe on the other side.

"Vom," Calfe said, "about time for that favor you owe me." Vom went to close the door and was stopped immediately by the tip of Calfe's boot. "That ain't right. You've tried to disappear, dancing around this city like a ghost, and I've let it slide. But it's time that I come knocking. So, I'm giving you a proposal. We can finally come to an agreement about Fiddler's old place, or I can make you the ghost you obviously wanna be. You know I have *people* for that."

Vom appeared to grit his teeth underneath his bushy black beard. He wiped the sweat from his bald head. "I've meant . . . I've been trying—" Frustration clawed at the words forming in his mouth. Rottgor was sure that the muscled dwarf was holding back his full annoyance. "I'm truly sorry, Calfe," he said, his voice suddenly cool. He straightened his back and smoothed out his fine silk tunic. "I think we can agree. You don't want to sully your reputation. Besides, you have students at the College of Boneskies, am I correct? I do hope they know about their professor's other activities. . . . Some might get caught in between your two lives. You're not the only person with *people*, Calfe."

"You're not making your case. My students know what I do . . . and I do it for them and my family. But if I hear that you tried to touch a hair on their heads . . . well, that building will be the least of your worries. Now let us in. I want to have my new friend in the place before nightfall."

Before nightfall? Rottgor choked. He looked over his shoulder. The sun crept over the City of the Undead, spraying pink-and-red rays across the darkening sky, creating long shadows across the green and moss-covered streets. Only a couple of hours of day remained.

"Good thing you packed light, friend. Makes moving a lot easier."

Calfe and Rottgor followed Vom into his home. A tall levia man bowed and closed the door behind them. He, too, seemed terrified of Calfe's presence, darting his eyes toward a nearby wall. The history between the two dwarves was thick, it seemed. Dwarvish families often held strong grudges against each other, and to have a prestigious elf house behind Calfe only added fuel to the fire. Rottgor knew bitter enemies when he saw them, those who were always one step from battle. Vom glared at them. A man used to second place and hating it.

They made it to a parlor room, a short walk from the entrance. The room was small, a long table topped with stacks of documents taking up most of the space in the center. A crystal chandelier hung from a golden chain, spinning refracted light in different directions. A fine red dwarvish rug lay beneath the table's legs, stretching between the entrance and a large window. Rottgor took a few cautious steps. He knew his way around parlor meetings—never as the guest, always as the silent muscle looming at the edges of the meeting rooms. *Five soldiers*—he counted a few steps in—*no, seven. Dwarves and levia.* The two people he hadn't initially seen hid behind the massive wardrobes to the left and right of the table, one no doubt guarding a secret exit in case of the worst. Rottgor sighed. *A bit sloppy. My guards would ne—* he stopped that thought. They weren't his guards anymore.

Calfe kicked the chair at the head of the table and plopped

himself into it, then lifted his feet and rested them casually on the table. Vom curled his fist; the soldier behind the right cabinet stirred. The master of the home gave a slight shake of the head—not the cleanest command. A true leader knew better than to tip their hand on the opening play. Rottgor knew that; Calfe knew it, too. The simple fact rolled over Vom's head. A show. Theatrics. That was all this was. If Vom tried anything, Rottgor was going to cause some trouble, though Calfe probably would beat him to it. Rottgor sat beside his new acquaintance.

"Now, where did I put the deed for that home?" Vom pondered aloud, leafing through the piles.

Calfe's eyes darkened. "Don't play games. It's right where I left it, the third pile from the left. You know better than to touch documents that don't belong to you."

"The Fiddler's place was a joint venture last time I checked, Calfe," Vom sneered.

"One that you pilfered before forcing the poor man out—"

Vom scoffed. "Man? Please. He was a walking corpse. What did he need all that space for? Oh, don't give me that, Calfe. Like you haven't done *worse*. And you want me to sell the fine place to *yet another dead thing*. Oh, I see what he is. The dead shouldn't speak, and they really shouldn't deal."

"Do you think I'm going to let you do this again, you bigoted, one-man clown party? I'm not asking you. We're past that. I gave you plenty of time to give it to me of your own free will, but here I am. You've pulled this time and time again. You steal from people, you threaten them, and you drive them out of town. And you expect me to treat you with any kind of respect?" Calfe's feet, once casually on the table, hit the floor. He leaned forward. "I *won't* ask again. We can talk about a price right now, or it'll cost you more than you're willing to pay. That's all I'm gonna say."

The two dwarves shot hateful glances at one another. Rottgor knew that during these times, a straight face was needed. He fell into that dark expression, the cold sentinel, eyes facing forward and mouth an indecipherable line. Vom glanced at Rottgor as though trying to find a weakness. He wouldn't find one. Centuries of experience stood between them. Rottgor had lived maybe two or three generations of Vom's family. With a couple of guards, flimsy negotiations, and hard glances, the dark-bearded dwarf might as well have begun pouring dirt into the ocean hoping to make an island. Vom made an annoyed click with the back of his teeth. "Ten thousand gold," he said.

And Calfe laughed in his face, then abruptly stopped. "Oh, you're serious. For a minute there, I thought you were my ex-wife, trying to ask for anything." Calfe rolled his shoulders. "No. Three thousand."

"Three thousand, you can't expect—"

"I can get it for *free*," Calfe reminded him. "All I would need is to bring a heavy rock to a deep river."

"Seven thousand five hundred," Vom said, clearly shaken.

Calfe didn't flinch. He cocked his head. "Getting there. Four thousand five hundred, and the ability to sleep well at night." Legal or not, he was going to get what was his. *That* was *a good deal*, Rottgor admitted, forcing down a smile. "I'll give you four hundred more for the restoration cost, but that's it. I'm doing this as a favor. Is that good for you, Rott?"

Rottgor nodded. Four thousand nine hundred wasn't even a dent in the pension he would receive every month for the rest of his life. Ten thousand wasn't, truth be told. Alas, this man—this viper—didn't deserve that much. Rottgor saw it in Vom's oily grin. *One hundred short of five thousand, just for pettiness.*

"What do you even want the old place for?" Vom asked,

searching for a feather and inkwell. "The last tenant squandered our investments. And this . . . *thing* doesn't seem to be anything but a foot soldier or a fancy piece of furniture. He has to have *you* speak for him. Don't tell me he's one of those who can't speak. Urgh. You have to think about us and our needs, instead of those without minds of their own."

"Our?" Calfe asked. "Your *bridge* tongue must be rusty." Calfe said the word "our" in *dwarvish*. "You meant that word. Funny, I don't remember you doing anything but hiking up that man's rent under my nose. Regardless, that's none of your business, Vom. This isn't going to be your property anymore. It's going to be his, and I'm going to watch over whatever he wants to do there myself. You've had your chance. Got it?"

"Got it, Professor." Vom's voice found its confidence once more, dripping with venom and hate. Calfe said nothing in response—not acknowledging him at all. "Here you go."

Calfe unfurled the long parchment, his eyes scrolling over the document. After the first reading, he went over the agreement, price, and possible pitfalls. The place had been officially named the Violent Lantern and was founded by a Bladeborn orc and his husband years in the past. It had since passed from hand to hand as both a home and a business, its most recent incarnation being the Fiddle and Fool's Gold. The deeper they went into the contract, the more Rottgor realized that the original agreement had put Calfe in a hole . . . leaving Vom holding the shovel. Calfe had paid for the upkeep and Vom had stolen the spoils, hiking up the rent and providing nothing for the tenants. Vom was an untrustworthy landlord. *They were friends once,* Rottgor realized, *before this.* The pure restraint Calfe had shown must have come from somewhere deep. An idea stirred in the back of Rottgor's mind. Nothing for sure, just a small sprout from a barely cracked seed.

After his thorough read through, Calfe amended the contract, striking out the previous prices and dozens of names.

"Read it over once more," Calfe urged Rottgor, "and make certain it's something you're willing to agree to."

Rottgor knew little of the legality of such contracts. Without Calfe, surely, the snake would have found him in the grass, as it clearly had for Vom's other tenants. So he read it over, asking questions to Calfe alone, then read it twice more. In the end, he was pleased. Calfe would be taking Vom's spot as the land's caretaker. That alone was enough to ease his concerns. "It looks good," Rottgor said, emphasizing every word in Vom's direction. The slimy dwarf recoiled.

"Good, good," Calfe said. "I'll sign here"—he scratched his name, then indicated to Rottgor—"and you will sign here, and Vom will sign it off and send it to the Hollowed Hall."

Vom raised his hand. "And *I'll* be getting paid." He sounded so proud of himself that Rottgor almost drew his sword and slashed him. "I am giving up a *valuable* property to a sack of bones. I swear . . . maybe the Worm King was onto something. Free will is wasted on the dead."

You're about to be a sack of bones. Rottgor shook his head, untying the leather satchel from his back. His fingers ran through his belongings, finding the cache of gold slips tucked within. He pulled out the exact amount, no more, no less. To a better person, a little extra wouldn't have been a big deal. For Vom, Rottgor hoped it all fell into a spike pit. "Here you go," Rottgor said, putting the stack of gold slips between them. He held his big hand over it. "All I ask is that I never hear from you ever again."

"That building is your problem now. Why would I even care?" Vom shrugged.

You care. You hate losing anything. I see it in your eyes. You're going to watch this place like a hawk. You're going to want to know what's happening. You're not new. There are always people who hate their fellows. This is my city as well as yours. Never forget that.

The arrogant confidence on the dwarf's face made Rottgor want to vomit. The price, though much lower than Vom had wanted, was a profit in his head. He had run that well dry anyway, and what good was a well void of water? The orcish blood in Rottgor's body, once so chilled, warmed in his body. *I'll embarrass you,* he thought. *You think you're getting ahead of me. You think that you got something out of nothing. All you see is a walking corpse.* Rottgor struggled to hold the emotionless mask upon his face. He reached for the feather and inkwell, his palm finally leaving the gold slips on the desk. He gave one more look over the deed, confirming Calfe's name on the line. Rottgor picked up the quill and dipped it into the ink. The smile on Vom's face grew with each letter Rottgor signed. *Four thousand nine hundred gold richer, this pig.* Rottgor slashed the last *x* of his clan name. *But you're not happy . . . are you?*

The former Fiddle and Fool's Gold, and long before that the Violent Lantern, was now the property of Razgaif Onyx-Ax. As he left Vom's house, however, there was a hot feeling on the back of his neck. He sensed eyes boring into him, and turned to look back. Vom's own mask had dropped, now showing pure contempt. Hatred. For what, Rottgor didn't know. *This isn't the end between us. Some people don't need a reason to hate.*

FOUR

The Little One

Calfe made good on his promise. Rottgor entered his new home as the three moons—Mari, Yari, and Awi—rose into the night sky.

Rottgor jammed the rusty iron key into the oversize keyhole of the front door of the Fiddle and Fool's Gold. The rain-rotten sign, painted with a gold alembic and tinkerer's tools, swung above the entrance, hanging from worn rings and determination. He hit the side of his forehead against the door for at least the third time, jiggling the key in the stubborn lock. Rottgor grunted, finally pushing the maple door open. A bell on the other side rang. Rottgor rubbed his shoulder, a bit of an ache running through his muscles. *Death Knight Rottgor. Taken down by a door.* He swore he heard Lady Cleo giggling in the back of his mind. He took the first step into his new home and smiled.

The taste and smell of dust struck him first. Floorboards creaked beneath his boots, moonlight spilling across the broken planks. The room had clearly been a storefront at some point. A counter stretched along the northern wall, with empty shelves holding abandoned bottles and casks. A few abandoned alchemy tools sat by a dwarvish metal stove and furnace. A large ventilation shaft rose from the back, its small fan powered by a minor wind rune scribbled on a glowing metal plate. Other than that, nothing—just a few abandoned chairs and tables stacked upon each other in a corner. Rottgor stepped through the open space, his brain churning. A small wish, one he dared reach for. He sighed.

"You see it, don't ya?" Calfe said. "Something you want to do."

"I think . . . ," he said, pausing, "I think I got something I wanna try. I'm not . . . sure if I can. I don't know where to start." Rottgor clenched his fist. "I hate this. I hate that I don't know where to—"

"You don't know where to start," Calfe repeated. "Gonna be a bit honest. I'm a businessman, no surprise. I had you down as a guy who came across some good gold and had nothing to do. Better someone like me notice than a scum like Vom." Calfe walked over to the chairs and unhooked one from its brothers, placing it on the ground. He took a seat. The pale moonlight at his back gave his face a dim shadow, but his stormy-blue eyes still shone. "Of course, I come to you as a friend. Or at least a person that could be one. I don't care what you do to this place . . . but I have a sense that we can do something glorious here."

Rottgor crossed his arms. He had decades left in this second life. He didn't *have* to fill them with purpose—he could waste them doing nothing. The thought tempted him but left him feeling hollow. What waited for him after his second death? This question always lingered. Necromantic creations walked a line between magic and mortality, their souls unraveling once the spells animating them faded like waning moons. *I don't want to waste the chance that I have.*

"I . . ." His sword hummed on his back more, cutting through his hesitation. "I want to pay things back. I've been in the city for hundreds of years."

"Urgh." Calfe snorted. "My knees hurt just thinking about it. Coming on my forty-third birthday, and I feel as old as time." His joints vocalized their dismay, popping as he stretched his limbs. "But truly, that's a good way to look at it. You've served the city, never lived in it. Two entirely different things. It's time to make decisions for you. . . ." Calfe's face fell. "All I can say is to live your life here. Use that now-beating heart and fill this place."

"I'm not going to take your kindness and sit on it, ser. I'm willing to do business." Rottgor rubbed his chin. Truthfully, it had been a thing he had been thinking about for a while. Having someone around with experience had worked out better than he'd thought. "But I do want to ask—if you go into business with me, what's in it for you?"

Calfe grinned. "Life changes, let's say it like that. I'll tell one day." He gave one final stretch, bones popping again like corn kernels. When he stretched his spine, he winced. An obvious old wound. "All right. There should be at least a spare bed that the previous owner left, but that's 'bout it. I'll send a furniture man over tomorrow. He's a good friend. Let me get back home, fella. Got people waiting for me. It was a pleasure. And please enjoy your first night."

The business dwarf left Rottgor to his own devices, closing the door behind him and cursing all the while at the old thing's reluctance. His footsteps receded into the distance, and after a while, Rottgor was alone.

Rottgor kicked his boots into a small corner by the door, then patrolled his new home. There was not much more to the open space—just a few things the owner had left behind. Dust trailed the soles of his feet, tickling a distant memory of a winter-chilled stone floor. That simple memory began creeping into the inner workings of his mind. He roamed, his slow heart picking up speed. He had never had a home before now, not his own, or at least he hadn't remembered one until now. His life, his people, and his very land had all been stripped from him the day his tribe had fallen and he'd died and risen once more. To let himself hope and see things among the empty spaces of a place all his own seeded a fear. One that had been a constant in his life and in his death. *You'll lose it all. Serve. Bend. Break.* The sword at his back sang its song of carrion flies and mosquitos, the taste of rotten fruit blooming on the roof of his mouth. *It will never be yours,* the blade seemed to say.

He pushed the thought aside and continued his inspection, his footsteps as light as a thief's. He knew no one was there, that it was his space, but being cautious was second nature. He found winding stairs hidden behind a back wall on the other side of the counter, and quietly climbed them. The second floor was more of a home than the first. Several rooms opened into a hallway at the top of the stairs, the doors closed and the floor bare. Rottgor checked the rooms—two bedrooms, a bathroom, a small kitchen, and a study—all sizable and all clean. He returned to the larger bedroom.

As promised, there was a bed and nothing else, save for a single pillow. Rottgor placed his satchel down and unhooked Malferioel from his back. The blade weighed on his quivering arms. He carried it over to the fireplace and placed it on a dusty shelf. He looked at his hands after. A burn. Rottgor stared, confused, frowning at the reddish mark on the gray of his palms. It stung, itching underneath his already-thin flesh. Was it the sword's reaction to him? Rottgor scratched at the burn. *Do you resent me, old friend?* He shook the thought away.

He escaped to the plain straw bed, collapsing onto his back. He stared at the ceiling, listening to the sounds of the street and night around him. Cicadas and crickets whistled their songs among the rumbling of the rolling carriages. The wind brought him mumbles of conversations. His mind wandered back to the castle, to his duty to the Ruinous Guard, to the people he knew and understood. Here, alone, he barely understood himself. *Is this all I am? A weapon once wielded, am I going to collect dust in an armory? Am I going to be the rusted sword in a long-forgotten treasury?* The bitterness hit his heart hard. Comfort wasn't happiness, only the absence of struggle. Rottgor turned over on his side, grabbing the lone pillow. *Who am I now?* he thought.

The itching in his palms gradually lessened, and he eased toward sleep. Little did he know that a long-lost dream would meet him on the other side.

The caves of the Onyx-Ax clan weren't known for their warmth, yet Razgaif remembered them fondly. He sat cross-legged by a burning fire alongside his five brothers and lone sister, their mates, and their children. They rarely had the chance to spend time with one another, each stolen by the battles of the warring clans. He, himself, was a decorated clan warrior, masterful hunter, and . . . head cook of the tribe. The little ones watched as he diced up large carrots, skinned chunks of boar meat, minced fragrant herbs, and swept them all into the mammoth-tusk cauldron. The sweet smell of herbs, vegetables, and meat mingled through the smoke, burning his eyes and tickling his nose. Their stomachs growled at the sight of it.

There were plenty of other dishes. Thick slices of sweet-potato and pumpkin-seed bread lay cooling on a slab behind him. At his back was an assortment of nettles, sorrels, and dandelions, both roasted and raw. To his side, apples, blueberries, currants, and wild orcish persimmons were piled on wooden plates alongside goat and mammoth cheeses he'd bartered from the farmers of the tribe. Last was his prized jewel: an elderberry-and-cloudberry-crumble pudding. The little ones weren't fans of fruits on their own, so he'd made something just for them. He remembered having his own sweet tusk, so he hardly blamed them. Razgaif smiled, patting one of his nephews on the head. The eagerness in the boy's round red eyes grew bigger by the second. His father, Razgaif's brother, laughed.

The voices were gone, the faces a little blurred. The pieces of his family began to slip. Still, he served them, a smile on his face. The family tore at his feast, big hands and little hands alike. Razgaif laughed, the only sound audible in the cave he once called home. His brothers wrestled for the last scoop of stew, while his sister took to her milk-thistle tea. Razgaif said something to her, and she chuckled, trying her best not to spit out her drink. An entire morning of cooking and baking, and it had taken less than thirty minutes until all the plates and pots were emptied. Orcs never left an empty plate.

Soon, the brothers and their mates went out for a hunt, and his sister returned to training the tribe warriors as their quartermaster. The little ones were doing as little ones did, playing. Some pretended to be warriors, some hunters, and even a few played as shamans or druids. Razgaif watched over them. He hadn't a mate, content keeping his siblings' children safe. "Uncle" served him fine. The kids always asked for their uncle's story as the Champion of the Onyx-Ax, and he was always content to provide and protect. Alas, the words were long gone, faded so far through history that there wasn't ink left on the page.

It was that fateful day.

That horn.

That war horn.

That blaring scream that broke everything and began the torture that was his life thereafter.

The dreamer shouted, telling them to run, to gather all the children and run. It didn't matter if they were regarded as cravens. They would live, maybe even a whole life if the gods deemed it fit. Razgaif did as he always did. He was the Champion of the tribe, the protector, the warrior of the Onyx-Ax. They needed him for any threat that their people faced. He walked over to the obsidian-and-redwood ax, Tremorwalker, and took it from its pedestal. No hesitation, no fear. Razgaif, Champion of the Onyx-Ax, stepped out of his cave to his death—which outlived everyone he loved.

Rottgor awoke to sunlight on his face. He stirred himself upward, the dream clinging hard to his grogginess. "I hate sleep," he decided, snorting through his nose. Living without it had been a boon. The foul mood leaked through him, souring one morning routine after the next. Before long, he was dressed and ready for the day, and not feeling even a wee bit better. Growling, he left the room, slamming the door behind him. The entire home shook at his thunderous rage.

For centuries, the burning orcish blood had slept, and was now reawakened by his new life. He found himself stomping down the stairs, his teeth grinding against one another. He stood in the empty shop, growling, and stared. The little things became unbearable. He scrubbed the counters and dusted the cabinets until they gleamed, and when that didn't fix his mood, he smashed a dusty and ugly fruit painting into splinters. Nothing *looked* right; nothing *felt* right. He wiped spittle from the corner of his snarling lips. "Pull it together," he told himself, hands shaking. "It was just a dream." The past remained the past.

Nerves sizzling, he forced himself to a seat. Tasks. There were plenty on his list. He still needed furniture, more civilian clothes, food, and perhaps tools for the kitchen. He froze. The kitchen. Rottgor growled once more, scratching his scalp under his thinning black hair. He hadn't thought of all the work his kitchen needed. His mood soured further. A passion he'd loved that had brought his family together was taken from him. *What else did you take from me, Worm?* Centuries gone, and there were pieces still left scattered. Rottgor breathed in slowly through his nose and out his mouth. The rage eased a little.

Someone rapped on the front door. Rottgor took one more deep breath, running his fingers through his now cold, sweaty hair. This "somewhat living" mess wasn't as glamorous as he'd been sold. He opened the door. A squat, dark elf in a carpenter's apron craned his head, peering inside the building as though a giant undead orc wasn't standing in front of him. He might have pushed himself in if Rottgor hadn't cupped him by the crown of his head. "Excuse you, can I get a name before you invite yourself in?"

"Mohek," the elf said distractedly. "Calfe sent me. Saying that you needed a furniture guy. I'm that furniture guy."

"And you didn't think about saying hello first? A good way to get an ax to the head."

"Wouldn't be the first time." Mohek waved him off. "Now can I come in?"

Bold. Rottgor stepped aside. Not like the carpenter was listening anyway. Mohek wandered in, taking stock of the place, already wielding his measuring tools. "Fiddler did well keeping the place up. A little wear and tear here and there. Nothing I can't fix up." Mohek leaped over the counter. "Gonna need to replace this stove, he burned this one out. Got any plans for it?"

Rottgor opened his mouth and closed it. The man was already on the other side of the room.

"I always hated these tables. They look ugly, some of my worst work. I'm glad they're collecting dust. Was I drunk when I designed these chairs? Urgh." He took one of them by a leg and slammed it down. It exploded upon hitting the ground. Wooden chunks flew, legs rolled. Rottgor bit his lower lip, reflecting on his own bubbling anger. His morning outburst suddenly didn't seem so bad. "All right, got that out of my system. What do you need . . . uh . . . ?"

"Rottgor."

"That's a scary name," Mohek said.

"Wasn't born with it."

"Thank the gods. I just thought that your parents had some twisted sense of humor. I've met an orc named Bluudragl, the nicest guy in the world, looks mean as the Depths, though." Mohek stepped over his carnage. "I'll clean that. Now, tell me what you want. I'll see what I got in my shop, make some, and send Calfe the bill. Don't be afraid to blow up his tab. . . ."

"Actually . . . ," Rottgor started, "bill it to Lady Cleo. She owes me a favor."

"The soon-to-be *Duchess* owes you . . . Wait, you're not . . . ?" Mohek froze. "I knew the name sounded familiar. Death Knight Rottgor? The Famine Blade? What are you—?"

"I'm retired—not of my own volition, I'm afraid," Rottgor sputtered out. "That's behind me." It wasn't. None of it was. Rottgor was who he was, who he had been for longer than he'd used his birth name. He clung to it: the Knight of Salted Fields, the Blade of Endless Hunger, Hollowed Stomach—all those nasty titles that people whispered under their breaths. The ones they said out of fear. The Ruinous Guard respected him, the Crown valued him, and the people . . . knew nothing more than was in the legends. Mohek's face told it all. "But yes . . . I'm that Death Knight."

"Ah, well I'll be. . . . Thanks for your service?" Mohek frowned. "All right, now that *that* is handled. Tell me what you want. Actually, don't tell me, write it down, I'm not going to pretend like I'm gonna remember. I won't care to remember. I want to get back to the making part." He pulled a small parchment pad and portable ink pen from his pocket. The dark elf tied his hair back. "I'm gonna check out the upstairs. Call me when you're done. Or don't. Just leave your notes on the table."

And gone—all his interest, *poof*. The wiry, muscled dark elf ascended the stairs, muttering up the steps. Rottgor swore he heard it long after Mohek had left earshot. *What an odd fellow.* He did as he was told all the same. He wrote everything he needed: tables, chairs, a new stove, storage, a nightstand, and a few comfy items to make the place feel more like a home. He was sure that Mohek would work something out. Unlike him. His logic fought its losing battle against his heart and soul, his body soon taking the winning side. His fingers quaked, trying to sketch through his ideas. The doubt reared its head. It always did, taking the voice of the villain he knew better than anyone. *It will never work*, the Worm King's guttural voice whispered, *you'll never see smiles again. They aren't yours, not anymore. Serve. Bend. Break.*

Rottgor pushed through.

His slow heart always knew what he wanted. The dream, the

memory of his lost family stolen from him. That was his past, forever set in stone. Honoring them opened up a deep fear in him, worse than the grieving. Guilt bubbled up soon after. Did he have the right to do this after all he'd witnessed, after all he had done? No. They wouldn't want that. Shele—his sister, whose name he hadn't dared think—wouldn't want him hesitating over the thoughts of the dead and gone. *Dive into it, don't think about it. Do it.* He drew until the ink went dry and his dreams were brought to life on the page. Embarrassment flushed his face. More than a few times, he thought to tear the sketches into pieces. He forced his fingers still, hearing the elf coming down the stairs.

The elf wandered over, taking back his pad and pen, grimacing at the lack of ink at first. When his eyes met the parchment, though, the grimace turned to wide-eyed excitement. Rottgor resisted snatching the pad back. *Too late. It's out there now.* "A restaurant, eh? Fancy yourself a cook?"

"Well . . . I was before. . . ." Rottgor stumbled over his words. They all sounded stupid. "Orc tribes usually have a designated head cook called a war chef. I was that and the Champion of the Onyx-Ax way back when . . . before . . . the . . ." His words trailed off. Ruin came for the Onyx-Axes soon after, and his people now danced on the edge of extinction. "It's something I wanna try."

"Well, you've got the right person. Besides, having an affordable restaurant that's not a tavern or an inn on Famine Street? Woo boy, that'll be nice." Mohek stared over the plans. "I guess I'll get to it. I'll spare no expense on this and your living quarters. It might get a bit noisy. My boys are known for their work, not for being quiet. We'll get it done as soon as possible."

"Sounds good."

"Got a name for it?" Mohek asked.

"Not yet. . . ." Rottgor kicked his feet. "I just convinced myself to do it today."

"It's no rush. Well, at least not until opening day. Someone will help you along with it. Better than the name for my company, I hope. Mohek's Builders. What a classic. I'm too lazy to change it now. Do as I say, not as I do." Mohek shrugged. "Well, good luck and pleasure to meet ya, Mr. Rott. I trust that the Lady will pay me well."

Rottgor laughed. "You have no idea how excited she'll be."

"Lady Cleo? Excited? I'm not sure if that's a thought I wanna think about, good ser. Have a nice evening."

Mohek left, whistling happily at what Rottgor assumed was the thought of the open check that would grace his pocketbook shortly. Any promise made by Lady Cleo never faltered. *A restaurant.* He pushed away the grief and the sorrow, holding down the doubt as best he could. He hoped he would love this profession as much as Mohek loved his. He followed the builder out, locking the door behind him. Wherever the dark elf had ventured, he was long gone, mixing among the crowds clamoring through the streets. Rottgor began walking.

The day passed quietly from there. The cool evening air brought life back to him, a spring in his step. The dream clung to him still, the day already nearly passed before it had loosened its grip. The restaurant was what pushed him forward. *Rottgor . . . making a restaurant.* He shook the head. His fingers itched. How long had it been since he cooked a meal? *Do I have the skill anymore?* The thought darkened. *The only skill I have is feeding the worms.* No. Rottgor exhaled hard from his nose. *I'm not my past. I'm not my past.* Only one way to find out.

He took to the market on Famine Street. The irony of his presence there still wasn't lost on him. Rottgor moved from stall to stall. At least his senses still worked. Quality ingredients meant a quality meal. His stomach growled loudly at the thought. He hadn't eaten all day. A bad habit he knew he needed to break. His hunger didn't leave him dizzy or lightheaded, but it did make him feel weaker. He had to eat something. *Fast and easy, then. A stew of some kind? Perhaps some chicken and rice. Herbs and spices for flavor.* His old mind churned. *Keep it simple. Nothing fancy.* He bought a few carrots and some honey from a fast-speaking dwarf, a few herbs and a bag of rice from a stern, gray-skinned rhino magiian, and cuts of chicken from a sweet-talking otamo. His biceps already ached from the weight of his purchases. *Better buy some bread to go with all this and head back.*

The moons danced above him by his last stop. While most of his purchases had come from wood stalls, this last shop was set in a small stone building on a corner. A large window opened onto the street. The wonderful, unmatched scent of fresh bread wafted out of the warmly lit building. A stocky magiian woman met him at the window, her hair half pigeon feathers and her skin brown and smooth. It was said that the sign of a good baker was their apron. Hers was covered in flour and spices, and her eyes were curious and powerful. Rottgor looked up to the sign of the shop: Meutras. Above the name was a beautiful drawing of a skull-faced lizard wreathed by orange marigolds and gladioli. The name and the animal seemed to come from the southern lands, the Plains, maybe. He smiled at the thought of that. New foods were a pleasure he hadn't experienced.

"Welcome, welcome to Meutras," the woman said, her Plains accent clear and sweet. "How can I help you? I haven't seen you around these parts. Rakuel Khrysan. I'm the owner of this place. The menu is to my right, and if you have any questions or need any recommendations, I'll be here."

Rottgor stared at the immaculate menu painted on a slick wooden board. He scanned it up and down. Grains, flatbread, sourdough, and rye, even a few foreign breads from the orcish tribes and the dwarvish nobles. Rakuel knew her craft. Mouth watering, Rottgor remained frozen with indecision. She saw that and acted.

"You can't go wrong with the grain breads, a fantastic accompaniment to any meal. It's a common choice for anyone new to my shop, and it's a safe one. Safe doesn't equal boring, though. There's a reason why it's a bestseller, enough sweetness and hardiness for the common folk. How about it?"

"Sounds good enough for me." Rottgor's stomach rumbled.

"The stomach doesn't lie. I have a couple of loaves coming out of the oven. Shouldn't be more than a few minutes. Please take a seat."

He sat on a bench right beside the window. The smell of fresh bread tempted him to widen his wallet further. He brought his focus to his surroundings instead. The night had settled, stars bright above and the air cool and damp. Necropolis rose from its sleep at night, its people wandering through the streets alongside the undead and summoned. A man strolled and chatted with a massive demon servitor as though they knew each other beyond their planes of existence. A woman drank a steaming cup of tea alongside a small army of skeletons and ghouls. Children played between the gravestones, laughing and spinning. Among them was a girl who wasn't playing like the rest. She hung behind one of the gravestones, looking in his direction—or rather toward the shop.

It's her. The one from the feast.

The little magiian girl was thin, her fragility showing through her frayed, oversize purple coat. Her skin was as dark as night, her eyes the color of finely cut rubies. Her white hair was a puffy little mess, unkempt but curly and beautiful in its own right. She tiptoed barefoot behind the gravestones, among the flowers and the taller grass, like an assassin watching her prey from the shadows. Or maybe she was more of a mouse, sneaking some cheese from a trap. She crept, slipping away from the kids her age, catching Rottgor's glance across the way. A yelp escaped her young lips, one that Rottgor could hear from the other side of the street. He laughed and looked away.

Rakuel's window opened once more. "Your order's ready, hon."

Stretching his back, Rottgor returned to the window. "Do you know who that little girl hiding behind that grave is?"

Rakuel squinted toward where Rottgor pointed. "Oh, you mean Astra. The girl's a sweetheart. Kind, though rebellious. I don't know much about her. Everyone on Famine Street knows to treat the kids and the homeless to any of their leftovers. She's been a hard one. Prideful. She can be shy, depending on the person. She never takes more than she needs." Rakuel pushed the fresh loaves over to Rottgor. They were nested in a small wicker basket, covered by a cloth. A soft, warming magic rose from the fabric. "I've included some of her favorites. Would you mind carrying some over to her? I don't believe she's eaten for days . . . again."

"Sure, I can try."

"She's good with strangers, but keep in mind, if anything happens to her, Zennexus will handle you accordingly." Rakuel's eyes went dark, her smile unmoving. "I mean it. Look up."

Rottgor did so. At the city's skyline, over the tall buildings, loomed a large shadow along the outside edges. He heard the cracking of stone and smelled marble. This aether was strong.

A *gargoyle* from the Stillness. The orphanage must employ their help to protect the children when the caretakers could not. Sleepless, hungerless creatures were quite the protectors indeed. *One beckoning call, and that gargoyle would crush me.*

"All right, all right." Rottgor slipped the baker her money. "Keep the change."

"Thank you for your patronage. And . . ." She pointed at him. "Serious, be nice to her."

Rottgor agreed. No matter how safe a city was, people remained dangerous everywhere. He took his time crossing the street, softening his stance from the shoulders down. He pictured his brothers' pups, who never made it to adulthood, never forged their *kallgr* or earned their *haogu*. He approached the small girl.

"How's it going?" he said, keeping his voice higher than usual. Up close, he could see she had about nine or ten seasons behind her, the gangly phase before the teenage one. Her ruby-red eyes stared back at him. Nervous, not scared. *Good.* Rottgor extended his hand. "My name's R—" His tongue hung on his birth name, yet his mind settled on what he knew. "Rottgor. How are you doing?"

She stared up at him. Children always had this way of seeing through a person, deeper than adults ever dared. Only the luckiest kept that when they were older. "I know who you are. You're the knight on that big fancy chair I saw at the ceremony who waved at me the other day! I'm Astra." She shuffled her feet, bare heels kicking crumbled gravestones. "I haven't seen you around these parts, Mr. Rottgor, but I guess you aren't at the castle anymore, huh? Your name sounds scary. Are you new to these parts? I could show you around."

"I am," Rottgor said. He kneeled and extended his hand, everything he cradled tumbling in all directions. Astra quickly jumped to grab his falling parcels. "Sorry about that. Old hands and all."

She laughed, her giggle a sweet sound. The sudden and inexplicable urge to protect burned through him. "It's not a problem, Mr. Rottgor. Old people are clumsy, especially someone as old as you."

Rottgor stifled a laugh. "We are."

"Finally someone agrees. You old folks act like it's not the truth." She stomped her little feet.

"Here." Rottgor lowered his basket to her. "The bread lady over there asked me to give you some."

"I saw you two talking." Astra sighed. "I couldn't bear to ask her. I already took too much, and I missed dinner at the orphanage." She took a loaf and some rye bread, then shook her head. She looked him over. "You need help. How about I help you take all that home?"

"I think I got—" The bags almost slipped from his hands. Rottgor caught them at the last second, using his legs to prop his groceries back to safety. He snorted. "I suppose an extra set of hands wouldn't be bad." She wasn't an orc, yet surely she should've been bigger for her age, right? Bread alone didn't help young children grow. But here she was, offering help all the same. "How about this? You help me take this stuff home, and I'll cook you something nice and warm." His stomach growled at the thought.

"I—I can't ask you to do that," she said. "That's—uh—"

"You'd be the one helping me. You've seen how clumsy I am. You said it yourself. Old people are clumsy. I'm going to end up dropping something." Rottgor froze. *I'm a stranger, no matter how esteemed,* he told himself. Conserving trust meant life or death for those on the streets. "If you need permission, ask anyone you trust to come along, or to come check up on you. But on my honor as a knight, I will never harm you in any way."

Astra folded her bony little arms, which were drowning in her oversize coat, certainly meant for a man twice her size. After considering, she nodded. "I trust you," she said. "You're a knight, a famous one, I think. I hope to meet more knights one day, y'know, like the ones that rose up against the Worm King all those years back and helped start this city."

"I hope I can live up to that." The horrific stories behind the heroic tales weren't meant for young ears. "How about you get your permission, and we'll talk more—if you want to."

"I want to," Astra said. Confidence overcame her previous shyness. "Let me ask Mrs. Rakuel and Ser Soz. And of course, Zenny."

"Go right ahead. And *eat*. You're too small for your age."

"Oh, we're starting with *that* already. *Already*. I've known you for five minutes. Five minutes. Urgh, fine." Astra took a bite of the warm bread, then continued speaking with her mouth full. "At least I know you are a good person. Only good people point out my skin and bones."

Rottgor looked down at his recovering body. "Do I have the right to talk about skin and bones?"

"Then you need to eat, too," she scoffed. Bread in hand, Astra walked first to Rakuel's window and then to one of Necropolis's Black Dread guards manning a gate not too far away. Rakuel nodded her assent, never breaking eye contact with Rottgor. The Black Dread guard—a hulking, black-winged levia man—appraised Rottgor from his station. The darkness of his miniature scales made his skin as black as soot, contrasting with his amber-and-bronze eyes. He stroked his braided beard. Seemingly satisfied, the guard murmured something to Astra and patted her on the back. Astra returned, smiling while munching on the last heel of bread. "Ser Soz said I can go with you, but if anything happens to me, the entire Black Dread will be at your door. He told me to tell you just like that. And Zenny, I mean Zennexus"—she pointed to the sky—"will be coming along."

"Noted. On that, you have nothing to worry about. I wouldn't harm you."

Together, the two traveled down the long road. Once she warmed up, Astra was excellent company. She was a bright young girl, knowing the world and city around her better than Rottgor did on some subjects. As he listened to her chatter, it became clear to Rottgor that he had a lot of catching up to do. He was out of touch—or worse, downright ignorant. Being a Death Knight had given him a reason for such blissful obliviousness, serving one purpose. Now he was exposed, the cover torn from his shivering body. Astra held a smaller bag using both hands, talking and walking, occasionally spinning on the heel of her foot. During one such spin, Rottgor saw she carried a dagger, a simple thing of scratched-up metal and unfinished bone.

"You've had to use that?" Rottgor asked.

Astra paused. "Only a few times," she admitted. "I never hurt anyone bad. But—"

"You've had to protect yourself, I understand." A dull silence came over them. *One of the safest cities in the world, and a little girl still has to know how to use the point of a knife.* "Do you think that Necropolis is a good . . . home?"

Astra tilted her head. "I don't have much to compare it to." She laughed. "But I do. I like it here. I feel . . . connected to it. Like I belong."

"That's good. Galelin would've been proud."

"The Knight of Boiled Blood?" Astra's eyes widened.

"The very same. In a way, I think you remind me a bit of him."

Astra let out an excited giggle.

A huddled group of workers and common folk caught their attention. They gathered around, torches held high. The light from the torches formed an uneven circle around a single man, one Rottgor recognized. Even clothed in a dark robe with a hood over his head, there was no hiding his voice. Vom. The dwarf stood on a small wooden platform overlooking his much taller followers, his voice as clear as a bell in the midnight air.

"And what have they done for you?" he was saying, with the confidence of a man who clearly spoke silvered words often. "Stealing your lives, taking your homes, living where you should be living. How is that fair? They have overstayed their welcome here. Their kind, the undead and the summoned—this is not their land. Why should they know happiness, love, and comfort when they aren't capable of any of it? Why should they take *ours*?" Vom paused, catching sight of Rottgor and Astra.

He stared.

He hated.

And then he continued as though he hadn't seen them at all.

The words cut deep. Rottgor had heard them before, a dozen times, but that didn't lessen their impact. He gripped the underbelly of his bag, the divisive rhetoric continuing on and on. Rottgor hastened his step. Astra glared over her shoulder as they walked away, her stare piercing the crowd.

"Why?" she asked, after they were far enough away. "Why does he say those types of things?"

Rottgor pondered a response, for his own sake and for hers. "It's hard to say, little one. Hate is easy. I found that it's the easiest and most contagious evil. A simple drop can poison a well."

"Does that mean that being kind is hard? It doesn't seem that hard. You seem pretty good at it!"

A warm memory stirred in his slow-beating heart. The little girl with eyes of rubies, a curious heart, and a soft floral trace of aether looked up at him and reminded him of that far-off memory within the caves a long time ago. Of his brothers and sister, of his nieces and nephews, and of a good meal waiting for all of them at the end of a hard day. But Vom had soiled it all. Bitterness coated the inside of Rottgor's mouth. All the terrible things his hands had been forced to do, all the people who'd once feared the Famine Blade. Was he truly stealing away someone else's life? *Happiness, love, comfort.* Were the once-dead capable of any of that?

FIVE

Unsteadiness

Rottgor's fingers trembled over the cutting board, the knife unsteady.

These are the ugliest carrots I've ever cut. Pa would be ashamed. The diced vegetables sprawled across the bamboo block, alongside the meat of the full chicken he'd butchered as though it owed him money. He groaned. *It's chicken-and-rice porridge—it doesn't need to look fancy.* His reassurance did nothing for his nerves. The broth simmered on the old alchemy stove, bubbling in a large cauldron he'd borrowed from a neighbor. The herbs released their aromatics, mingling with the rich fragrance of the bones as the scent wafted through the room. He took his chances, sweeping the meat and the carrots into the cauldron with the flat of the knife. He poured the rice in last, and the contents coalesced into a brownish soup. "I hate it," he muttered, looking down. "I don't know why I thought this was a good idea."

"It looks fine to me!" Astra sat on a stool Rottgor had set up at the counter, swinging her little legs and watching the simmering porridge.

"A watched pot never boils," he told her.

"What do you *mean*? You're watching it. . . ." Astra puffed her cheeks.

"I'm also the cook. It doesn't apply." *Though it is taking a lot longer than I remember.* His palms were damp, cold sweat trickling down his wrist. He hadn't cooked for anyone, himself or another, in years. *One step at a time.* He stirred the porridge. "Where do you come from, Astra?" he asked. "You seem to have quite a lot of people looking out for you." Rottgor glanced out the window every now and again, seeing the form of Zennexus patrolling the premises.

"I've always lived here," she said matter-of-factly. "My ma and pa left me at an orphanage when I was young. They died soon after. My family's cursed. It got worse with every generation. My pa didn't even have a last name until he met Ma. It didn't stop the curse. I like to think that by leaving me, they were protecting me from whatever it is, or was—or whatever. Or maybe they didn't see much in me." Her voice cracked toward the end of her story, her face hardening and eyebrows furrowing. "I don't mind, though. Them being dead, I mean. They weren't the best people, from what I gather." Astra gave a big smile that flaked at the edges and broke at the eyes. There was a deeper darkness in those last words. *They weren't the best people, but she survived. She survived in ways only an orphan knows how.*

The world never seemed less cruel, no matter how much time passed. Rottgor had lived more than his share of lifetimes. The more he lived, the more that simple realization became the truth. The least he could do was to make a meal for her. *You bear your curses,* the dark voice in his head whispered, *ones that end in a shallow grave.*

"We bear our curses," he repeated aloud. Astra hung her head. No need for both of them to be sad. Rottgor stirred his wooden spoon through the now silky porridge. The sight of it dragged them both out of their stupor. The bright lights returned to those ruby eyes, a sight all cooks craved.

"All right, rules," Rottgor started. The young girl groaned at the sound of the word "rules." "You gotta promise to eat slowly. You haven't eaten enough full meals, and it'll probably upset your stomach if you eat too much at one time. Does the orphanage feed you?" She frowned. "They do, but they don't have enough, do they?" She nodded. He went to pat her head but then thought better of it. The paternal instinct was strong. *You don't know this girl—you just met. Don't get attached. And anyway, you're not worthy of attachment; it all ends in ruin. Your last family can attest to that. . . . Or they could if they weren't all dead.* He pushed those thoughts aside once more, focusing on what he had left.

Rottgor ladled the porridge into the wooden bowls he'd received from Calfe and a few neighbors, giving them equal portions for now. Next, he cracked the pepper and sprinkled the ivory sea salt atop, garnishing each bowl with some chives and garlic shavings. He set aside some of the sweeter breads for dessert, letting them absorb a bit of the honey he'd bought at the market. Astra knocked her feet together when the spoons came out. He passed her one.

"Remember what I said," Rottgor told her again. "Eat slow, and you'll get some more if you're still hungry."

She nodded. "Thank you for the meal, Mr. Rottgor."

He hadn't heard that in ages. A smile crept on his face. "Now eat up."

Rottgor watched her dunk the wooden spoon in the porridge and stare at her first bite. She frowned and tried again. It still wasn't a perfect-enough bite. She scooped up a better one this time, getting a huge chunk of chicken and a small hill of rice.

Satisfied, she opened wide and stuffed a big gulp in her mouth. She hissed for a bit, her tongue dancing from the heat.

"Ow, ow, ow, ow," she murmured through her full mouth. To her credit, she didn't go fast after that. She kept her pace steady, scooping, blowing, and chewing. Rottgor got her water to go alongside the porridge, which she drank without complaint. He soon joined her. The silence between them was delightful, one of a quiet, simple dinner.

Alas, the doubts crept in. *I could've done more.* The chicken was cooked well, but was not flavorful enough for his liking. The herbs didn't come through as much as he'd wanted, and the texture of the porridge seemed off. Rottgor mused on the recipe a bit more. Not strong enough; it didn't have the orcish punch he wanted. He took another bite. *Should've gotten butter, maybe levia soy sauce.* Another bite. *It needs oil . . . and better rice. I should've gotten the Sunland rice and the ginger.* Rottgor deflated, taking another bite. *I can't open a restaurant if this is the mediocrity I'm going to serve. Why did I think these old soldier's hands could do anything but—*

"May I have some more?" Astra asked, breaking him out of his thoughts. She held up her empty bowl. "Please?"

Rottgor gulped. "Did you like it?" he said. "Also, I told you to eat *slow.*"

"That was slow! And of course! The food at the orphanage isn't the best usually. It's not their fault. They don't have a lot of stuff there. This was amazing."

"You're saying that because you're hungry." Rottgor suppressed his smile, grabbing the bowl and getting her seconds. "It could be better, and I'm sorry about that."

"Could be better for you, maybe—doesn't mean it's bad for me," she countered. "It's a wonderful meal, Mr. Rottgor. You didn't have to do this. I appreciate the time you put into it."

Rottgor bit his lower lip, tusked mouth quivering. *She's not wrong.* He turned his attention back to his own bowl, slowly taking another bite. Somehow, it didn't taste as bad now.

They finished before the bells outside sounded the end of the first night watch. The crowds hustled, relieving those who worked at the beginning of the night and leaving it to those who worked toward the dead of it. Rottgor swept up the pot, the bowls, and the spoons, leaving Astra munching on her bread. She looked out the windows, taking in the traffic of people heading home.

She sighed. "I'm going to have to go, Mr. Rottgor. Ms. Thess doesn't like it when we come in too late."

"Ms. Thess?"

"She watches us! She's not mean or anything, a little strict about being on time, and studying, and taking too much food, and—" Astra rubbed the back of her neck, the list growing larger in her eyes. "But I get why. People are dangerous, and she doesn't want any of us getting hurt. But, I want to *do* things. Studying is boring."

"Can't say I don't agree with her." Rottgor tossed the dirty dishes into the sink. "Do you need me to walk you home?"

"No, no, you've done enough, Mr. Rottgor. I've been out later than this. Much later . . ." That little darkness, that unbreakable will to survive. *Where have I seen that before? I'm going to have to get her a better knife at least.* "Besides, I would have to lead you to the orphanage, and that will take time that I don't have. . . ."

"Are you saying I'll be in the way?" Rottgor asked.

Astra nodded, grinning. "I'm saying that you'll be in *my* way."

"That honesty, keep it. I want more of it." Rottgor straightened his shoulders. "Well, if you ever need anything to eat, come by. I'm . . . trying to make a restaurant from this old place."

"A restaurant?" Astra's eyes went wide. "I'll be happy to come! I don't have a lot of money, though."

Rottgor held down a chuckle. "Did I say that *you* have to bring money? That's what working and rich customers are for. But please do come."

"I will!" Astra said. She jumped off her stool, making no sound when her feet hit the hardwood floors. The second bell, louder than the first, rang from the outside. "Oooh—no! Bye, gotta go, Mr. Rottgor. Thanks for the meal. I'll be back, I promise! Ms. Thess is gonna kill me this time. I'm going to have to write on the board again, or do the dishes, or mop the floor, or—ahhh, I hate it. Zenny! Fly me home!" The young girl droned on and on, rushing through the front door at a blinding speed. Rottgor barely heard the ding of his own doorbell by the time she was gone. That made him crack a smile. *Be safe, little one.*

Rottgor took the rest of the night to clean, washing the dishes and wiping down the counters. His mind drifted back to the dream of a restaurant and the words of the young girl who'd crossed his path that day. He sat where she once had, staring at the midnight crowd through the window. On the sill, he placed his inkwell, quill, and parchment—he would need to get one of those dwarvish pens someday—and he let his imagination roam. The quill danced across the page, writing down line after line, as he searched deep in his memories for lost recipes and potential restaurant names. The former came easy, and he was soon filling the pages from margin to margin with ingredients and ideas for dishes. . . . The latter stumped him. As the sun began to rise, he realized he'd made no progress on names and felt that he'd been blankly staring at the parchment for hours. Rottgor gritted his teeth, ink-stained fingers rubbing the sides of his temples. *I don't know what I'm doing,* he thought, flipping through the pages. All he knew was that he wanted this dream more than anything.

He missed the smiles of friends and family satisfied from a good meal. His heart warred with whether he deserved them or not. Surely, it didn't matter. *I made a promise to Cleo to live.* He didn't know *why* he'd promised that, nor what made him do any of the things he'd chosen to do the day prior. Was this how life was supposed to be? A series of irrational choices? The past centuries all blended together, years when he'd never had to make a choice. He barely remembered anything from hundreds of years of service, besides the battles and skirmishes in the name of the Dukes and Duchesses of Necropolis . . . not to mention the years before that as a mind-trapped thrall. The uncertainty of his new life shook him. His fingers began to move the quill again on the page. The words became sketches . . . of his space at its best, filled to the brim. *I want this,* all of him decided. *More than anything I've ever wanted.*

Sleep overtook him soon after, head aloft on the windowsill.

The threads of light greeted him in the darkness of his sleep. They wove together, binding into one soft ball, warm as summer sunlight. Aether poured through him. His waking mind rustled and reached. The power continued growing. A land of trees heavy with persimmons, stalks of wheat sweeping against the wind, fish schooling under a riverbank by the caves, and wild buffaloes grazing stretched all around him as far as the eye could see. The power apexed. It didn't hurt. Quite the opposite, it comforted him. *You're freer than you know,* came a whisper in the voices of a thousand orcs. *The dead cannot control you. Not anymore.*

"It's a nice place, Rottgor. I almost envy you."

Rottgor watched his fellow Six Shadow walk through the door of his new home. Tytli looked around, quietly taking it in. She looked a little out of place, a diamond within a sea of copper coins, stunning where everything else seemed mundane. Before long, she was smiling at him with half of her face, the blackness of her corrupted side unmoving, as always. "You're planning something here. Not just a home. What is it?"

"A restaurant. Maybe." Rottgor stumbled with his words. "I always wanted it."

"Were you a cook in your past life? You . . . never told us that." Tytli clasped her hands behind her back.

"I was, I . . . always enjoyed it."

"I suppose being undead stole that from you, too. How much more can one man steal? One death wasn't enough."

"You've given more than one death in return, Tytli. It's over. You can rest."

"*You* can rest!" Tytli clutched her chest. "None of you ever understood what was stolen from me."

"Will you ever feel better, Lili? Will it ever end?" Rottgor went to put his hand on her shoulder, and she recoiled.

"You know it's not that simple," she snapped, shaking her head. "I'm happy for you, I truly am, Rott. You're allowing yourself to move on. But I can't. I still have people to protect. I made a vow. Until I'm sure—"

"You'll never *be* sure!" Rottgor roared. Tytli frowned and straightened her back. "I know *I'm* not," he whispered.

Tytli wandered over to his stack of papers and leafed through them. "You always did take Galelin's side. I don't know how he did it, how he kept smiling after all he had seen and all he had gone through. I always hated his optimism. Perhaps I envied it.

How do you look on the bright side when you can't bear to look at brightness? But here you are, following in his footsteps. In a way, I'm glad you're not following mine."

"How could I have followed any of you when I stayed where I was?" Rottgor took a seat. "I've been stuck. I've been too scared to take a step forward. I don't want to live the rest of my life a statue."

Tytli sighed. "It's better than living your life as a blade." She paused. "I didn't mean anything by asking you to join me. I needed to know where you stood, and you gave me your answer. You deserve your peace. I haven't earned mine yet."

"I don't think I deserve mine either. You know what he made me do. But we can't keep staying where we were."

Tytli, the Fallen Queen, conceded their discussion. She looked around once more as though envisioning the pieces of the restaurant that Rottgor had scribbled down. "I've heard that orc cooks are some of the best in the land. I hope that one day I'll enjoy a meal alongside you."

"My hearth is always open to you."

"And I cannot provide anything in return but my sword. If any harm comes to you or your home, I'll come running." She extended her hand and opened her palm. Bees and wasps formed at her fingertips, swarming together and forming the familiar Deathblade Soshadyel. The whiplike blade clanked against the floor, giving off the melodic buzzing of the gathered swarm. From the rafters, the flies and cicadas from his own Deathblade reached out to its sister. "We made a vow, one of many that day. Some of us are gone; others missing. But we're here. Promise me if anything goes wrong, you'll call me."

"I will."

Tytli clutched her palm once more, and the blade disappeared. She turned and headed for the door. "It was nice seeing you, Rottgor. You're looking better." Nothing more to say, the Fallen Fae Queen left his home, and left him missing the comradery he once had among the Shadows.

Rottgor awoke to the taste of sweet honeysuckle flowers.

He was sprawled against the windowsill, morning sun hot on his face. Once again, he hadn't made it upstairs after his dinner the previous night. His body ached, bones stiff. The taste in his mouth remained, pulling back memories of him and his younger brother, Jal'l, exploring the forest outside their mountain cave homes, sucking nectar from blooming flowers. Deeper still than the memory was a new power radiating from inside him. Something had changed, so deep that he couldn't recognize it. He closed his eyes, reaching toward the center of himself. Magic reached back. Rottgor recoiled, stunned, losing all balance on the stool where he'd slept, the legs slipping underneath him. He crashed to the floor.

He lay there for a moment, staring up at the lights. Pain crept up his spine and back, but there were no serious injuries. Turning on his side, Rottgor gripped his knees to his chest. His mind rushed, piecing together the parts. Did he dare reach for the magic again? His stomach lurched. The power was still there, but *Festrain*, his rune of famine and mold and corpse flies, was gone. In its place was something glorious, strong, but a bit out of his depth. He opened his eyes, stretching his fingers out. A gentle aether rose from the tips of his black nails, curling upward into the air. He had grown accustomed to the foulness of his aether, suppressing it within battle so as not to cause his allies trouble. The smell of this one was sweet—of pumpkin bread in the oven, of butter and cream, of soft cuts of roasted boar meat, and of wine. He shook, curling deeper into a ball. It was all new, terrifying, and powerful. Discovering magic and runes was for the young. And this . . . this wasn't anything he knew. *It'll pass.* He had to trust what Lady Cleo had said. His rune was waking, growing, thriving. "By the Depths, what am I afraid of?" he spoke aloud. "This is a good thing!"

Rottgor brought himself to his feet, wincing a little at his aching back. He made himself a simple breakfast of sliced toast and roasted vegetables. He'd just finished his last bite when someone knocked at the door.

"You in there, champ?" Calfe's voice called. Then, he shouted to someone else, "Mind your business, Caroll. I can yell where I want to. No, I don't care that it's early in the morning. Maybe you should get out of bed like your husband does when you aren't home. Eat ya breakfast." Rottgor opened the door. "Hey, ugly, how's it going?"

Calfe strolled in, wearing a bright-blue satin robe, fine trousers, and soft brown leather shoes. He puffed at a vaper atop a small wooden box. An aroma of hard candy tickled the nose. Rottgor stepped aside, letting in the half dwarf, who took a seat at the bar.

"Mohek's gonna be sending your stuff over today. He said something about you making a restaurant. You cook?" Calfe arched an eyebrow. "A dead man can cook?"

Rottgor gave a sloppy half grin. "I wasn't always dead."

"Well, I guess you gotta eat now, so that works out. Got a name for it yet?"

Rottgor sighed, staring at his notes still on the windowsill. "No. I don't have a name for it yet."

"Can't help with that." Calfe shook his head. "I can't even name my books."

"You're an author? What do you write?"

"I don't wanna talk about it." The half dwarf's face turned red around his nose. He gritted his teeth.

"It's lewd, isn't it?"

"I like to think I write steamy romances." Calfe crossed his arms. "But . . . you ain't wrong. Copper novels, at best. It brings in some extra gold." He gave an overdramatic cough. "Mohek thought you were kidding when you said to send the bill to Lady Cleo. She responded within hours and gave more than asked, speaking of her high hopes for you. I didn't know that you had such a benefactor."

"Hundreds of years of service makes that happen." Admitting it aloud sounded sadder than anything else. "Guess something good came from it all."

"Great way of putting my life into perspective. Got a few hundred years in me, thanks to the elf blood. Urgh. I don't wanna think about that. Put me down early." Calfe drifted over to the window by the bar. "What's this?"

"Do you do this to everyone?" Rottgor reached out, trying to snatch the parchment back from the smaller man. Calfe darted away with it in hand.

"Only to people I like."

The former knight stopped bothering after a while. The half dwarf was too fast and far too slippery. Calfe spun, landing back on the stool. He scanned through the notes. A certain warmth filled Rottgor's gut. Embarrassment? What was it about having a simple restaurant that made him as shy as sheep? The newborn rune within him stirred once more, the flavor of dried venison, brown sugar, and salt on his tongue this time. *This is gonna take some getting used to.* Calfe gave one last sweeping look over the notes, leafing through one page and back to another. By the time his business partner put the notes down, the taste had inched closer to full-out cooked meat over a spit. "Good stuff. Suggestion. Lead with your big dishes—things you're good at, a few experiments that will catch some eyes, and smaller things you know will sell to the crowds. Small menu at first, then expand."

Sounds like a plan, a better plan than I had . . . which was none. They discussed the smaller aspects of the restaurant—potential themes and colors Rottgor hadn't considered. The more Calfe talked, the more Rottgor visualized the plan. He jotted down more notes. *Home.* That was what he wished for more than anything. The obsidian caves on the edge of the continent called his name, though they were long gone—collapsed and desolate, the remaining pieces of his once-proud clan scattered. To create a place that recalled those dark stones and reconnected with his tribe's long-lost traditions—that was his goal. As they solidified the details, the soft morning sunlight gave way to the harsher rays of noon. Another knock came at the door, this one softer and more polite than Calfe's.

"Mohek's Builders," a deep voice said from the other side.

Rottgor opened the door to three large fellows. The first was an orc like him—big, brawny, and dark orange. A Bladeborn. The second was a smaller but wide-set magiian man from the north, pale-skinned and purple-bearded. The last was bigger than the other two combined, an otamo construct made of metal and looking a bit like a large furnace. Where the other two carried one piece of furniture each, the large otamo carried two large pieces on his back. The orc man, whom Rottgor assumed to be the supervisor of the trio, tipped his leather cap. "I have an order for a Mr. Rottgor."

"I'm him."

"Ah, a fellow orc. Always nice to have some orcish business. My name's Nagu. Purple beard is Erling, and the steam giant is Duff. We'll be furnishing your place." Nagu straightened his vest. "We, of Mohek's Builders, pride ourselves on quick and effective work. We'll have your stuff ready to go within the day, or we ain't the best movers in the company." In unison, the three nodded and began their work.

The movers shuffled in and out of Rottgor's home one at a time. They left every decision to him and placed each piece swiftly and with care. Duff was the strongest lifter, carrying things that required at least three or four men. Erling, the technical designer of the group, hardly spoke. But what he lacked in words, he made up for in design and flow. When Rottgor or Calfe couldn't decide on a specific placement, Erling pointed. Somehow, it worked. The day trudged on, the movers and the owners working in tandem, filling the space and the upper area with everything they needed. Rottgor was sure that he hadn't ordered *all* of this. It smelled a bit of Lady Cleo's meddling. An open paycheck from her meant she was going to put forth her opinion—whether he liked it or not. Not that he didn't need it. She ordered parts that he hadn't bothered considering. *Thanks for that, Cleo.*

By the evening, the three men had kept their promise. The once-bare area was filled, the builders' wagon now packed with the things that Rottgor no longer needed. Duff shrugged out of his metal suit to rest, revealing his true form as a slender water-elemental otamo. His suit, he explained, ran off the steam of his own body. Nagu and Erling gave the thin elemental a splashy pat on the back.

"Well, you're some of the best movers I've seen," said Rottgor.

"Best believe it," Nagu said, through panting breaths. "Only the best for our customers. Besides, I've never been *paid* that much. I couldn't let the Lady down. I wouldn't want the Ruinous Guard to take me in."

Rottgor laughed. "Believe me, if you had disappointed her, she wouldn't send the Ruinous after you." *Much worse, more than likely. The Slicksters, probably, but he doesn't need to know that.* He stepped around his furnished kitchen, smiling. "You're staying for dinner?"

"I wish we could, mate, but we still have an order on the clock." Nagu sighed. "But we'll come back."

"I guess that's good." Rottgor stroked his chin. "I gotta figure out what to serve our otamo friend here."

"Do y'all even need to eat or drink?" Calfe asked.

Duff nodded. "We need sustenance, but not in the way you need sustenance. There are ways we can trigger our 'taste buds.'" His high voice came as a bit of a surprise given the heft of his suit, but it was pleasant, like a forest creek that had somehow gained speech. "There's plenty of cookbooks for our people. If I see any, I'll send them your way."

"Same here, ser. We only want the best for you. Mr. Mohek might be an odd one, but we'll drag him along, too, once this place opens." Nagu saluted. "Well, enjoy your night, Mr. Rottgor, Mr. Calfe. If you need anything, please visit us on Blood Street. Our workshop ain't that far from here, so come on by anytime. All right, suit back up, Duff, we gotta go."

Duff dove back into his suit, filling it until the slits of his helmet oozed steam. He huffed, rolling his big, armored shoulders. "All right," he said, his voice much deeper now that he was inside his metal body, "all suited up, boss, and ready to go."

"Erling?" Nagu nodded toward the quiet man. He nodded back. "Sounds good. Good luck, sers. We'll be on our way."

The Mohek's Builders left as they had come, coordinated and

professional. Rottgor was sure now that he didn't want to work with anyone else on this building. He turned to Calfe. "Where did you find them?"

Calfe laughed. "If you have a good foundation, you tend to find people who want to see it grow. Mohek is one of my only true friends. My dad used to say, 'If you can count your friends on your hands, consider yourself lucky. Those will stick with you.'"

"Sounds a bit lonely," Rottgor mused.

"It's not," Calfe responded, somber. "The numbers don't matter. You can be surrounded by people, and not one of them may care. Don't confuse loneliness with a lack of people. One or two friends can care more than an apathetic crowd."

"I hope you'll consider me among those chosen few, then." Rottgor straightened his back. "You can stay for dinner, if you like."

"Not tonight, I'm afraid, I got a date with my lady. I already missed it once this week, and I don't want to lose my head. But, how about this? I'll come visit on opening day."

"Sounds good to me." Rottgor extended his hand. The half-dwarf businessman and professor took it without question. "See you when it opens."

"Of course. Have a nice one, Rottgor. Don't get into any trouble that I wouldn't get into."

Calfe took his leave, heading back to wherever the mysterious fellow went after his day was completed. *Home, I assume. Odd to think that.*

The building went quiet. The bustling of the night life was comforting now. He admired his home, all put together for the first time. The tables, shelves, and chairs were all made of a slick gray-and-black wood known as grim walnut, harvested from a towering tree of petrified bark from the eastern side of the continent. They'd chosen some darker rugs and tapestries from the San Isthmus—skulls, vines, and flowers woven upon black-dyed wool. That motif extended to the table covers and the tattered banners of the Onyx-Ax, showcasing an obsidian ax gripped by the midnight-black knuckles of an orc. Looking at it brought a bit of pride into Rottgor's old heart. The Champion left in him moved once more. He paced around the kitchen.

The builders had provided most of the main things he needed. A brand-new set of kitchen tools lay across the rune-forged stove. A plethora of mugs, bowls, plates, and silverware stuffed the once-empty cabinets, and large barrels were installed in the western walls by the stairs, waiting to be filled with drinks of all kinds. By far the most amazing invention was an elvish-and-dwarvish creation, a large mechanical wooden box etched with cooling ice-and-water magic meant for storing all types of perishable foods. That meant he could stock a good amount of food for eating and testing, and for the dreaded opening day. Thinking about the prospect was worse than those fleeting moments before battle. Rottgor supposed opening a restaurant was a battle, too, in its own way. And like any good warrior, Rottgor needed to prepare.

Which meant meditation, learning, and rest.

He climbed the stairs to his quarters on the second floor. Though now furnished with all the essentials, his room still didn't feel like his own. Rottgor lay on his bed. The sheathed sword hung still over the fireplace where he'd left it. The rotten smell permeated the leather, so strong that it clawed at its owner's nose. The buzzing, however, was worse. He was sure it had gotten louder, hundreds of thousands of locusts and corpse flies all crying out to him. Rottgor stared at it, stared at his past, that blade that had both terrorized and defended these very lands. He thought about how easy it had been, how effortless to obey commands—an obedient lapdog. The blade was a reminder of those centuries. When his nightmare had ended, his dream never began. That was his biggest mistake, and one he clung to even now. The horrid stench and sound kept him company for the rest of the night. But this time, something else fought back.

SIX
Old Habits

Silkmaster Kao presented him with his *haogu*, the traditional robe-like jacket of the orcish clans of the Tusken Ring. She, half Duskgrave and half Onyx-Ax, had worked on the piece with extreme care—the latter tribe was often cited in history as the originators of the tradition. The older gray orcish woman opened the jacket for him, and Rottgor pulled his arm through the first sleeve and pushed the jacket upward and around his shoulders. The feeling of the soft fabric brought memories of his old linen—now turned to dust. He straightened the two sides, looking at the embroidered symbols. The *haogu* was the canvas for the life of the orc, a constant painting of their skills and accomplishments. Kao had said nothing and asked nothing of him, yet this *haogu* spoke of a deep knowing.

The right side of the *haogu* showed his life before: a life of white printed chains and dried lilies. These were things he knew. The captivity of his own will, the deaths he'd brought, the decay that had come from his touch—those were etched in his soul. The other half spoke of a story he hadn't known. Honeysuckles lined the edges, and at the bottom a deer grazed among stalks of wheat.

Across that arm and the rest of the body was an *orken* symbol that repeated to a larger version on his back, one meaning "abundance." His throat went dry; the man in the mirror reflected a foreign image. Kao came up behind him, pressing her hands against his shoulders and adjusting the *haogu* to sit perfectly.

"The magic is strong in you, my boy," she said, in a voice with a softness rivaling that of the materials she worked on. "The moment you stepped foot in here, it washed over me. It was the warmest thing I've experienced in a long time." She straightened his thinning hair, resting the limp black threads on his shoulders. "You will recover what was yours. It's happening now, bit by bit. Trust in yourself. Let go of those chains. You've done it before."

"I know, but I keep coming back to it. Chaining my wrists and ankles."

"What's your name, child?" Never once had she asked. She'd simply taken his request for a *haogu* and let him be.

He tensed. "Rottgor."

She shook her head. "Your real name, son." She grabbed a bit of his hair on the back of his neck, tying a small orcish bone through the makeshift ponytail.

"Razgaif," he managed to say.

"Why do you hold on to the name that is not yours? Why, when it has brought you only pain?" The Silkmaster touched the side of his neck that retained the scar of the wound that had first killed him. He flinched. The pain was long gone, but still, in his mind, it gushed blood. "Why hold on to it?" she repeated.

"It's . . . my redemption."

"How is it redemption when you were given no other choice? How can you repent for a mistake that wasn't made by you?" The older woman sighed. "You may be older than me—I sense it—but you do not know life as you should." She walked away, heading back to her counter. She turned and searched him with her knowing eyes, off-white like silk cocoons. "You can cling to what you believe is your absolution all you wish. There's only one constant, and that is change. Fight it all you wish. It will not falter." She leaned on the counter. "Think about it."

"How . . . do you know so much?" Rottgor asked.

"There's much a person's aether tells." Kao waved it off. "But do not worry about that, Onyx-Ax. Do not worry at all." She giggled. "I know who you are. Do you?"

Rottgor wordlessly paid for the *haogu* and ducked out of the tent. His mind held on to the old orc's words. The new rune still gave him pause. Perhaps it would have been better if he had ridden into the distance, taking the blade and serving the land as he always had. *That would've been the easy way out.* Cleo wanted happiness for him, not a quiet retreat. *Fight for it.* His greatest fear wasn't his true death—it was following his dream.

Roaming the market now, he wasn't sure where to start. Placing orders made his plans feel too real, a silly folly. The market stalls had multiplied since the last time he'd walked the roads. Plenty of stall owners who recognized him called out his name, offering to sell everything from herbs and meat to pantry items.

By the time afternoon rolled around, he still hadn't made any clear decisions on the exact ingredients of any of the dishes in his starting menu. "I can't do this. Why did I think I can do this?" he mumbled, confidence draining from his body. Rottgor found a bench in the market that was half covered by oak leaves. He dusted them aside and sat, twiddling his thumbs. Aether pooled on his palm. "Abundance. What does that even mean to a man of death?" he said to no one. Kao had felt it the moment he'd stepped foot in her tent. The life within him soared to the surface, uncontrollable and swift as the wind.

A myriad of flavors overpowered his senses.

He wrestled his magic as best he could. The more adept mages in the market noticed, and a few warlocks from the different colleges came to his side, led by a young blonde-haired woman. The undead, with their powerful runes, were always in danger of losing control. One misstep. One horrible misstep, and they were a danger. He overcame the surging power and waved the young woman away, thanking her for her vigilance. She bowed, and she and her group melted back into the crowd. Rottgor clutched his chest, taking a long breath. His magic subsided.

"Mr. Rottgor?" A familiar voice spoke out. "It *is* you. Hi, Mr. Rottgor."

Astra appeared from a break in the crowd. She wasn't wearing her large coat, having swapped it out for a lighter cream-colored dress. Her bare feet danced across the cobbled roads, as Astra kicked up with each step. The soles of her feet were well worn with calluses from what was surely hundreds of walked miles. A child shouldn't know the pain of developing calluses as hard as leather. She danced over and sat beside him, swinging her little legs, her toes barely hitting the ground.

"Whatcha doing here?"

"Trying to buy some food for the restaurant."

"Unsuccessfully," she observed, raising a judging eyebrow.

Rottgor grumbled, "Unsuccessfully. Too many people—too many roads. I just wanna—"

"Scream, if you need to. Sometimes I need to. Ms. Thess and Zenny say screaming is good."

Rottgor let himself howl. The crowd shrank away. He did feel better.

"See? Better! Here's the plan. I can introduce you to some people to help get you started." Astra smiled at him, clearly thinking the world of him. Rottgor's urge to protect her came back tenfold. "There are people I like, and there are people I don't. We'll avoid the people I don't like. Then I won't have to kick them in the shins."

"That's a good way to live life. The not-kicking-people-in-the-shins part. Keep to that." Rottgor patted her on the shoulder.

"I can't promise that. Some people need a kick in the shins."

Rottgor rubbed his temples. "I'm not against having some guidance."

"I'm happy to help." Astra stood back up. "All right, where do you wanna go first?"

"I'm . . . lost," Rottgor grunted, crossing his arms. "I don't know where to start. It's *annoying*."

"Okay, new plan, since that one didn't work. We're going to all my favorite spots, and we'll just walk around. That's the best kind of journey, not knowing where you're going and figuring it out as you go. Follow me."

Rottgor looked up and she was gone. He could just see her cream dress disappearing into the crowd. He leaped from the bench and followed the magiian girl through the winding streets. She moved faster than a mouse mazing through a cornfield. He found a way to keep track of her after a while, watching for the white puffs of her hair. They came upon the first of Astra's favorite stands, and she quickly began to sweet-talk the vendors. They hopped from one stall to the next, ideas blossoming clearly in his head as they went. Everything came together, order after order. He started imagining full pantries, stocked with wonders. There were things he hadn't seen before, cultivated in this new age. By the time they finished their shopping, it was nearing nighttime. They had worked their way through merely a quarter of the fruitful market. But it was more than enough. Together, they sidled up to a small tea stand for a snack. Rottgor ordered himself cold milk tea flavored with coconut while Astra ordered a purple drink made of... yams? A delicacy in the Sunlands, to his knowledge.

They strolled through the street, sipping tea from the gifted wooden cups. Rottgor enjoyed the sweetness of his drink, the subtle flavor of the coconut at the back of his mouth. He hadn't had one of these in years, and hadn't remembered it being so flavorful. Had he even liked coconut when he was alive? A strange strength came over him, a spring to his step. Astra noticed and smiled, rocking back and forth on her heels. "Having fun? I am. Were you always here? In the city, I mean."

"Well, not always, but long enough for it to be the only home I fully remember."

"Then take it. I don't see why not. It's yours." The childlike simplicity of her advice shocked him. He'd held on to so much of his time as a Death Knight, and not enough of the person underneath. The wall between those two sides remained. He glanced at the sleeve of his slightly oversize *haogu*.

"It's hard. I'm so used to not being... me?"

Astra blinked and cocked her head. "You sound like you when you talk to me." She gave a cheeky grin.

"I—" He didn't have a counter to that.

"You're overthinking it. I think. Maybe. I'm not sure."

As he mused, his body suddenly stiffened. An odd feeling came over him. He knew it well. Years of protecting the Duke and the soon-to-be Duchess had made him alert to all dangers, instantly. Rottgor sniffed the air, noticing a disturbance in the breeze. He clutched the hand ax he had brought along. Not a weapon of a warrior, but a weapon fit for a merchant. The small ax, at least, made him feel like a proper orc... but he wished for a real weapon of his people for protection. His guard up, he guided Astra a little ways off the street, the feeling of an impending attack stirring in him by the second. Astra seemed startled by Rottgor's sudden change. Her mouth pursed in question. Just then, a scream tore through the streets.

The guard in Rottgor swelled. He drew his ax from his cloth sash, his body moving by muscle memory through the short streets. Never too far from Astra, but far enough to see everything around him. An undead man and woman stood pressed against a wall in an alley, and a third person held a knife that glimmered a frozen white in the moonlight. A knife of holyglass. It was an obvious robbery. Though one of the safest cities, Necropolis wasn't without its crime—and the undead and summoned were frequent targets. Some of the living thought the undead less worthy, or far too dangerous. This thinking had led to fear and hatred, which he'd seen in Vom's eyes when they'd met. Rottgor sprang into action, launching himself between the undead couple and the living bandit with the holyglass knife.

Rottgor struck out with his ax, half as swift as he'd been at his full power. The curve of the ax hit the man on his wrist, knocking the holyglass knife from his grasp. The thief yelped. Rottgor pivoted, heaving the man up by the hook of his ax and bringing him over his shoulder using sheer power. Rottgor slammed the thief to the ground, cobblestone cracking against his back. Rottgor was stunned. He shouldn't have had that amount of power, not anymore. The man groaned, still conscious. *Still have a lot of fight in him, it seems.* He turned to walk away.

A beam of holy light shot from the dagger and grazed Rottgor's cheek, burning hot. The thief staggered upward. Blood leaked from the side of his bloated lips, and his sunken eyes were reddened at the corners and blackened around the bottom lids, beneath matted and oily hair.

"Abominations," the man spat. All but a few of his teeth were missing. The pain of being tossed around didn't appear to bother him—he was a fanatic, a radical adversary of the Unwreathed and the Languished, born of the constant worry of an undead horde losing control. He had heard of these radicals before. They committed minor attacks around the city on the undead—occasionally the summoned, too, if they were foolish enough. The Black Dread managed the issue . . . but Rottgor couldn't stand by. What if they came for his home?

The man lunged at Rottgor, who kept to his feet, avoiding lethal force. The man was fast for being injured. Adrenaline? That or hate. Both were good motivators. Another beam of holy light grazed Rottgor once more. He despised how slow he was moving. The speed and power of the Death Knight augmentations were something he was used to. Now, he was weaker than an average orc without training. That was something he would need to fix. Too late now. He'd gotten himself in this mess; he had to get himself out. He rushed forward, avoiding the holyglass knife—one of the few things that could kill the undead. At least it wasn't a full-length sword, which were a pain. Rottgor slipped through the man's defense, slamming the blunt side of his ax onto the man's dominant hand. The arm crumpled and fell limp. Still, the thief fought back.

A long arc of light streamed from the swing of the holyglass knife's blade, long enough to tear through Rottgor and the couple he was protecting. He had no choice; he would have to take the brunt of the attack. Without armor, without proper defensive weapons. He wasn't sure if he was going to survive. *I was so close.* A feeling of helplessness surged through him, the bright light blinding him. He expected pain, the blazing heat tearing his undead flesh from his bones. But it never came.

Time froze. Astra stood between them. Her arms were outstretched, her face serious, thick threads of red aether swirling around her. Bones rose from the moist ground of the alleyway, reaching up around her ankles. The joints of the fingers cracked over and over again. Roses. Moist earth. Baked bread. All smells from her aether, all reaching through the veil of death and pulling life from the other side. *A necromancer.* Rottgor had seen plenty and knew hundreds. But he'd seen none like her for a long time. Her magic tingled on the surface of his mind, calling out to him in whispers. And for a moment, Rottgor felt a deep fear: the fear of being controlled.

The worst never happened.

A bone shield surrounded them, dancing around his body and the couple's, covered by a red liquid that smelled like a strange mix of blood and roses. Astra stood to the side, holding up her shaking hands. Her aether was stronger than almost anything he'd felt, Lady Cleo's magic included. The magiian girl held the holy light—the mortal enemy of necromancy—at bay. The bone shield didn't buckle, not in the slightest. A bone spear formed within one of her hands, collagen and marrow pulled from the dead world around her into a thin sharpened point. There was a darkness in her gaze, flashing within those once-innocent ruby eyes. Her new friend was in danger. *She's willing to kill for me. No. I will not let her innocence fade this early.*

Rottgor acted quickly. He moved fast and without remorse, slashing his ax across the thief's chest. The wound was far from fatal, he knew. He had killed a thousand times and knew when a blade of any kind severed mortality. The zealot fell to his knees and then onto his side, breathing but unconscious. Rottgor exhaled.

"Thank you," the couple said in unison. They were two

weaker ghouls, milk-colored and saggy-skinned. One cut from the holyglass blade and they would have been ash. The two scurried off without another word.

 Astra came to Rottgor's side. To his surprise, the ruby-red eyes were as hard as her shield. She fisted her hand and the bones collapsed, dissolving back to dust. A chill went down Rottgor's spine. He had seen plenty of necromancy before. But seeing it in one so young, teeming with power that came from instinct alone, was a humbling moment. She looked down at the wounded body. Behind the smile, behind the fun, curly white hair, was an orphan unfazed by blood and gore. And she was willing to kill. Had she before? Orphans had to do terrible things to survive. Rottgor stared at her. Nothing, no fear or panic on her face. She looked up at him with a smile. That terrified him more.

 The Black Dread soon came through the crowd, undoubtedly sent by the couple. Soz was at the head of the guards, fully suited in his gleaming black armor. He closed off the alley, two of his soldiers taking both of the entrances.

 "Another one, huh?" Soz said. "They've been popping up now and again. The Light of the Chosen, they call themselves. A small group, unhappy with their lot in the city. Feel like the living should always be above the dead. Any happiness in the afterlives of the undead means unhappiness for the living in some twisted way, as if happiness is a finite resource. It's odd, though. They normally don't have holyglass. That's expensive. We'll keep an eye out for them. . . ."

 Soz exchanged a serious glance with Astra, who shook her head.

 "Keep an eye out for our friend," he said. Rottgor wasn't quite sure which of them Soz was talking to, but they both nodded.

Soz then scooped up the man from the Light of the Chosen, tossing the criminal across his shoulder as though the thief weighed nothing. "We'll bring him to the healers and question him there. Remember, don't get into trouble. You're citizens, not heroes. I can't have regular people doing my job. Not good for the yearly evaluation. Have a good day and *stay safe*." He stressed the words. *That* was for both of them.

Soz and his guards took the culprit's body away, leaving Rottgor and Astra in silence, the splatter of blood and the dust from the bones all that remained of the scuffle. Rottgor cleaned his ax with a cloth and replaced it on the loop of his sash underneath his *haogu*. The tension in his shoulders eased away. A brief encounter. A brief moment, and then normal life snapped back into place. How odd it was, realizing that in one moment, life was on the line, and in the next, it moved on as though the danger had never happened.

"You're all right?" Rottgor asked the orphan girl. She said nothing. Not at first.

"I'm all right," she said at last, her voice even. Her aether still hung from her small body, the immense power leaking from her hands, but much softer than before. It was as red as her irises, a gentle mist smelling of sugarcane and the iron of blood yet also of the blooming of roses and spider lily blossoms. A gentler type of necromancy, this was. One that spoke to souls. But the sheer power remained unmistakable. Whatever family she had come from had power indeed. *Why does it feel so familiar?* Astra flicked her hands the way people dry them after washing, and the magic was gone. "You're not scared?"

"Of what?" Rottgor asked.

"Every person I've shown my rune to gets . . . weird. Like when they see it, they've seen something wrong."

"Here in Necropolis, where necromancers might as well grow on trees?" Rottgor crossed his arms. She didn't need to know that he saw her as different, too.

"They keep saying I'm . . . different. I don't know what that means. And not like different in a good way. Different in an 'I'm too scared to explain' kind of way. I've learned not to ask. But . . . I saw you in danger and I knew I had to help." The smile returned to her face. "I'm glad you're not scared."

"And I'm glad that *you're* not scared, but . . . Astra. Were you willing to kill that man for me?"

"I—" She looked away. "Yes. Yes, I was. I don't mind you knowing. You're my friend. We just met, but I don't want you to go away." A shadow soared above them. "Zenny's going to give me quite the talking-to, but I had to do something. I had to act."

"Astra. Don't. Your hands don't need to be bloodied. Not bloodied like mine. I didn't want to show you what I've always been." He felt the weight of his ax. "Let's head back. I'll let you rest up at my house. The restaurant. Whatever it is."

"Still haven't decided on a name?" Silence. Astra giggled. "All right, we're gonna decide today."

"That's a lot of pressure." Rottgor nervously rubbed the thinned hairs on his head.

They made it back without any further disturbance, aside from a brief panic when they realized they had dropped their newly acquired wooden teacups somewhere in the alleyway. Rottgor unlocked the door, fumbling his old key into the rusted hole. It swung open. A homey warmth struck him on the other side. He'd never understood the feeling of coming home, not truly. The castle was a place to stay, but stepping into a warm home, kicking off his boots, and hanging up his jacket—these actions brought a feeling he didn't know he'd craved. Astra followed him, eyes wandering from one place to the next, absorbing all the new things. A sense of pride made it all worth it. He took his place behind the counter, where he was most comfortable.

"It's okay, Zenny. *We're* okay," she shouted through the door. "I promise I won't do anything reckless."

"He's welcome to come in if he's worried," Rottgor offered.

"Zenny prefers watching, but he thanks you. Tight spaces are hard for him to get into." Astra laughed.

Rottgor placed his ax on its hook above the fireplace and washed his hands as thoroughly as possible. The kitchen was his space, not the space of the warrior. Quietly, he began making dinner. Astra's eyes widened as she watched him work. The pantry and the icebox weren't stocked yet, but he still had a few things to work with. He settled on a quick soup using the ingredients he had already chopped from previous meals. He made a quick broth from boiled chicken bones and herbs, thickening it with a bit of the bread he had left. Before long, the soup was done. He sipped at the warm liquid. *A little more salt.* He stirred the cauldron, adding salt a pinch at a time. The aromatics brought the soup together, infusing the leftover chicken with flavor. After a few more testing spoonfuls, he was pleased. He scooped some into bowls for the two of them.

Rottgor presented one bowl to his small friend. She took it, cupping the big bowl in her hands. *To think those small hands used so much magic not even an hour ago. Those same hands that were willing to kill for me.* He supposed his own hands had also moved on from hacking up enemies to stirring soup. Life was an unsteady thing, tottering between little moments of joy and terrible seconds of survival. He pulled two spoons from the drawer under the table and handed one to Astra. Her smile was infectious, and Rottgor wished he had it around more often. Together, they had their simple meal, one that somehow tasted better for the company.

"About that name," Astra began. Rottgor grunted. "Hey, I said that I was gonna help with it."

"Well, what I've been doing hasn't been working." He sipped at the soup, chewing on a softened parsnip. "Been hoping that something might just pop in my head."

"Ideas don't work like that, Mr. Rottgor." Astra rolled her eyes. "You gotta think about them."

"It's hard," Rottgor muttered.

Astra took a sip of the soup. "Well, got any place that you remember? Like a place you want to return to?"

He considered. All the memories of his homeland, the caves on the edge of the continent, were long faded, the years of battle since having leeched away his proudest and happiest memories from before his death. The scar on his neck burned a bit, a reminder of the grimmest memory he had left from the land of his birth. "No," he said, after a time. "Nothing great."

Astra made a soft sound at the back of her throat. She saw the sadness, no matter how well he tried to hide it. The little ones always knew. "I'm sorry."

"No. It's not your fault. I haven't . . ." His words failed him. "There's a lot I haven't healed from."

"Do we ever stop healing?" she asked, half to him and half to herself.

Wise words for one so young. How hurt are you, my friend? "I guess we don't." Rottgor finished his soup, got up, and returned to the table bearing the whole pot. He placed it between them.

"Maybe name it after a dish you're good at. . . ."

"Don't know what that is yet." Rottgor searched the catacombs of his mind once more and found only dust. He had a few dishes he needed to try, but nothing that was worth naming his first establishment after. His tusk rubbed against his upper lip. "I've written a few down, but none of them struck a chord."

"Think simpler." Astra pointed at him with her spoon. "Something catchy. Something that will get everyone, undead, summoned, and living alike. Something they could understand."

Rottgor pondered. He hadn't thought of that. Having a place not only for his heritage but where all were welcome. The city needed that. He wasn't used to the tension he could now feel within the city. Life in the castle had softened him in a way. The quiet protection he'd provided the nobles and councils numbed him. He never listened to any of the conversations, never on the level he should have. No matter how safe it was in theory, Necropolis was still a city. The citizens had their issues and their differences. To have a place for them to sit down, and a roof to shelter those conversations—that was his dream. A bit idealistic. But worthy. He straightened his back. "We're getting somewhere. I don't know where, but somewhere."

"That's the fun." Astra chewed on a chicken bone, peeling the last vestiges of meat from it. "Maybe," she said, "you can draw from a new experience. How would you say this is going?" She stretched out her hand toward the empty restaurant.

"It's going . . . great and not great." Rottgor rested his forehead on the table. "It's been a lot to deal with. I'm not used to it all. I keep wanting to run away from it all, to go back to things I know. But I also just wanna go wild and make a lot of mistakes."

"I know what you're talking about!" Astra exclaimed. "It's called a midlife crisis. Or at least that's what I think they're called. . . . One of my teachers is having one, that's what Ms. Thess said. Just doing a lot of silly things for the sake of excitement and because he's old."

"Well, I'm old and kind of dead, so that works out." Rottgor groaned. "Guess I'm going through an afterlife crisis." He laughed at the silly joke. Astra didn't. She stared, mouth agape. "What?" No reaction. She continued staring.

"There it is!" she exclaimed suddenly. She pointed, jumping up and down endlessly. "There is it! There it is!"

Rottgor stared back, furrowing his brow. "There what is?"

"The name for your restaurant, silly! The Afterlife Crisis."

SEVEN

Svadagd

Some runes were named by the person, while others came through visions or whispers from the earth, or from goddesses and gods themselves. *Svadagd* was his.

A new strength accompanied Rottgor through the weeks leading up to the opening of the Afterlife Crisis. Plenty of duties were still on his list, and no doubt things he had forgotten about. All the while, changes were happening in his own body, too. Over the days, Rottgor's body began to rebuild itself—his twiglike arms and hollow body thickened, and his hair regained its strength, allowing for the orcish braids he'd once worn, a reflection of the promise he'd made to Astra to never harm her. He ate what he could. Oddly enough, a lot of his missing teeth began sprouting from his gums—an odd feeling as an adult. Weeks later, he was already a new man, a bit more alive than dead, much like an abandoned house overrun by nature, partially collapsed but holding a certain kind of beauty and teeming with life. *Almost myself, whoever that is.*

Rottgor paced around the kitchen, watching the next batch of recipes as they cooked. Over a dozen times, he had made these recipes, his staples for the restaurant. The more he worked, the more his old skills returned. Rust fell away, leaving the gleaming tools of his natural talent shining through. But talent alone meant nothing. He worked, and *Svadagd* grew. Fresh bread, herbed lamb, stew, and pies. Then, of course, there were his persimmon cheesecakes and elderberry-and-cloudberry-crumble pudding, signature dishes from his past. He had reclaimed his weathered title of war cook, he decided, a memory of warm laughter and happiness he held in his heart. He rubbed his eyes.

The front door opened, a light ding of the bell catching his attention. Calfe strolled in. Rottgor hadn't seen the skinny elf-dwarf during the preparation for the opening, only exchanging letters back and forth during that time. Blood caked Calfe's cheeks and hands. His shaved head and face were covered in bruises, and his right eye was as black as the night sky.

"What happened here, friend?" asked Rottgor as he grabbed his first-aid kit and set it on the counter.

"Oh, this?" Calfe gave a gory grin, teeth bleeding. "Business. Vom business . . . They've been lurking around here, checking out the place. We had to have a . . . conversation about it. Nothing to worry about. You should see the other guys." He laughed as if he weren't bleeding all over the place. Calfe rummaged through the first-aid kit with the ease of a man who had done so a million times, perhaps using far-less-desirable supplies. "You sprang for the nice kit. Old Man Tallwisp always has the nice stuff."

"It concerns me," Rottgor said, returning to his dishes, "that you have first-aid preferences." *Vom business? How has he been protecting the place?*

"It's nice to know what's most effective in case of . . . *emergencies.*" There was a darkness in the way he said the word. "Again, it's no issue."

Rottgor drew a small basin of cold water and slid it toward Calfe. Washing the blood from his face with multiple handfuls of water, he began to look like himself again. The seriousness in his eyes faded the moment he bandaged the bridge of his nose. "Don't worry, I'll replenish your supplies. It's nice to have friends and investments you can depend on." His shoulders relaxed and he blinked. "What the Depths happened to you?" he asked, noticing Rottgor for the first time. "You're huge."

"Still not quite what I was in my first life," Rottgor admitted.

Calfe's eyes widened. "You were *bigger* than this?"

"Much bigger actually. I could crush men with my hands."

Calfe's bruised brow twitched. "Why did you have to put it like that?"

"Well, I was a Champion once. Had to keep my strength up." The fondness of that memory brought a smile to his face. "I feel better, unlike you, probably."

"Eh, believe me, I don't feel bad. Just tired."

"Why not stay for a while? As you can see, I have plenty on the fire." Rottgor dusted the flour off the belly of his apron, sauntering back to the myriad items cooking around him.

The lamb was finished, having been in the oven since the break of dawn. Rottgor slipped on his oven mitts and pulled the meat from the blaze. A delightful smell spread through the Afterlife, filling him with memories he forgot he had. He hadn't eaten lamb meat in centuries and barely remembered how it tasted. Rottgor felt his hand trembling from excitement. He popped a slice into his mouth, and it melted. Pride swelled in his chest like a swarm of butterflies. Wheat-gold aether swam around his feet, then rose up to his shoulders and back down his arms. He knew, then, that this was what he was meant to do.

"Try this," Rottgor said, cutting a large slice of the lamb and placing it on a plate alongside a piece of pumpkin bread and a few roasted vegetables. "It'll help with the blood loss."

"Won't say no." Calfe grabbed the plate. "Got a drink with a bit of a punch?"

"You're asking for a *drink*? It's not even noon." Rottgor shook his head but poured his friend a heaping dwarvish ale he'd procured from a brewery on the other side of town. The orange-brown liquid punched the senses with its hops-infused fist, then caressed them with tangerine and cinnamon. The alcohol did nothing for Rottgor, but it tasted wonderful. He handed Calfe the tankard, which the elf-dwarf took graciously. The moment of truth—the first bite that all cooks and chefs feared. When Calfe's fork pierced its prey, he seemed noticeably surprised by its softness. Ceremoniously, he started his meal.

Calfe said nothing, only ate. Bit by bit, he tore through the lamb, the vegetables, and the soft, orange pumpkin bread within minutes. The ale came last. He chugged the tankard in true dwarvish style. Life itself rushed into those swollen and flushed cheeks, somehow easing his whole demeanor in mere moments. The smile on Calfe's face was all that Rottgor wanted.

"I don't give a lot of compliments." Calfe leaned back, patting his stomach with one hand and pushing the plate back with the other. A satisfying burp escaped his mouth. "But that was a bloody good meal. What did you do? I feel great."

"Uh . . ." Rottgor ran his fingers across the lines of his palms. "I cooked like I always have."

"I felt it when you were plating this food. There's something strong in you, a gift. I . . ." Calfe collected his thoughts. "It's something I haven't experienced. You said you're going through changes. I mean, I see it." He gestured up and down. "Maybe you can get someone to help you understand your rune a bit better."

Calfe was right. The sudden changes to his body needed addressing. It wasn't unusual for food to hold magical properties. Pretty much everything held magic, from animals to plants to clothes to food and drink. But he hadn't expected such a power within him. His big hands trembled so much he almost forgot the rest of the food. He quickly turned away. He didn't want Calfe to see the warm tears in his eyes. *Famine and rot were all I knew. Poisoned blood from a venomous blade, salted earth from the soles of my feet and the palms of these hands. Flies. So many flies. Life and abundance are things I don't understand.* He pulled the crumbles out of the oven, and warmth permeated his cold body.

"Can you do me a favor?" Rottgor asked, now that he had gathered his courage and faced his friend once more. "Look after the place for me. I'm heading up to see the Lady about this rune."

"Lady Cleo?" Calfe arched an eyebrow. "I don't envy that."

"She's not bad. Ambitious and educated, but not bad." Rottgor pulled off his flour-stained apron and hung it on the hook above the cabinet. "Scary, yes," he admitted after a while. "Very scary."

"All right, I don't have anything better to do . . . today. I should lie low anyway. Y'know, for safety." The mousy half grin returned, still a little pink from blood. Calfe laced his fingers together. "Don't worry about it. Your home is safe with me."

"You're not who I'm worried about. I'm worried about the other guy."

The two men laughed.

Lady Cleo took his audience within her wing of the Blackspear Château. He was wearing some of his better clothes: a black silk doublet, fine brown pants, leather boots, and a half cloak featuring a carrion crow holding a scythe, signifying his former status as one of the Death Knights of the Realm. Two of her guards, the Slicksters, met him at the door. What people thought of the Ruinous Guard was the reputation the Slicksters should've had. They were the cold, unfeeling guards of the heir apparent, protecting them at all costs. They wore masks of iron, with a weeping trail of green paint, and robes of midnight and moss, secured by a silver clasp in the shape of a death slug, from which they'd gotten their name. The two guards gave a reverential nod, an unusual departure from their typical statuesque demeanor.

Rottgor entered Red Willowhall, the wing of the Château that served as the heir's abode within the castle. There, he'd watched Lady Cleo mature through the years, developing into the witty, clever, and dangerous woman they all knew—and either adored or feared. From those times, he knew Willowhall better than most. The Slicksters bothered him little, though their knives and shortswords remained in sight at all times. Rottgor began moving through the twisting hallways, passing countless rooms, under grand archways, and between the tall, twisted pillars. Sunlight poured in from the stained glass windows, splashing the white marble in a storm of red petals. He kept to his path, heading toward where he knew she would be at that time of day: the gardens.

He took one final turn, leaving the hall's coolness, and headed toward the palace's namesake. The rays of the setting sun streamed over the tips of the towers and rested on the lanes of willow trees below. A path of spotty stones snaked, splitting three ways. The middle path led directly upward and to another part of Willowhall. The one to the right was a dead end, leading to the fish pond, and the one to the left—where he was headed— ended at a private sitting area meant for the current Lord or Lady to take in their most treasured guests. Under the weeping leaves of one of the largest willow trees was Lady Cleo.

"Thank you for your input, Baroness." The Duchess ended her conversation at the sound of his footsteps, a bright-red ball of fire disappearing. She turned to Rottgor.

"I'm glad you can join me this evening. I was finishing a conversation with Baroness Yavari, my other dear friend. She has a few hundred centuries of rune studies of mortals, more than I do, and I needed her advice. Please, sit." Lady Cleo offered him a chair facing her. He took it without question. Contacting a millennium-old demon, the Progeny of Pain and Baroness of the Burnt Rooms, for a chat and some counsel was quite the Duchess's move.

"Now . . . ," Lady Cleo said, taking him in. She plucked one of the fig cakes from the table between them. "I've never seen someone adapt to the shaping so . . . well. Neither has Yavari, from what she told me." Rottgor looked away. "I'm serious, Rott, you look amazing. It's only been a short time. I hope to see it continue."

Rottgor grumbled in embarrassment. "About that . . . my rune?"

"*Festrain*?" Lady Cleo asked.

"Not anymore," Rottgor started. "Does the shaping . . . change runes? I don't know what I'm asking."

Lady Cleo waved her hand. "You don't have to know. I've figured it out."

"Rude."

"Direct. Do you want an answer or not?"

"Continue, milady."

Lady Cleo poured herself some strawberry wine from a carafe, offering Rottgor a silver goblet. He took it, tasting it for the first time after seeing it offered to hundreds of guests from this world and others. Sweet, light, and fragrant. What came next was far less pleasant. Lady Cleo heaved a giant, fleshy tome onto the table. Rottgor groaned. *A blood tome.* The warlocks often complained about their first run-ins with the ancient artifacts. The brown book thrashed on the table, already snapping its teeth through its binding, a reddish-purple tongue lolling from underneath its lock. Rottgor stared at the book and cocked his head.

"Why?"

"You were a Death Knight. A little pain isn't going to end your world," Lady Cleo said, annoyed.

"I didn't have to worry about stubbing my toe for hundreds of years. Imagine how it felt when I woke up one morning and *that* happened. Day almost ruined."

She bit her lip. "That's fair. Sorry for your loss. Now open the tome."

Rottgor realized that the wine was the offering, and this was the price. Sighing, he flung the leather strap open. The blood tome bounced across the table, thrashing and drooling. It was oddly almost cute, wandering around the table, its thuds slamming little dents in the wood.

"Still," Lady Cleo commanded. The book obeyed. "Open up." Again, it listened, sitting on its spine like a dog would. It opened its mouth. Gods, it had so many teeth. Rottgor groaned again. "Now, put your hand on the page." Rottgor puffed his cheeks. She rolled her eyes. "I can't believe you went through several wars."

"Weapons are different. War is different."

"They are both pointy." Lady Cleo grabbed him by the wrist and slammed his palm on the page. Rottgor roared. The tome slammed shut.

It didn't take as much blood as he'd thought. The book opened back up within a second, leaving the page stained a dark reddish black. Seeing his blood brought Rottgor a bit of comfort in a weird orcish way, its color now a bit closer to its living hue than the stilled liquid of the undead. What came out on the other side, however, shocked him. The blood tome spat the page out, the creature coughing and shutting itself. The torn parchment glowed green and gold, his aether filling the page and then spilling outward to the world around them. Honeysuckles, persimmons, smoked fish, and baked piecrust hung within an emerald smoke.

Lady Cleo gasped. "An Abundance rune . . . They—wow."

"What does that mean?" Rottgor muttered.

"I'm going to have to tell my colleagues. They are so rare." Lady Cleo smiled, the excitement of an academic breaking through her usual stoic demeanor. "You must tell me what it does. You have to learn more. This is yours; this is the orc behind the Death Knight." She shook off her excitement. "I apologize. I've . . . only heard about runes like this in study. Not a lot of life runes around here, I'm afraid. Anyway, before I have you kidnapped and taken to the College for study, how is the restaurant?"

Rottgor rubbed at his hand, the pricks already healing. "You mean the restaurant that you paid for? That one?"

Lady Cleo laughed, getting the rise she wanted out of him. "Why half-step when you can leap? I promised that I'd support you as long as you put battle behind you, and you did. I need to know everything. Where is this restaurant? What's the menu? What type of cuisine is going to be served?"

"It's the Afterlife Crisis Restaurant on Famine Street. You're welcome to come when it opens."

"Oh, that's *implied*, sweetheart, but I don't want to hamper your success or facilitate your failure in the first weeks by showing up and scaring away your customers." Lady Cleo hid her sadness between sips of her goblet. She was right, of course. The publicity that came with her name was a tightrope, one she didn't wish for him to walk. Besides, she wanted it to be his success, not the pandering of people who wanted her favor. Then there were her enemies.... "I do expect to be treated at one point or another, however."

"Of course," Rottgor said, surprised at his confidence on the matter. The answer pleased her.

"One more thing," Lady Cleo said. "I've heard that you've acquired a bit of a helper. A girl."

"Yeah, her name's Astra. She's taken a bit of a shine to me, it seems."

Lady Cleo made a soft sound. "Look after her." More words flashed across her eyes, not making it to her lips. "I trust you can do that. It's not an order, nor a promise—a simple request."

"She's a good kid. I can do that." Rottgor stood and bowed. "I must go, Your Grace. I still have quite a lot of business to take care of."

The redness of the setting sun fell across Lady Cleo's face, shadows harsh around her brow. She brought her glass of strawberry wine to her lips. "One thing I want to make clear," the soon-to-be Duchess of Death said to her former knight. "I won't accept failure at all. And next time, dress more comfortably. I want a friend, not a former knight, to visit me. You know better than that."

Rottgor returned to the Afterlife Crisis to see a freshly painted "Help Wanted" sign, courtesy of Calfe, and a newly washed door. Rottgor shouldered into the restaurant to see the two scoundrels at work. Calfe and Astra leafed through the parchments before them, one at a time.

"This one didn't even put the right date down," Astra said, frowning, her face unusually serious. "And they expect a job?" She placed it aside in what Rottgor assumed was the reject pile.

"Take your time, people."

"I guess this one's better." Calfe groaned. "Relevant job experience. We can teach him, but he misspelled every other word. I get it. Spelling's hard. But ask someone for help." Another application put aside.

"I like this one. She has the experience." Astra handed him the paper.

Calfe glanced over it, taking a long drag from his dwarvish smokebox. "She also expects her weight in gold for payment. We said good pay, not a small fortune."

"She cares! That's what matters!" Astra shrugged. Calfe thought for a moment, puffing rings of smoke.

"All right, we'll consider her. Having someone with that experience is good, and she deserves a little extra pay if she can step up." Calfe put the application in a separate pile.

Rottgor slumped into the large chair next to the fireplace. "You two have that handled, it seems." The business aspects bored him to tears. He knew the principles of running a business, of course. With hundreds of years of life experience, he'd picked up this and that from the lords he'd served—specifically Duke Jamis, a former jewel merchant before he'd taken the throne. But that didn't mean he'd developed a taste for it. His heart was in the cooking, and everything else was a mere necessity toward the end goal. He looked around, seeing the empty tables, the tapestries of his lost clan, the countless vacant shelves awaiting trophies from his hunts. He needed this. He craved it. *A little longer, just a little longer.* He leaned his head back, closing his eyes.

"No ser," Calfe said, stirring him awake, "this is *your* restaurant. You're gonna have to live with your staff for as long as your doors are open."

Rottgor groaned.

"Stop being a baby," Astra told him, easily chastising a man centuries older than she was. "It can't be *that* bad."

In comparison, most things weren't as bad as dying. He conceded.

Getting up from the comfort of his plush chair, he joined them at the table. They had organized the potential employees into three job categories: servers, assistant cooks, and cleaners. He would rather have a smaller staff of close-knit employees than a large staff of unreliable ones. The fear of failure struck him once more. *Look at you,* the voice of the Worm said, *can't even make decisions on your own. It's okay. You're not built for it. Your knees are meant for bowing, your hands for salutes. Serve. Bend. Break.* A feeling of a thousand maggots curled up his spine.

No.

Rottgor steeled himself against the doubt wriggling its way into his mind. He inhaled. The cool feeling of air circulated through his rejuvenated lungs. The aether came rushing back again. *Svadagd* fought back. It cut through the fog of his mind. His eyes ran across applicant after applicant. As his courage settled, the taste of his aether strengthened, this time piping-hot beef smothered in gravy. A calm came over him. *Never doubt yourself, my child.* He didn't recognize the voice but remembered it all the same. His tiredness slipped away, and in its place, he felt a fiery determination. The stack of documents was no longer that daunting task.

He listened to the surprisingly professional back-and-forth

between Calfe and a girl perhaps shy of a decade. Astra knew things. The schooling of orphans in Necropolis was a serious business to the Crowsilks. Duke Jamis had lost his parents when he was young, long before his Dukedom, and ages before his Lichdom. He made sure any orphaned child received a fine education, and it came through clear as day with Astra's wit and cleverness.

Rottgor joined Astra and Calfe in their constant discussion, the middle ground between the hard and nonsensical Calfe and the optimistic yet practical Astra. A few hours passed and they conquered the task. They shook hands after their long duel, an odd friendship forged from rounds of reasonable debate. Rottgor's respect for them grew.

Rottgor gave one more hard look over the candidates they would interview. People of all kinds: mortals, undead, and those traveling between the planes. *A good mix,* he decided, *the foundation of this city.* Just like the black stone, worn cobble, and graves it was built upon. He took a deep breath. *Seven potential employees.* It appeared to be enough for a starting crew.

"Thanks, both of you," Rottgor said.

Astra gave that childlike smile Rottgor yearned to protect. "It's no problem. You fed us."

Rottgor looked over to the kitchen. They'd done their work. His morning experiments were almost gone, and the rest had been put aside in the dwarvish icebox. The cook's pride hit him hard. The *orken* word *siefu mak* came to mind—"chef's stomach," or more loosely translated in *bridge* as "pride of the filled belly." It was the ultimate goal of any *siefu* of an orc tribe. He hadn't felt it in years. It reminded him who he was. "I'm pleased," he said to the both of them. "It's better to have other people enjoy your meals than to eat it alone. Take whatever you like home with you.

I cannot eat this all." Truthfully, he could. However, that was not his way.

"I wasn't going to ask . . . but my wife and kid wouldn't mind me bringing some food home."

"Wife and *kid?*" Rottgor arched an eyebrow.

"Wife and kid. One kid. For now . . . Another one's on the way. . . . Don't look so surprised. Goddess. I'm not *that* bad." Calfe rolled his eyes.

"You're just a little . . . abrasive is all," Astra said, already building her plate. Rottgor eyed the vegetables pointedly. The young girl sighed, defeated. "Somehow you're worse than my teacher." She scooped some vegetables onto her plate.

"Good. Y'all be safe on your way home. There's some dangerous people around."

"I'll walk her home. It's on the way."

With the time the two had spent together working at the restaurant, they had bonded as friends. Given Calfe's bloody entrance this morning, Rottgor trusted him to take care of Astra. The comfort brought a smile to his face. "Both of you, stay outta trouble. Keep to the main roads. It's late."

"It's not my first time on the streets of Necropolis." Calfe looked at Astra. *A parent's look.* She looked away. "*You* should be home by now."

Defeated twice, Astra held up her plate, ready to go. Calfe took his own.

"Check behind the counter," Astra called as she walked out. "I left you some presents. Okay, night!"

The two left without another word, the satisfying ding of the bell ushering his guests away.

Rottgor did as he was told. He peeked around the back of the counter and saw two large chalkboards. One was the menu written in a flawless print of black-and-white paint. A small tear formed at the corner of his eye. *You didn't have to do that.* The weight of it all rose from his heavy shoulders. He hung the sign above the counter, the moonlight and starlight catching the words in the dark, pride consuming his every thought. *That girl,* he thought.

The second board stole away the little breath he had left. He stared, his throat dry. The restaurant sign was a thing of dreams. The back was painted with a gold moon and stars. On the front, Astra had taken his vision to life, seeing it through the lens of a young girl, and made it a wonder. Her studies of the Onyx-Axes were clear. In the drawing, she'd depicted his fabled black-bladed Champion's ax dug blade first in a plot of dark dirt—a grave. A large hand resembling his own tore through the grave, glowing the faint yellow of his new rune. The restaurant's name topped the image. This time, Astra's paint strokes were as harsh and beautiful as the dance of a sword, with perfect lettering from the top word to the bottom in the same gold as the moon on the back. He held it up. The painted moon somehow glowed like its real-life counterpart. The Afterlife Crisis. The sign in his hands made his dreams feel real. He laughed, losing his ridiculous battle to keep the tears at bay. He continued to hold the sign, the spirits of thousands of his lost clan cheering within his soul. Rottgor prayed for his own family and thanked his new one.

One thing bothered him. The washed door. *What happened while I was away?*

"Astra. Why was the door washed yesterday?" Rottgor asked in their brief time together the next morning as he practiced a few recipes. That day, it was cranberry-and-orange scones. He'd failed miserably on the first batch.

The young girl didn't answer at first. Whatever had happened, it seemed to bother her more than she cared to admit. "They were painting mean things on your door," she said at last, deflating. "I hoped that you wouldn't notice."

They? Vom.

Rottgor gave a long sigh through his nose. This wasn't out of the ordinary. The hate from the living for the undead was contagious, and all it took was one in the group. And then, like wildfire, those feelings spread and burned everything around until nothing remained. "What did it say?"

"Nothing you needed to see, just more bad things about the undead. They saw something new happening here and weren't . . . happy about it. Some people say nasty things about other people. I don't like it when they do that." Astra gave herself a tight hug. Her anger came through once more. Children always came to this realization, one day or another, sooner rather than later. That cruel moment when they started seeing not just the good in people but also the worst they had to offer. "Why do people have to be mean to each other? It doesn't make sense. Don't they also want a happier world to live in? I couldn't bear to see the world like that. It hurt to read. It hurt a lot."

Rottgor frowned, wiping his hands clean of flour, butter, and eggs on his bright-green striped apron. Whatever words they'd smeared on the door, it hadn't gone away with a fresh wash. *She wanted to protect* me. Warmth gathered in his cheeks. Embarrassment? Pride? *I'm a grown orc who has lived centuries, and this girl barely touching ten summers wants to protect me.* He didn't know how to react. Flattered? Yes, he decided. She had done this twice already. But why? What did he do to deserve such a kindness? Such loyalty. A fear settled in his gut, that he would be the one to push her toward whatever darkness she held at bay. And darkness was there. He saw it in every breath she took, no matter her good intentions. One didn't step on the streets as an orphan and experience joy alone. Little kids deserved their childhood. He knew that better than anyone. "Astra," he repeated, "you don't have to prove yourself to me. You're my friend."

"I know," she whimpered. "But . . . I don't have a lot of them."

"I don't see why not."

Astra stared at her feet, kicking a single leg. "People find me scary."

"Well, I know all about being scary to other people." Rottgor rubbed the back of his head. "What they think doesn't matter as long as you don't lose yourself. You're much too young for that."

"And you deserve more than how you're treated." Astra's little face scrunched. "You're doing amazing. *This. All of this. It's amazing.* I want to see it full of people. I want to eat here. I want to see your sadness disappear. And I'm starting to see you like a da—" She pressed her hand over her mouth.

"Like a what?" Rottgor cocked his head.

"Never mind. Never mind. Never mind. That was stupid. I'm stupid." Astra turned on her heels and sprinted to the door. "Stupid Astra. Why would you assume that? Why would you *say* that?" Rottgor reached to her, but she was already gone, fleeing through the door and pulling it closed behind her. The subsequent bang rippled through the air. Rottgor clenched his teeth, staring at the closed door and empty restaurant. *What happened there?*

"At least you could've stayed for the scones." Rottgor sighed, wiping his hands on his apron once more. "I'll save her some."

"No one asked you to come here," Rottgor said, not looking up.

"Oh, I can't visit?"

The door of the Afterlife Crisis stood wide open, the night air whistling through. A man in silver stood in the doorway, his gaze sweeping across the restaurant floor. Vom strolled in, stroking at his long black beard, a crooked smile on his face. He readjusted the rings on his fingers and closed the door behind him, still smiling.

"We're closed."

"Oh, I didn't notice." Vom twirled a rusty golden key around his finger. "I just happened upon this spare and was wondering where it went. This was the first place I thought of. Silly me. As a gesture of good faith, I'm giving it to you."

"After you defaced my property? I'm not blind, Vom. I see that you hate me."

"You make it sound so personal. And that wasn't *me*. I have zealous followers. I cannot be blamed if they took my word vigorously. The curse of being such a good speaker—sometimes people take your words and dash off down the road with them. But . . . my words stand, I'm afraid. I promised not to have another undead tenant after the last. What do the dead need with a roof over their heads anyway?"

"We didn't ask for this," Rottgor said softly, his anger building. "Most of us are trying. We were brought from death and thrown into this world. Some of us lived hundreds of years here, trying our best, and living the rest of our existences the best way we know how. How are we to blame when the living *brought us here* in the first place?"

Vom slammed the key onto the counter. "You were meant to serve."

"I'm *serving* our people."

"You know what I mean, you insipid pile of worms. You have no value. Our land is meant for the living. You are a tool. We pick you up, then when we're done, we put you back in the cabinet where you belong and forget about you until we need another bolt for a creaky door. Nothing more. Play pretend all you want."

"Pretend? Pretend!" Rottgor leaped up and soared over the counter in a single hop, landing on the other side. The floor quaked beneath his weight. "I've spent hundreds of years working to build this city from the ground up, protecting this city and *never* living a moment in it. This is the first time I've ever felt something other than the crushing weight of responsibility. This is the first time, my first chance, to get to be here in the present. And you . . . your blatant ignorance astounds me, so let me define 'insipid' for you."

Rottgor closed the gap between them, standing over the dwarf as a towering beast of an orc. Vom had forgotten what he was, it seemed. The dwarf's legs trembled. Rottgor stomped even closer still, his feet crushing the man's toes, even in their thick boots. Spittle dripped from Rottgor's lips and down his beard as he growled.

"It's something flavorless and bland, and something as flavorless and bland as you doesn't belong in my restaurant. *Get out.*"

Vom bit his quivering lower lip. He shrank back in his billowing silver robe, wringing his hands. He had a weapon, a gold-hilted short blade meant for self-defense.

But he didn't try for that. Instead, his fingers twitched a spell. Rottgor looked at his hand. "Don't do that," he warned. The magic dissolved in an instant. "I don't want to see your face around here again. And if I find you or any of your followers defacing my property, I won't need a weapon. Understand?" Vom stepped back, a noticeable limp on his injured foot.

"I understand," Vom muttered. All the bravado and courage were gone at the sight of the half-dead orcish chef who would smash him as easily as he could a walnut. Red-faced, the merchant-landlord grabbed the hem of his robe and scurried off, flinging the door open and slamming it closed before the giant orc could change his mind. Rottgor swore he heard Vom's mutterings of revenge long after he was gone.

Rottgor picked up the key, his jaw tight. Whatever Vom had whispered, it didn't matter. For now, the Afterlife Crisis was his.

EIGHT

Recruitment

The five employees (and six little helpers) sat in a ring within his study, an odd group of choices but a confident bunch—an undead dwarf, a fae fox from the Glimmer Glade Veil with her six animal companions, an orc-vampire, a demonkin from the Burnt Rooms, and a patchwork abomination. It sounded a bit like the beginning of a joke. To Rottgor's surprise, none of them seemed as nervous as he was, tapping his large foot endlessly underneath the table. They waited for his words. Little did they know he was still searching for them and probably would be for this entire orientation. The undead dwarf puffing at his pipe was the only one who noticed.

After years of being among some of the most stoic guards in the empire, it came as a pleasant change to have more relaxed colleagues. They all were gathered within his study for the orientation. A heatless gold flame brightened the room from the fireplace, the aroma from its magic matching the smell of pumpkins, nutmeg, and cinnamon. Food, drinks, and notes were sprawled on the circular hardwood table. Sitting on the tall brown chairs, the employees studied and talked among each other. Rottgor nursed his tankard, a brew brought in by one of them crafted for the undead and tasting of both apple and orange blossoms—otherworldly. The warm buzzing tingled through his head and body, so foreign and pleasant that he almost didn't recognize it.

"Well, I see everything seems to be in order," said a tall, dark-skinned magiian fae woman named Bao Summersweet, or rather affectionately called Bao Su, reading over the notes provided. She was a beautiful woman, warm-skinned from the Sunlands yet ethereal in a way that must've been from her father's land of the Glimmer Glade Veil. She wore the robe of the Sunlands, printed much the same way Rottgor's *haogu* was, but with tea leaves, grapes, and fanlike symbols. Her three foxtails swooshed behind her, and her fox ears stood tall amid her chestnut-brown hair. "It appears we have a lot to learn." She pressed her fan against her lips. "Nothing my little creatures and I can't handle, of course." Gathered around her in their handmade aprons, two birds, two rabbits, and two raccoon bears all gave little nods.

Rottgor coughed, masking the uncertainty in his chest. He put on his best boss face, suppressing the pesky emotions. He reclined in his chair, lacing his fingers together. "The grand opening will be happening in a week. I wanted to give us a bit of time to get to know one another, and see what you are capable of." He took a long draw from his tankard, his chest inflating by the second. He rolled his shoulders. "From what I understand, we need to get the word out long before the doors open. We need to draw people in."

"I'm quite the promoter," Clyth the Forever said, with a quick bow. A resident of the realm of the Burnt Rooms, he had red skin, a long and forked tail, and dark wings, but he possessed the smooth demeanor of a man who walked this realm frequently. A blue hue caught in the normal demonic yellow tinge of his eyes.

Rottgor was sure Lady Cleo had sent him their way. He didn't have proof, however. Clyth smiled in his charming way, somehow making his sharp teeth look inviting. "I've already had flyers printed, but having free items will draw the crowds. Nothing too expensive, but something intense, iconic. No free alcohol. We're a restaurant, not a tavern, so making that distinction is important at opening."

"I see your point," Bao said. "We have to establish it early as a nice restaurant. But not too nice. Those places are dreadful. I'd rather lose another tail than work somewhere like that."

Flynn Stillsun winced at that. The skinny undead dwarf gritted his teeth, chewing hard at the stalk of wheat between his teeth. He was a former soldier, not unlike Rottgor, raised from the dead in his peaceful village to fight a war that hadn't been his. Underneath his shock of messy reddish-brown hair, his eyes glowed with a hard intensity. He was to be the assistant cook.

"You're not wrong," Flynn said, his voice deep. "I've worked for restaurants like that, too. I came here to make good food, not that fancy mess. The moment you ask me to make one of those one-bite plates, I'm going to break all your windows and jump out."

"Noted," Rottgor said.

Clyth's gloved hands tapped at the table, gathering their attention once more. "As I was saying. We need something worth giving away. Something that will draw the crowds in. I suggest a portable dish. That will draw the working class in, which seems to be the crowd you're fishing for."

"Free samples, are you sure that's wise?" Rottgor arched an eyebrow.

Clyth wagged his finger. "Getting people into the door is just as important as making the sale."

"Huh." Flynn rubbed his beard, sitting upright for the first time. He stared at Rottgor with a knowing look. Rottgor considered handheld, portable snacks that might hit the spot. *A pastry of some kind? A pie?* He cocked his head at Flynn, who nodded.

Bao frowned. "Please speak with your mouths. Stop doing that."

Flynn grinned. "Doing what?"

"I have no clue what you're talking about," Rottgor agreed.

Bao rolled her eyes. "Speak up like proper normal people. You can't even speak with your minds like I can, and yet you know stuff about each other. It's creepy. But please continue, Clyth. Your plan sounds wonderful."

Clyth gave a short bow. "As you wish, my lady. Now, to promote the place, I would normally suggest using the rather illustrious career of our dear owner, but he has made it clear that he doesn't want to do that. It's his retirement, and using anything from his past will be a disservice to what he has built here. So, instead, I'm going to suggest we make friends with the fellow stallkeepers and restaurants in the area. Knowing people is more than half of success. All of us should make an effort to spread the word at any job or establishment we are currently working at."

The young orc-vampire at the table grumbled. Lord Waldruk Nightswallow. He was a midnight-black half orc, born from the union between a vampire of the Nightswallow coven and a high warrior of the Onyx-Ax clan. His red eyes drooped. Yawning, he revealed both fangs and tusks. He swept back his blond hair and rubbed at his handlebar mustache. *Calfe, I hope you know what you're doing with this one.*

"Is there a problem, my dear?" Clyth asked, adjusting his glasses. "I can repeat myself if you missed something."

Waldruk curled his lips. A glitter of anger came upon the

demon, a soft fury. Similar expressions spread around the room. Rottgor shook his head, then squared his shoulders, straightened his spine, and relaxed his core. His size filled the chair. The corpse he'd been when he walked out of that black armor was long gone. The darkness of his original coal-black skin now overtook the gray patches, reminding him of the Champion he'd once been. The fledgling vampire, however, didn't budge. Rottgor furrowed his brow, remembering his time as Commander.

"You're welcome to leave," he said, a hint of a threat on his lips. "I don't want my time wasted, and neither does anyone else. I hired you out of respect for your coven, as well as your grandmother Kao. I *expected* a Nightswallow and a proud orc. A gifted man who would take this job seriously. Not a boy."

That clearly stung. Rottgor saw it on the man's face.

"Respect the little things," Rottgor told him. The saying shook him further. Professor Kloss Nightswallow, one of Lady Cleo's instructors and one of Waldruk's fathers, often said those words—a personal motto of his. "Now, listen to Rib-Digger."

The last employee, Rib-Digger, nodded his bulbous head, raising his big eyes from the notes and books he had spread before him. The ghoulish creature of quilted purple flesh, hooks, and meat gave a soft, warm smile of broken yellow teeth. Patchworks—undead made with one mind but a body of many broken, dismembered parts, mostly from other family members—were ancient, now forbidden. The few that remained lived peaceful existences after years of abuse from their Fleshmeisters. Rib-Digger was one such patchwork, one of the few individuals in the city older than Rottgor himself. Strangely soft and knowing, Rib-Digger had the look of a great-grandfather caught in the body of a weapon far past its prime, long strands of lifeless brown hair on his head, and a neat beard covering his bulbous and flayed chin. The patchwork man pulled his suspenders over his giant belly and smiled, the two large teeth he had left managing a hopeful but stern expression. He motioned to Waldruk and spoke with a strained voice, no louder than a rustle of leaves.

"Follow. Need help. No help, balance ledgers instead."

Bao gave an inappropriately timed laugh. "Sorry, I found that funny."

The room returned to quietness. Clyth readjusted his glasses and fixed the ruffles of his loosened collar. "Well, that solved that. Thanks for taking charge. I was getting quite warm at the blatant disrespect." He scooped up the kettle with his tail and poured the fragrant fireblossom tea into a well-used porcelain cup. He sipped. "Let's get on to the rest of it, shall we?"

They continued planning. As they spoke, Rottgor felt the nerves rising in his throat. *It's real. It's becoming real.* The little orc pup, the part of him he'd thought long gone, squealed his excitement. He held that feeling, nursing the battered child that had never quite recovered from his death. Rottgor—the Death Knight, the Famine Blade, the Hollowed Stomach, and the Thrall of the Worm King—was reaching to a dream he hadn't known he'd wanted. Or . . . rather, that he hadn't dared to hope for.

Orientation completed, the new employees departed, leaving Rottgor alone with Rib-Digger. Together, they organized what was left, little things here and there that Rottgor had bought from the markets. He hung up the last item of decor in the open kitchen space, a wreath of purple flowers, bison bones, and flicks of onyx—made from the remaining threads of the Onyx-Ax clan in the city. A sigh escaped him. Rib-Digger arched a big eyebrow underneath his thinning ribbons of brown hair.

"There's a lot happening," Rottgor explained to the giant flesh monster. "Being happy feels . . . weird. I keep expecting . . ." The *worst*. Always the worst. A dread hit him every time he smiled—fear that someone would take it away.

Rib-Digger shook his head. "Go. On. I. Listen." Lifting a table out of the way, his employee plopped on the ground, feet outstretched, staring at his new boss. Rottgor forced his shoulders down and cleared his throat.

"You're one of the few who understand it, I think. Fighting back from the pain of your death, put under the control of someone else. You're not yourself. You're awake, watching your feet take steps, your mouth move, your hands wield foreign weapons that are not yours. Freedom meant nothing after a while, and the sword became my blanket." Rottgor thought of the Deathblade on his mantel and rubbed the burn on his palm from the poison. "Cleo had every right to push me out of the nest, and I'm happy she did. This—" He drank in his home, his work, his new life. "I don't want this to go away."

Rib-Digger's kind eyes seemed grim, darker than their normal soft blue. "No. Go. Away. Protect."

"You're right. It's worth protecting . . . but can I?" The buzzing of locusts and flies swarmed his ears, and he swore he smelled the foul stench of the sword's aether. *Protect?* The voice of the Worm King, a man who had long met his fate, came to him. *I dearly hope that you protect it better than you did me, traitor. Perhaps you'll lose it all like I did.*

Those souring words in his head were interrupted by the ringing of the doorbell. Astra skipped in, stopped, and stared at Rib-Digger. Her eyes brightened. Not exactly what Rottgor expected from a girl seeing a patchwork for the first time.

"You're Rib-Digger, right?" She walked up to him, eyes filled with amazement. The patchwork soldier stared back at her, a bit of a red blush on his cheeks from embarrassment. "You're amazing—no offense, of course. I read your application, but wow. I know you've probably gone through a lot. But my word, you're amazing." She rocked on her bare heels, staring up at him.

"Thank. You." The flesh golem shrugged his large shoulders. "Who. You?"

"Astra. I'm a friend of Mr. Rottgor's. You're gonna work here?"

Rib-Digger tapped his meaty fingers together, nervously laughing. "Yes. Cleaner. Fixer."

"Oh, so you're good with fixing stuff. I wish I was good at fixing stuff. Maybe I'd get yelled at less." Astra laughed, too. Her childlike giggle warmed the room.

Rib-Digger turned his big head toward Rottgor, the seriousness back in his eyes. "Must. Protect." He pointed to Astra. Astra pointed to herself.

"I know, friend, I know," Rottgor said.

"It's a pleasure to meet you, Ribby."

"Ribby?"

"Can I call you that? Does it make you sad?" Astra quickly asked, horrified.

"No. Yes." Rib-Digger shook his head. "No. Sad. Yes. Ribby."

"Okay! Then it's nice to meet you." Astra extended her hand.

Rib-Digger took her small hand. His hand engulfed the young magiian girl's—her hand wasn't in sight. He kept it gentle, not daring a squeeze. Astra didn't appear to mind in the slightest, seeming more enthralled than anything. That childlike wonder awoke the orc pup healing within Rottgor's tattered being. *She deserves the best, but I'm not sure if it's me who can give her that. Me?* A thought struck him, one he feared to linger on. *Fatherhood.* His throat went tight, his typically slow heartbeat rushing. No. He didn't dare think of that. Him. A father. Sweat came upon him, dripping down his brow. Why would he think such foolish thoughts? These hands, this soul, weren't fit for such a task.

They barely knew each other. And him. Being a *dad*. What type of tomfoolery was *that*? He heard his brothers' and sister's jaws drop from the afterlife. He had been a good uncle, but that had ended poorly, hadn't it? *Stick to the restaurant,* he told himself. *There are things you aren't built for. Being a dad is one of them.* Astra smiled at him all the same.

The little rascal added a personal touch to the chalkboard, drawing a rabbit that reminded Rottgor of his childhood pet, Perin. She wrote "Chef's Special" in her beautiful handwriting, decorating it with green and purple vines.

"I saw him in a dream and . . . seems very appropriate now," she explained, as though it was a normal occurrence. "Been practicing drawing him ever since. Don't know what brought him to me." Astra picked up one of the rabbits that Bao Su had left behind to work, a smaller white one, and held it. It bounced happily in her arms.

"Hm," Rottgor grunted. Nothing was out of the realm of possibility in their world of magic—including prophecy or visions. The dead spoke, the undead lingered, and the dreams that connected them all thrived. He put his hand on her shoulder. "It's glorious, my friend. You didn't have to do all this."

"It's no problem, Mr. Rottgor. You've been nice to me, and I can't just sit by and get stuff for free. Besides . . ." She paused. "Never mind. I'm glad you like it."

Rottgor didn't pursue her thoughts. He was more afraid than curious. They let the conversation die. Rib-Digger looked back and forth between the two, rolled his knowing eyes, and lumbered off to the storage room. The uncomfortable silence stretched on. Plenty to say and not a word spoken. Rottgor found his retreat, circling the counter to the kitchen. The awkwardness faded with the scent of roasting vegetables and braised chicken. What caught her interest and relieved their clumsiness was his rigorous kneading of dough, then his cutting and placing each disk in small metal pans.

"What are you making?" Astra asked, walking around the table and standing on the rung of a barstool to see the counter.

"Savory pies. It's the best way I can describe them. Some with meat, some with veggies. I wanted to give it a try before bringing Flynn in. Make them smaller and easier to take around. Something to draw in a crowd." Rottgor tapped his flour-coated fingers on his cheek, a long line trailing down his face as his war paint once had. These pies were like bite-size memories of his old home. *They're cute,* he thought. "Perin's Pies."

"Awwww!" Astra's eyes got their ruby glitter once more. "What if the vegetable ones had little ears?"

Rottgor pinched what was left of his dough into triangles, placing them on the top crusts of the ones filled with carrots, onions, frost peas, and a hardy blue orcish potato known as the lungs of the clouds. He presented them to Astra and earned a round of applause. He gave a bit of a bow. Finished, they popped the pies into the oven, and the waiting began.

"I appreciate everything you do, Astra," Rottgor admitted after a time. She was peering at the oven window, watching the crust turn golden brown.

"And I you," Astra said. "What made you talk to me that first time?"

"I don't know," Rottgor told her. He actually didn't, not the first time he'd seen her. There were plenty of children her age there, and he saw them, too. Yet there was a connection there.

That small piece of him that knew she needed someone and that she was someone he needed. He had been right. The *why* still escaped him. Fate? Destiny? A simple longing for a friend? The hope of a family? He didn't know. The moment she stepped into his life and the moments after gave him a joy he didn't know he could have. A blessing. *A fatherly one—no.* "I . . . I just did. You're a great kid, Astra. Don't grow up too fast."

"Urgh. Adulthood." Astra shook her head and stuck out her tongue. "I'll try not to. Adults sound *so* boring. All you do is work and mope around."

"We are boring," Rottgor admitted solemnly. "That we are."

The wonderfully sweet smells of the pastry alongside the savory fillings made concentrating on any meaningful conversation difficult. On her stool, Astra swung her legs, her attention back on the small oven window. And then, like lightning on an otherwise sunny day, a flash of familiarity struck him. Time slowed. He watched her, confused. Her red eyes were still beautiful and innocent, yet somehow familiar. His heart rushed. *Who? Who does your face remind me of?* His fingers shook, his throat felt dry. His death wound festered at his neck, burning, itching, biting. A howl of pain escaped his lips. Rottgor collapsed to the ground. The faint sound of Astra's scream fell on dulled ears.

Darkness reached out to him: an abyss and a familiar friend, Tytli. The pain spiked further. His body writhed. A voice on the other side of the pain reached out once more, through the tenuous connection all Six Shadows had from their shared past. *"Rottgor . . . ? Is that you? Did you feel that? Rott . . . where are you? Who's doing that to you? Is there one I missed? There can't be. His bloodline is gone."* Tytli's voice, though panicked, eased his worry. The gaping blackness of his mind broke against the tide of light-made bees, wasps, and butterflies, all swarming and cradling him in his fear. *"Stay where you are, friend. Don't leave me. Don't give in,"* said Tytli. *"I'm coming. Hold on."* Then, nothing.

He awoke, panting. Astra was hovering over him, holding his large hand. A cold sweat poured down his face, still an odd feeling after years of undeath. He heaved his body up, the heat of the still-burning oven warming his skin.

"I'm all right," he reassured Astra quickly. His tongue ran across the roof of his dry mouth. The worried look on his friend's face didn't fade. Somehow it got worse, tears appearing at the horizon of her eyes. Her hands tightened around his fingers. "I'm okay," he told her once again, as well as himself. "I—I don't know what happened." The moment stirred a fear all the undead held: having their freedom ripped from them. As much as he hated admitting it, he was afraid. No sword, nor fist, nor tusk, nor claw could save him from his mind being taken. He knew that from experience. He held Astra's hand a little tighter. "I'm fine. Don't cry."

They gathered in the silence that followed a storm, dried tears on their cheeks. He told her what he'd seen and experienced, the cold and the agony. She listened. Never once did she interrupt. The panic on her face fell away, giving way to determination.

"I'm sorry," he said. "You didn't need to see me like that."

"No." The way she spoke sent a shiver down his spine. "Don't apologize for crying. Everyone should cry. That was scary and we cry at scary things."

Rottgor nodded, then realized the pies must be done. He hurried to the oven to pull out the fresh pies. Rottgor fanned them cool and gave her one. To his surprise, she chose one without the meat, tapping her fingers on the crust ears. Rottgor took one of the Perin's Pies himself. He handed her a spoon and held his own. He ran the back of it against the crust to test its flakiness. Though his heart still raced and his mind remained scattered, this small joy lifted his spirits. The two friends broke through the crust, white steam billowing from its core. They scooped the flaky crust, soft vegetables, and thick gravy into their mouths and put the fear behind them . . . for now.

NINE

Opening the Doors

Rottgor wished he were preparing for the comfort of battle, donning his black armor and holding a blade made of rot, rust, and metal. His armor now was a gray apron, and his weapons were his kitchen tools. The restaurant was immaculate, unlike the chaotic battlefield he knew. But inside Rottgor, the criticism mounted, the inner voices victorious against simple logic. *Will it be enough?* More questions and only one answer . . . opening that door.

"You're going to pace a hole in the floor I just shined," Flynn snapped.

"That *we* just shined," Bao said, cocking her head.

"You didn't do *anything*. Your cute lads did."

"Delegation is a *job*." Bao batted her fan at him. "And they aren't all boys."

"They're still lads." Flynn took a puff of his pipe.

"Waldruk, are the coffers filled?" Rottgor asked, earning the classic look a young man gives to his elder.

Waldruk folded his arms. "You mean before or after the thousandth time you asked?"

"All right, tensions are high," Clyth said, interrupting.

"It's not the only thing that's about to be in the rafters," Rottgor muttered.

Clyth patted him on the shoulder. "Boss, keep it together."

"Together," Rib-Digger said. He was the only one who seemed to be keeping it together. He removed his little glasses and closed his novel, a riveting historical romance. "Will work. Believe."

Rottgor paced a metaphorical (though almost literal) hole in the ground, hands clenched. His nerves spread to the rest of the crew. "This better work. Did we check—"

"Yes," Flynn snapped again. "We did. If you ask one more time, I might explode."

Rottgor groaned.

The morning bell rang.

Clyth's loud voice announced the opening of the restaurant from the other side of the closed door. He played the crowd, riling them up for a good meal. Inside, breaths lay on pins and needles. Knees knobbed against one another. The door slid open. The first crowd surged in.

"Welcome," Rottgor found himself shouting, adrenaline taking over. He hoped his thunderous voice sounded more inviting than terrifying.

Clyth slipped in, steps like ice sliding across the slick floor. He bowed, ushering in their first customers. The crowd wasn't too thick, a reasonable amount for their first gathering—free food brought people in, as Clyth had said. Clyth guided them toward the Perin's Pies. They'd set up a heating station engineered by Flynn and his clan. Clyth was careful, bringing out each of the pies using thick mittens and placing them on the small table for the samples. The customers gathered, including workmen and workwomen from the docks, warehouse movers, and guards from the first watch. A warm meal was all any of them wanted.

The first man, Johas, a warehouse worker Clyth flirtingly charmed his name out of, took the first cautious step forward. *A high-elf worker at that. Perfect.* Johas took in the decorations and the atmosphere, seemingly appreciative of the good ambience.

"Come, my fine, fine-looking ser. You look famished. You might find some simple comfort among these pies if I'm too spicy for you." Clyth winked. Waldruk, from behind the counter, groaned, face notably red.

As predicted, Johas chose one of the free Perin's Pies while perusing the rest of the menu. He cracked the rabbit-eared pie, and a wisp of steam emerged. The crowd gave an impressed hum.

Here it came. The first bite in his new restaurant. Rottgor tried not to be that chef, watching unblinking as his clients ate, searching for a reaction. He studied his first customer's expression as he blew on the pie, then bit down. His bright-turquoise eyes shone, and he began munching.

"Nicely done," Johas said to no one and to everyone. "Can't find a good vegetable pie around here that tastes like somethin'." He bit down again, clearly enjoying the flaky pastry. Rottgor had added a dwarvish root vegetable known as the loot root, which lent the filling a satisfying tooth feel.

The rest of the crowd began to dig in.

Bao danced among them, her little animals right behind her. "Of course, may I recommend the cider or a light juice to go with the pies? I'm a fan of the grape or the apple, but if those are too sweet, tea is available." Her voice had switched effortlessly from its even, aloof tone to one crafted for conversations among customers. "If you need anything, and I mean *anything*, wave over one of my sweet peas, especially the brown raccoon bear. His name is Brae." The little raccoon bear waved, holding a small scroll of parchment and quill. "He will take any order, but of course, he can't talk unless you're an animal speaker. If you are, you'll find his conversation lovely."

"I wish she'd talk to us like that," Flynn said under his breath. Bao's ears and tails twitched, but her smile remained the same.

Rottgor huffed a laugh. "She heard that."

Before long, the hungriest of their first throng decided to sit down for something more. A few left, holding their free pies and snacking away. The satisfied talk told him they would be back. The animals were indeed a help, darting through the rafters, little aprons flying. The orders came flooding in. Customers were approaching him, asking to meet the restaurant's chef. A few recognized his name. One man, a shaped undead like Rottgor, stared in amazement as though Rottgor were an unseen treasure of the ages.

"*The* Lord Commander Rottgor, the Famine Blade?" he asked. "A chef and owner of a restaurant? What happened?"

"Nothing, friend," Rottgor reassured him, the thickness of his Onyx-Ax accent coming through, soft and long on certain words. He'd missed it. "I chose a life I wanted, and this is what I wished for."

"Huh," the undead man said, nodding. "Sounds nice. I've just been moving from job to job since I left the city guard about one hundred and four years ago. Don't know quite what to do with myself. I find myself going back, wishing I never left. It was easier." He shook his head. "Never mind my rambling."

"I don't mind it. I understand."

That one conversation broke the ice. The living and the undead struck up conversations with one another. Soon they were arm in arm, delighting in their shared comradery. When the conversation faltered, Rottgor kept it going through his tireless work.

The inaugural special—an orcish red-beef-and-tomato stew by the name of *maborrt*—caught the eyes of many. He'd made a big cauldron of it the moment the craving struck him that morning. Rottgor gave the stew one final taste, dipping a fresh ladle through the sea of red liquid. The sweetness and spiciness from the tomatoes and the spices filled him with warmth, cut through by the rich, slow-cooked beef. The spice wouldn't be for everyone. He'd learned *that* from Waldruk's mild overreaction to the burn of the chilies on his tongue. Serving it with the option of a dollop of soured cream from the Plains cooled that heat, and the sweet, rich bread he served alongside was a crowd-pleaser. He slid the first bowl to Thomme, the former knight who had started the conversations.

"Thanks for the order, ser. I hope you enjoy." Rottgor cleared his throat, turning to the entire restaurant. "Be full and be merry," he shouted to the Afterlife Crisis. An eruption of cheers answered him. Joy, unlike anything he'd ever felt, filled his gut. Living. That was what this was. He hadn't felt it that strongly in all his days.

He and Flynn worked the ovens and the countertops, rushing from one to the next, speeding through dish after dish. Getting a smile from the stone-serious Flynn was the biggest treat of all. Their work slowly developed toward a competition of sorts. They made a show of it. Flynn's knife tricks, the constant flicking and juggling, got a roaring cheer. Rottgor matched him, blowing fire into the air, his aether turning the flames a shimmering gold. He laughed at the playful annoyance spreading across his assistant's face. Of course, they didn't miss an order during their performances.

The end of the early-lunch rush gave them a moment of reprieve. Rib-Digger returned chairs to where they were supposed to be, buffed the tables and floors, and prepared them for dinner. Waldruk counted the coins and slips, focused and surprisingly quiet.

"Take a break," the lordling vampire told Rottgor. "I'll watch the floor."

"You're taking this job well for a nobleman," Flynn said, slapping Waldruk on the back.

"Seeing Clyth talk to the customers and all of you having . . . fun . . . made me—" He frowned. Flynn and Rottgor leaned in.

"Made you what, Wal?" Rottgor arched an eyebrow. The half orc grew redder around the nose.

"Made me feel like I belong," he muttered.

"I hope you chase that feeling," Clyth said, winking. "And maybe, just maybe, I misjudged you." That made Waldruk's whole face turn a blazing-hot red. He turned away.

Rottgor retreated upstairs to the large seat in his study, taking a bit of time for himself. He leaned back, a smile he once dared not to have creeping up the corners of his mouth. The day was going better than he'd hoped. But he knew there was no sitting in battle. "Tonight's another challenge."

When he went back down, he was met with an interesting sight. Astra stood in the doorway, alongside five other children and an adult high-elvish woman. The woman glared around the Afterlife as though the floor were a horrid bog and a step onto it meant her doom. Her thick, curly platinum-blonde hair fell across one of her shoulders in a tight ponytail, with some covering her eyes. She gathered the children around her.

"Astra," Rottgor said. A new type of happiness rose in his chest. Her big red eyes found his. She clapped.

"Mr. Rottgor!" She started to run toward him, but the elvish woman put a hand on her shoulder to stop her, then took her first steps forward, keeping the space between her and the children, and Rottgor.

She cocked her head. Her dress, though a simple green and brown, somehow made her appear elegant and noble. Intensity brimmed from her pupilless eyes. She approached Rottgor, still cautious, and stretched out her hand, which he took.

"Guardian Thesselie Armatius," she said, by way of a stiff introduction, her *bridge* tongue sharp. She didn't blink. "Astra has done nothing but rave about you, Mr. Rottgor. And I mean *nothing*. Even work seems lost on this child since she came across you. So, I figured, the children and I had no choice but to visit your establishment. Please take us to our seats."

Astra gave Rottgor an apologetic glance, which he waved away.

"Of course, Guardian Armatius." Rottgor felt his voice become lighter and more pleasant, a tone crafted for customers. Bao was rubbing off on him. He walked them through the Afterlife, explaining all that he could. Astra soon joined in. Thess arched an eyebrow, letting them talk all the same. He sat them at what he considered the best spot in the restaurant, a small dais flanked by a window that gave a good view of Famine Street. He pulled out the chairs for the lady and the children while Clyth handed out silverware, menus, and plates.

Astra leaned toward Rottgor to whisper, "I'm sorry about Ms. Thess. She's not a fan of new people." He nodded his understanding, avoiding the teacher's steely gaze. *I see why Astra always needs to be home on time.*

Thess looked up sharply. "We would like plates of your appetizers and the finest juices and water you can provide. Nothing too sweet or salty, please. The children's health comes first." Thess stared down at the menu as though the parchment spoke ill of her. "I would like to try your braised beef steak, mashed potatoes, and honey carrots. Any *good* quality tea or coffee as a drink for myself."

"That's more than possible." Rottgor knew what he would serve her. "I'll bring everything out promptly. You aren't short on time, are you?"

"We are not. I decided to make a whole day of it. Please take all the time you need." Thess looked over to Astra, who sulked in her chair, arms folded, lips pursed. The elvish woman sighed. "You can accompany him, Astra. I suppose I should know better than to expect a cricket not to hop. Please do not get in the way of his cooking our meals, my dear."

"I won't," Astra told her, then scooched out of her chair and rushed to the large orc's side. She bowed low.

Thess waved them away. "Go now. Just because we *have* all day doesn't mean we want to *be here* all day." She paused. "No offense, of course. You have a fine establishment, Ser Rottgor. You should be proud."

Rottgor gave a brisk nod. "I am, my lady. I am. I'll bring the drinks and the meat pies out as soon as possible."

Rottgor turned, holding back his smile. Astra followed him around the counter, bouncing with every step. "I'm sorry about Ms. Thess," Astra said again, looking over her shoulder. "She's . . . a lot, a lot of a lot actually, but she's nice to me! I always feel safe with her." An odd pang of jealousy hit Rottgor's stomach. *Why?* He growled, annoyed at his feelings. *She's safe and happy. What could I provide?* He swallowed the ridiculous thought. "I'm happy to see that it's all going so well," Astra continued. "It's good, you deserve the best."

"You do, too, little one." He patted her head. "You, too."

She watched him work. Rottgor brought out the best slab of

marbled steak from his collection. He seasoned it simply, with fine salt and pepper alone, then seared it slightly before transferring it to the oven. He worked on the carrots and potatoes, and started boiling water for the tea. The popping bubbles of the boiling water were a music of a sort. The song pushed him along, each step of the recipe a joyful, simple exercise he loved. The glazing of the baked carrots, the mashing of the boiled and seasoned potatoes, and the basting of the fine steak imported from Lladad reminded him of the joys of every day. The dish came together on the canvas of the fine wooden plate. Nothing fancy. He'd promised Flynn they wouldn't do that there. Astra looked over at the finished meal, a small grumble of hunger rumbling from her stomach. Rottgor tilted his head and grinned.

"What? It looks good," she muttered under her breath.

"I'm not going to let you starve in front of your guardian. She would rip me apart." Rottgor patted her on the head again. She kicked a foot against the counter. "One more thing."

Rottgor prepared the tea he had bought from the Sunlands importer. It was what they called an azurlong tea—widely referred to as blue tea. The tea steeped faster than most, taking on a purple-blue color and smelling like hibiscus and raspberry. Its delicate floral notes might win the stern woman over. Once the tea was ready for serving, Bao Su swiftly took the kettle and cup and accompanied Rottgor, who was carrying the steak dish, back to the table.

Clyth and Bao had already served the children, giving them quite the spread of food and drinks, including the Perin's Pies. They munched delightedly. Thess's face revealed no expression, her brows, eyes, and lips straight, impregnable lines on a face as blank as new parchment. Rottgor hoped that the meal's preparation hadn't tested the patience of the stone wall of an elf. She turned her head sharply at Rottgor's approach, as though she heard his thoughts. Her face softened—if only a bit.

"Great timing," she said. Rottgor couldn't tell if she meant it genuinely. She delivered all her words with the same blank affect. *Best to take it as a compliment until proven otherwise.* He placed the plate down before her, and Bao Su quickly served the tea alongside it.

Thesselie Armatius straightened her back, gazing down at the food. Unceremoniously, she picked up the knife and fork and sliced into the steak, revealing a beautiful reddish interior. "Nice. You've chosen medium rare, a safe but sensible choice when not specified. I wanted to see if you were a *sensible* man. It seems you are." She brought the slice to her lips and ate it in the same emotionless, rigid style. She said nothing. A long time passed. She continued through the rest of the meal—no reactions. "Astra, please sit down. Your food will grow cold," she said at last.

"Well, how is it?" Astra asked, obviously for Rottgor's sake.

"Oh." Thess frowned. "It's divine."

"Really?" Astra glanced at Rottgor. Her mouth was open, her eyes so big they seemed to fill her entire face. She began bouncing once more, putting her hand to her mouth. "She . . . she complimented you! On the first meeting! Guardian Thess! Compliment! First introduction! Compliment!"

"Don't be ridiculous, Astra. I give plenty of compliments." Astra and the rest of the children all pursed their lips. "I suppose . . . I may not say it to them all the time, and I am"—she paused—"a bit on the stricter side, but credit is important. You have a fine restaurant here, Mr. Rottgor." The cold sincerity caught him off guard. She took a sip of her tea. "And a fine choice of tea to complement it all. Now, Astra, *please* come sit down, stop bouncing, and *eat*. That *is* what we came here for."

"Yes, ma'am," Astra said. She grabbed the hem of her shiny pink dress and curtsied to Rottgor, dipping deep, a noblewoman's practiced motion. *There.* A moment of sour familiarity struck him. Though Astra was nothing but genuine, innocent, and cute, a brief drift of memory pulled him away. It was of a woman in a similar pink dress, skin as warm as the sunset sky, a sinister smile on her red-stained lips. His heart skipped, remembering the venom in that woman's eyes, the same ruby red as Astra's. He stepped back, throat suddenly dry. The memories stabbed at his skull. He knew now where he had seen her face. A wave of fear rolled down his skin as he watched the young girl take her seat next to her guardian. Mistress Isobel Denholm—the Paramour of Skulls—one of many consorts of the Worm King known as the Silk Worms. Her face was etched all over the young girl's features. History had spoken of her as the cruelest outside the Worm King himself, and Rottgor knew from experience how true that was. And now he realized it at last—the Paramour's blood and the Worm King's blood ran through Astra's veins.

Time froze.

He stepped back again. No. Surely, he was wrong. The light was playing tricks on him. He would've known it immediately. He had lived in this city for centuries. *It's impossible. We made sure.* The Worm King's heirs had all been removed. They had all shown the cruelty of their parentage and had been eliminated. Rottgor stole one more glance at Astra. *I have to be wrong; I have to be. No. No. No.* But small things started to make sense: her aether, her rune, the draw he felt to protect her. Was it all fake? Was it the draw of the Worm King's thrall once more? He could almost feel the tyrant's cold hands snaking up his skin.

"I need to go," he said to no one in particular. He was sure that all the restaurant could hear the panic in his voice. He didn't care. *Not again. Not again.*

The door swung open the moment he decided to head upstairs to collect himself.

Tytli Bhihadra, the Fallen Fae Queen, stood in the doorway. She strode forward, the heels of her sandals clanking against the wood floor. She had lived thousands of years before that fateful day when the Worm King had stolen her life and her will. Their eyes met from across the room. She sighed in relief.

"Rott," she said, loud enough for the whole restaurant to hear, "you look great."

"Lili... I—" His voice failed him. "What are you doing here?"

"I felt it," she explained. "I felt his will on you once more. I thought it was a dream... but I didn't wish to risk it. We made a promise, did we not? As long as we live, we will come to each other's aid. And if it happens to us both, we will break his will together. Now, where is the scum hiding...?" Tytli reached out her hand. A cloud of bees, wasps, and butterflies wrapped around her wrist. The insects solidified into the familiar golden sword-whip, appearing of honeycombs bleeding blackened honey—her Deathblade, the Soshadyel. Rottgor had seen it a thousand times, seen that coiling sword slice through flesh and bone, leaving corpses full of venom wasps and terror hornets. Suddenly, that same blade was pointed at Astra. "There. You. The spawn. I will eliminate you."

Astra stood on her chair, face still, body quivering. She drew her little dagger. A storm of rose petals erupted around her, and from them emerged a skeleton clad in the tatters of a red dress, its bony fingers tipping a hat made of black feathers and spider lilies. *There. There she is. Isobel Denholm.* Rottgor saw her now, felt her once more after all these years. Though Astra looked scared, there was no mistaking that will—to kill for what was hers. A bone spear appeared in her hands. *Astra* . . .

Tytli showed no hesitation. A blink of an eye, a falling raindrop, a flash of light from a cloud—nothing compared to her speed. Rottgor acted without thinking, Malferioel appearing in his hand. The poisoned blade ate into his flesh, burning his large palm. He'd seen Tytli's speed and knew how she moved. He stepped between them, knocking the sword-whip away. The restaurant was awed. Some customers ran for the door; others cowered beneath tables. Tytli frowned. Malferioel and Soshadyel, sister blades, had never crossed paths. This was new for everyone.

"Explain yourself, Rottgor," she demanded. "I won't ask again."

He didn't have an explanation, and she knew it. "Trust me," he said.

"It's not you that I don't trust, friend. You know that."

"Lili . . ."

"Stop it, Rott. Too much is at stake. I can't risk it, *we* can't risk it. You know you cannot stop me now, not as you are. Your body is strong, your skill is there, but your will is not." Tytli's frown deepened. "I do not smell *Festrain* on you either. And your hand—holding the hilt pains you. I see your skin sizzling from the poison. I cannot falter. Look at her. Look. At. Her. Do you not see what she is capable of? Who she is? What she might *mean* for this city, this world? You're not blind, or are you to her? She cannot be allowed to live. This city isn't enough to contain such an evil. You cannot unsour milk."

Rottgor heard a confused sobbing and trembling at his back. He couldn't bear seeing its source. "You know that is not true. There's no evil born within a person. It's made. A little kindness goes a long way."

"And all it takes is one bad day to change all of it." Tytli glared around the room momentarily, seeing the disarray she had caused. She sighed. "Are you willing to risk that? I'm not. Spawn of Isobel Denholm and the infamous Worm King. I will spare you and her for now out of respect for an old friend and the people here. But I *will* fulfill my duty. Do not question my resolve. Many of your kind have met my blade for their sins, and you are no different." She dissolved her blade, returning it to the bees, the wasps, and the butterflies that had formed its long blade. "Rottgor . . . ," she whispered, stepping closer. "You may be under the influence of that child. And if you are, even subtly, I have no choice but to make good on our oath."

Tytli walked away and out the door, leaving Rottgor's new life a bit more broken than when she'd arrived. The Afterlife Crisis erupted in whispers. Rottgor dropped his Deathblade, palm peeling and purpled. He ignored his pain; Astra's was far beyond it. Turning to face the table, he saw her staring from over Thess's arms, which were wrapped around her, eyes red where they shouldn't have been. Fat tears rolled down her face. The looming skeleton was gone, returned to dust now scattered on the wooden floor. She looked at him in a way she hadn't before, not with anger but with pure and genuine sadness.

"That's not me," she told him. "I'm not controlling you. . . . I swear it to all the gods. I will never control you. I wouldn't do that . . . would I? Would I? No, I wouldn't. Please believe me." The worst part was that he believed her, but saw only the vile woman in the spider-lily hat.

TEN

The Wormling and the Honeycombed Woman

Rottgor questioned his happiness every day after he'd first opened his doors. The business's initial buzz cooled to a comfortable pace, and Rottgor enjoyed his life and doubted it at the same time. That morning was no different. He hadn't heard from anyone, least of all Astra. He hadn't seen her in weeks. His worry mounted. He had sent letters to Thess, only for them to be brushed aside. Rottgor dreaded the moment he and Tytli met once more, a shadow that continued to hover over his joy.

Then there was the fear he denied. The true reason he hadn't marched up to see Astra was because of the courage he'd lost as the once-infallible Death Knight. He remembered seeing Astra through the crowd that first time, a moment of connection there. Of course, there'd been the alleyway, the feeling of her magic on the surface of his mind. He'd feared her then, lying for her sake. The final straw, the final breaking of his strength, was seeing the skeleton behind her—the hat of spider lilies and feathers, the tattered red dress, the slightly broken neck from her death. It was her.

Isobel Denholm, that vile woman. She didn't deserve a place among his thoughts. Cruelty of that magnitude didn't deserve remembrance. Astra shared her features, an almost spitting image aside from the slightly darker skin. The cheeks, the eyebrows, the shape of her eyes, the texture of her hair, and the curve of her lips when she smiled . . . If she were at a healthier weight, there would've been little doubt. And yet . . . Astra had none of that falseness. Isobel never smiled from happiness. Never cared. Love wasn't why she'd enjoyed the company of her King. The little one was genuine; he saw that in her, felt it in her tears. But what if that cruelty was a part of her, too? Rottgor's heart wished it to be untrue, but his mind refused such logic.

Mind clouded, Rottgor began his day. The morning was cool and refreshing, with pale sunlight easing in from the opened windows of the restaurant. He wandered into the main area. Bao Su waved from the counter, while Clyth worked the floor and Flynn cooked for their new regulars. Rottgor stuffed his hands into the pockets of his silver sleeping robe, not changing out of it in favor of a more presentable outfit. Clyth finished his rounds, headed to the back of the kitchen, and brought out a pot of coffee and a mug. Rottgor sighed, steeling himself for the man's words.

The waiter said nothing. He kept his face cool and neutral, which made Rottgor feel worse. Clyth set down the mug on the table in front of his boss and poured the dark-roasted coffee with a perfect and practiced arc. The smell lifted Rottgor's spirits, if only a little. He cupped the hot mug with his hands.

"Are you going to say something?" Rottgor asked him, breaking the silence.

Clyth placed the coffeepot down and laced his fingers together. "What is there to say that I haven't already? Trust her, Razgaif."

Rottgor's eyes snapped up. "I've never told you my living name."

Clyth placed a single finger to his lips. His long black nail hissed smoke, his fang-toothed smile curling up at the edges. "Never mind that, boss. Do what needs to be done."

The triumphant ring of the front doorbell caught Rottgor's attention. Calfe strolled in, pulling down the tails of his long leather vest over his dark leather pants. Dozens of little knives stretched across his hairy chest. He smoked from his box, the scent of grape hard candy heralding his steps. As usual, he knew everyone. Rottgor swore he knew the whole city at this point. Calfe gave a lopsided grin, looking Rottgor up and down.

"Casual, aren't we? Should've gotten you some slippers."

"I do have some. Didn't feel like wearing them." Rottgor groaned, immediately realizing how sad he sounded. He drained the rest of his coffee and poured himself another piping-hot cup. "You've heard, haven't you?"

"Flynn told me." Calfe invited himself to the empty chair beside Rottgor, and Clyth fetched him a clean mug. He poured himself a cup of coffee. He placed his smoking box down and held his mug up.

"You know what happened with Astra," Rottgor said.

"Yeah . . . maybe don't have all that drama in broad daylight and maybe word won't get around, eh?" Calfe paused. "My boys and I have been keeping an eye on her, since she means something to ya. She hasn't left her home in weeks. Not that the director of her orphanage would allow it. She's been under lock and key for a while." Calfe soured at the taste of the bitter coffee. "No sweetness? No cream? What's going on with that? You must be really off your game." He helped himself to the cream and sugars on the table. A metal spoon clanked against the side of the mug over and over, Calfe's eye contact unbreaking. "You're happy about the restaurant, I see that. But something's missing. I've been there." He gave a smile, seeming more fatherly than Rottgor would've expected. "Be greedy, don't settle."

Rottgor understood. The Afterlife was his dream, yes, and it still was. But that dream might not have started without Astra. "I'm stupid."

"I knew that already, but explain," Calfe said.

"I have to go see her."

"There we go. That's what I wanted to see."

Rottgor got up without another word. He dashed to his living quarters and dressed more appropriately than he had since opening day. The *haogu* felt right on his shoulders. What stumped him was his weapon. His Deathblade had betrayed him. The buzzing of flies rang through his ears, amplified by the hum of cicadas. Malferioel knew its sister blade skulked the city, its only sibling left. *And it resents me for it.* No, he wouldn't bring the sword. Not now. If need be, he would summon it. He walked out of his bedroom with his simple hand ax at his hip. The sword hissed displeasure from across the room, a spurned cat calling to its neglectful owner. *I should invest in a better civilian weapon. A* kallgr . . . *or better . . . my Champion weapon.* Now more than ever, he missed his obsidian ax.

Rottgor returned downstairs to Calfe, who had somehow struck up a deep conversation with Rib-Digger. The giant patchwork sat cross-legged on the floor.

"You're right. The Languished and the Unwreathed have been making good strides since Lady Cleo began transitioning over. Duke Jamis is a nice guy-lich-person and all, but his granddaughter has that *flair*. He could delegate; she could lead. I like that. Good role model for my daughter." Rib-Digger nodded his approval. *Politics.* Rottgor had enough of that.

"Before. Council. Idiots," Rib-Digger added.

Calfe threw up his hands. "Absolutely. Lord Pitmore and Lord Rustway couldn't make a good decision to save their lives. I swear they are behind—oh, hey, you're back."

"Hi." Rib-Digger waved.

"Save me," Bao Su said from the other side of the restaurant.

"Sorry if I'm interrupting a gentlemen's discussion." Rottgor gave both of them pats on the back. Calfe almost fell out of his chair; Rib-Digger didn't move an inch. "I'm heading off to the orphanage."

"Do you even know where the Living Vine is?" Calfe asked.

Rottgor gritted his teeth. "Lady Cleo mentioned it once. I've never thought to—"

"I swear. You've lived here for how many years?"

A warmth filled his cheeks. "Centuries."

An awkward silence stretched between them. Rib-Digger snorted. Calfe coughed. "How many centuries?"

"In his defense," Bao chimed in, "after the first century, it all sort of becomes unsavory time slop."

"*Unsavory time slop.* That's a fantastic way to say that." Waldruk rolled his eyes. "I'm suddenly glad I'm not like the rest of you."

"To answer your question, Calfe, two and some . . . all right? After you live undying for so long, the world around you becomes a blur. Or . . . a time slop. Things go, things pass, and nothing changes, except everything does and it's actually you standing still."

"I suppose that will happen after a while." Calfe, compared to Rottgor's centuries, was young. But his wisdom and maturity were on the same scale. Calfe, no doubt processing their age gap, had a glazed expression, which dissolved after he caught his bearings. "Well. You can't miss it. It's on Hive."

"On Hive?" Rottgor's throat tightened. The street was named after *her*. After Tytli.

"Irony or fate—can't decide." Calfe shrugged. "The gods have a sick humor. I swear they do." He whispered his next words as if the gods themselves were listening to their conversation. "But, yes, Hive. You'll want to look for the building with the stone gate and the plum trees. It's near the end of the road. You'll know it when you see it. I'm sure they will let you in."

There was a caution in Calfe's voice that Rottgor wasn't fond of. *A peace offering. I'll bring a peace offering.* When his mouth failed, his cooking didn't. Simple. He had to keep it simple. The muse gave Rottgor the inspiration he needed. Between the orders he helped Flynn with, Rottgor cooked the kids and the staff of the Living Vine a meal of pumpkin bread and an assortment of cooked meats, roasted vegetables, and fresh fruits. After everything was prepared, Rottgor pulled one of Flynn's inventions from the cabinet. The large box was much like the dwarvsh icebox, but it was small and compact, made of metal, and wrapped in hard leather. He layered the food within it and slung the box over his shoulder. *One more thing. Kopsug.*

While making one of his special blends of apple cider, Rottgor had created *Kopsug*, a cauldron that shimmered with his aether and was bound to his will, ensuring the food within replenished endlessly, for a day at least. It had become one of his favorite tools.

"Flynn! I'm gone!"

"Boss!" the dwarf shouted back. "That's fine. Huh. You're bringing *that*." Flynn made his "Flynn noise," as Waldruk called it, a sound somewhere between a growl, a grunt, and a huff. "Well, *Svadagd*, is it? An interesting rune. Could save a lot of people, be a good thing for the world."

Rottgor flexed his fingers. He corked the enchanted cauldron with its lid and hefted it over his shoulder. It felt like it weighed nothing, given his renewed orcish strength and size. Razgaif. He was more Razgaif now than Rottgor, like nature reclaiming a long-fallen building. A refreshed determination rolled down his chest.

With a gold cauldron and a box of food over his shoulder, Rottgor stepped out onto the road. An ax rested at his hip.

It took a little under a day or two of travel to tour the entirety of Necropolis, with the constant twists and turns of its black roads. Becoming a bit less recognizable as Lord Commander of the Ruinous Guard allowed Rottgor the luxury of walking among the residents. Truly, he hadn't left the bubble he'd made for himself in quite a while. *Comfort is my weakness—I've weakened my guard and stilled my blade. I used to live for the fight.* He shook his head. Necropolis never appeared so beautiful, the day never so sweet. He slipped through the crowds, another person in the sea of people going about their day. A few asked him what the cauldron was about. Some asked what he did for work. A giant orc carrying a cauldron drew some attention, which only grew as his feet carried him down Famine, then turned onto Blood, and finally made it to Hive.

Hive was a residential-and-social district. The black stones of the street transitioned to honey-colored pavement, snaking upward through myriad homes and shelters. Small lanterns lit the way, attracting fire moths and sunset-colored butterflies. Long-armed lemon and lime trees stretched heavy over graves and memorial sites of long-lost warriors both on and off the battlefield.

Rottgor searched for the gate that Calfe had mentioned. He'd failed to say just how many trees and gates there were on the street. Rottgor inhaled, the sweet smells of the ripening citrus fruits gently hitting his senses. At least if he was lost, it was a pleasant day for searching.

At the end of the winding path, the Living Vine Orphanage stood tall, its gray-stone towers and broad-faced windows peeking out among the green foliage and lemon trees. Overgrown vegetation cascaded down the stone pillars on both sides of the iron-piked gate, which itself remained clean and bare. Two guards flanked the gate, armored head to toe in gray and silver. The man on the right, an elf of many years by the look of his salt-and-pepper beard, nodded.

"Ser Rottgor," he said. His tone held the sweetness of molasses and the fury of a stoked flame. Rottgor knew that these guards were not from this world. Behind the kindly squint and the lines under their gazes were eyes of stone. Light did not hit them. They were something deeper than the otamo, summoned from another world to protect these children. He bowed. "It's about time that we met face-to-face. I am known as Zennexus, or Zenny, as you may have heard the little one call me, and this is my brother Gosladau, or Go-Go. We're the protectors of the Living Vine. Please come in. Lady Thess would like to speak with you."

Zennexus walked forward, heavy footsteps sounding, far heavier than his elvish form would suggest. He smiled and his body flickered. *An illusion or a veil*, Rottgor realized. Through the threads of light, Rottgor glimpsed the form behind his veil—a granite gargoyle with wings of silver and a diamond beard. Rottgor blinked again and Zennexus was back to normal.

"Ah, you can still see me." He laughed, booming a bit. "We

keep this form for the safety of the children and . . . they tend to get rowdy when we're in our true form." Zennexus eyed Rottgor up and down. "You'll understand when you get there. Gosladau, I'm escorting him to the Lady."

Gosladau gave a sharp salute and opened the gate. The metal spikes slowly dislodged themselves from the ground, then raised, showering the entrance in a flurry of leaves and flowers. Together, Rottgor and Zennexus walked underneath the arch and toward the main building, a road of gravel and planks of wood stretching ahead. The gate closed behind them.

The Living Vine Orphanage stood on a hill overlooking the city. Rottgor and Zennexus hiked upward, passing the lemon and lime trees. The house looked like more of a nobleman's home than an orphanage of any kind, but Necropolis and its leadership had made use of the noblemen's buildings that were claimed by the state. Bronze statues and plaques honoring the previous owner, Lady Willa Mossdraft, were scattered throughout the courtyards and along the road. Heirless and widowed by her wife, an elf from Thess's bloodline, Willa had given her estate to the children of the city, now and forever more.

"It appears that the Honeycombed Woman is still looking for her prey," Zennexus said, breaking the silence. "I've been keeping a watch on Astra for a long time. Lady Cleo put in a special request for her safety. Now I know why."

The Honeycombed Woman—a name Tytli had earned from her enemies, those who'd managed to survive. She had vowed to end the line that had terrorized her. Was killing a young girl for the sake of what she *may* become justice? Rottgor swallowed his doubt. "I can see her?"

"Of course. She . . . has been terrified about what she may be capable of. I think you're the only person who can talk her out of it." Zennexus searched him up and down again. "She believes in you. Believe in her." He took a deep breath. "Do come in. That cauldron and box are gonna throw out your back. Do you wish for me to take care of it?"

"No, I got it," Rottgor told him. Other thoughts clouded his mind so much that the weight was nothing. "Just lead the way."

The orphanage's interior was modest. They passed plenty of empty rooms, long-forgotten studies and social areas, and small pieces of history from the Lord's estate. Life emerged the moment they hit the living area. The large room served as a space for the young orphans' classes. Thess stood before a chalkboard full of different equations and notes. All the students watched. They dared not interrupt her. Rottgor gulped when they made eye contact across the room. She paused, squared her shoulders, and collapsed her pointer.

"That is enough for now," she said. "It appears that lunch has arrived, courtesy of a friend of one of our own." The entire classroom turned to Rottgor, hungry eyes all around him.

"Rottgor!" a few called out. He remembered their faces from opening day. There were a lot more kids than he expected, including a few orc pups. *I'm not worthy of their smiles.* The words pained him more when he realized that Astra wasn't among them.

"Pleasure meeting all of you," he said, pulling the cauldron and the box from his shoulder and opening both as though they were treasure chests. "Please take anything you like. Food makes you strong." The assortment of food and the bottles of pressed apple juice excited the children. Thess watched her students reach for everything given, making sandwiches and partaking in the fruits and vegetables. Thess's workers brought out plates and silverware, corralling the children back to the dining area. Thess fixed herself the last plate after all the children had their fill. She motioned for him to follow. Zennexus stayed behind.

"Astra hasn't been out of her room in weeks," Thess explained softly. "I've tried to get through to her. Zennexus, too. Nothing has worked. More concerning are her bouts of anger. Sometimes her room is a mess, torn apart by her monstrous skeletons."

Rottgor frowned. The thought of her curled up in her room, weeping and scared, wrenched his stomach. Then there was the other part. The anger that crept through her blood, the ire of a Denholm. Rottgor and Thess passed dozens of closed bedroom doors. Small, flameless lanterns signified whether the resident was in or not. Thess remained silent until they made it to what Rottgor knew was Astra's room. The door was painted purple and covered with little blinking stars. Thess tapped on the door.

"Astra, are you there?" the director asked. Concern and consideration came through in her question, unlike her normal stern tone. An indecipherable sob came back. "A friend brought us lunch and you have to eat." More stumbling on the other side. "And I have a surprise for you."

That got her moving.

The door swung open. The small brown-skinned girl looked up at them, the whites of her eyes almost matching the reds of her irises. Her hair was frazzled, uncombed and knotted, and her shoulders slumped so low she might as well have been on the floor. She stood, still wearing her nightclothes, bravely wiping tears from her eyes. That all changed when she saw Rottgor standing behind Thess. A glimmer of hope seemed to rush through her. Her features brightened, her slumping shoulders rose, and a shaking smile replaced the broken sadness that didn't fit her face. *Tytli, you claimed one bad day could break her, yet you gave her more than just one, and she is still her sweet self.*

Astra pushed past Thess and latched onto Rottgor's leg. A hug. A solid, strong hug that reminded him of his nieces and nephews from long ago. A tear ran down his cheek.

"Having a rough day, little one? Sorry it took so long." Rottgor kneeled and returned the hug. "And I'm sorry about everything that happened."

"I'm not controlling you. I swear I'm not," she muttered between sobs. "I didn't know. I never knew. I'm sorry."

"It's not your fault. It's never been your fault." Rottgor patted her on the head. *What a burden we put on her.*

"But . . . but . . . ," Astra stammered. "What if I'm evil? What if I'm secretly terrible and I don't know it? I'm not always nice. Sometimes I get mad. What if that means I'm bad? What if she's *right*?"

"No." Rottgor put his hands on the little girl's shoulders, swallowing them with his palms. He lowered his head, staring her right in the face. "No one's born evil. That is and will always be *your choice*. Your blood has nothing to do with it."

Those simple words. That was what she needed to hear. The small cracks building across her face broke all at once into a maelstrom of tears. She fell into his arms, head on his shoulder.

"I'm sorry," she said to him. Or maybe to everyone.

ELEVEN

A Heart's Confrontation

"My family was mean and did terrible things to you," Astra said, sharing half her sandwich with him.

"Not only me, but yes. Your great-grandfather and great-grandmother treated us awfully...."

They spent the evening together, having a little picnic in her room. Bare aside from her bed and a single drawer, which showed noticeable claw marks and smashed edges. Her army of old and new stuffed animals were scattered everywhere, quite a few torn apart. *Her anger is a terrible one.*

"I don't remember much about my parents. My dad always talked about how we came from a once-powerful family. He wanted to bring us back to *glory*, whatever that means." Astra took a small bite of her crust. "I never thought he meant *that*. Denholm." The name sounded foreign on her tongue. "My father didn't speak much of our family. He said we had enemies, and that they would come for us if we said our names."

"It's true, we would've," Rottgor admitted. *Lili would've.* "Or at least we would have kept an eye on you." *Do the Duke and Lady Cleo know?* No doubt they did, given Astra's story and Zennexus's words. Very little information slipped by them, and a surviving line of the Worm King and the Denholm . . . They had to know. "Were your father and mother kind people?"

"No, they weren't," Astra said. "Mom was better, but not by much. They spoke only of some kind of glory. But at least they cared enough to leave me here." *The Duke had seen the man's madness and put an end to it.*

"Did you love your dad?" Rottgor asked. His throat clenched tight. He reached for a cup of apple juice and drained it.

"I don't think I had a choice." She said the words so matter-of-factly that it wrenched at Rottgor's heart. "For a while, I missed them, but . . . I don't know. Was it bad that I didn't cry at my dad's funeral? Or even my mom's? They weren't kind, but they weren't mean to me, either. Am I terrible? Maybe I am—"

"Don't make me tell you again." Rottgor's sudden sternness surprised both of them. They stared at each other. Rottgor coughed. "You're a good kid, I mean. I won't repeat myself."

Astra lowered her head and finished the rest of her sandwich. "Is that why your friend is after me?"

Yes, Rottgor thought, the truth refusing to leave his mouth. Tytli didn't see it the way he did. He likely wouldn't have either— even a few months ago. For the Ruinous Guard, duty came first, and that meant death to anyone who threatened the royal line. The unquestioning coldness of fealty felt foreign now. Life wasn't black and white, good and evil, not anymore. Tytli had been stuck in her ways since Isobel Denholm had ripped her eye from her socket. *Understandably so.* Tytli had vowed revenge, and that stood to this day.

"I'll speak with her," he said. "You'll be safe, I vow. But you have to promise me one thing, too."

"Anything," she said. The glow of her smile came back. *That smile.* Isobel Denholm never knew happiness. Those features she'd passed down to her descendant mattered little when such a difference shone through. *Isobel, whatever Depths you're burning in, I hope you see that your cruel line has borne kindness, and I hope you're choking on your anger.*

"Keep smiling, and get back to your studies." He patted her on the shoulder.

"That's two things"—Astra put up two fingers—"but . . . I can do that."

"Well, wish me luck. I have someone I have to talk some sense into." Rottgor got up from the floor, joints in his knees popping. He winced and whistled. "Old bones."

"Well," she said, seeming to hold in a giggle, "you're about a million years old."

"Aye, now. Watch your mouth." Rottgor tried stifling a laugh, but it surged out as a hearty chuckle. The moment struck another chord of forgotten memories and faces long returned to the earth. He missed, remembered, and grieved them still—but a new flower was growing in those memories. The taste of honeysuckles and warm campfire smoke struck his senses. *Home,* he thought. Calfe's advice—*Be greedy*—circled his thoughts. *Fight. Fight. Fight.* His orcish blood churned. *Protect your happiness.*

Rottgor knew now, seeing her, that his happiness wasn't a lie.

He left Astra to her studies, much to her and his dismay. He gave the rest of the children and the faculty a goodbye, and hefted the cauldron and cooling box onto his shoulders. Back straight and determined, Rottgor began his trek to the Afterlife. The long road framed a setting sun, a pink sky, and purple clouds hanging over the crowns of the tallest stone buildings. The calmness of the city and the warmth of its people washed over him, but not enough to bring down his guard. Beneath the other scents of the city was the faint smell of wildflower honey, sweet and floral. His heart raced and his pace quickened. Tytli was still in the city. She was close. *Why haven't you made your move?* It had been weeks, and she wasn't the careful type. *Unless . . .*

She, too, had her trepidations. That was also unlike her.

Rottgor followed the scent of her aether through the crowd. *Close.* The stinging began. Before his shaping, he had never experienced her aether. His once-deadened skin had given him immunity to the dreadful power of the other five Shadows, which meant he had never felt her ire before. He remembered once in his childhood when he'd shaken a persimmon tree and loosened a hornet's nest. The moment the nest crashed down, he was stung from head to toe. Her aether was no different. Perhaps worse. The more of her aether he weathered, the worse the little pricks underneath the surface of his skin became. He pushed through the storm, following the path she made for him. *You're calling me. Why?* He shuddered. Breadcrumbs and cheese often preluded the broken neck of a rat. He steeled himself for whatever would meet him at the other end.

Lost in thought, Rottgor barely noticed the sun's pink hues as he followed the dark alley to a quiet courtyard. The stinging stopped. Rottgor rubbed his biceps, the pain easing away. No swelling, no redness, only the pain. He saw her across the courtyard. Tytli sat on a weathered park bench, runelight lanterns casting a glow on her face. Soshadyel, with its honeycombed surface, rested on her lap. A thin silver veil covered her face. A black lotus replaced her missing eye, petals weeping down her face. Her other eye sharpened at his approach. "There you are. I've been expecting you."

"That's why you haven't made your move. Me?" Rottgor took a few cautious steps forward. She didn't move.

"Grimstone, Oron, Iliss, Jaggath . . . What would they say if we didn't at least talk first? I forgot about our pact. We've made too many promises in our lives."

"Grimstone would beat us to death." Rottgor gave a soft laugh. He remembered their leader, Ser Galelin Grimstone. The short, powerful magiian knight, stepbrother of the Worm King, had brought them together under one banner. He imagined the furrowed brow against the stone-skinned face. *I miss your advice, Grim.* "They wouldn't want us fighting."

"They wouldn't." The same glimmer of remembrance crossed her face as well. "But they aren't here anymore, are they?" She gave a faint, forlorn smile, then grabbed Soshadyel by its hilt and rose from her seat. She whipped the sword across the ground, slicing through the stone at Rottgor's feet. Honey splashed against the nearby grass, as black ichor, wasps, and bees built along its blade. Rottgor had seen the insects work plenty of times, but this was the first time he had reason for fearing them. "Are you going to stand in my way, my friend?"

"Will you make me?" Rottgor asked.

That gave her pause. "You've always been a man of duty, Rott. Never really speaking or making the big decisions, but always someone we learned to come to. You were our foundation and you never wavered." Her wings extended, broad and beautiful in their decay and battered state. More petals landed on the floor. "But this man before me is different. Not the Rottgor the Famine Blade I knew. Did I ever know you in the first place?"

"I wish you had," Rottgor admitted. "After breaking free, all

I knew was servitude. I didn't have a place to go back to. I didn't have a family. I was the worst rotting corpse among us." He laughed so weakly it barely reached his chest. "I looked strong, but I wasn't. I didn't know who I was. I was content watching life pass me by as I degraded into nothingness. Then I was given this chance. Lili, I don't want to give this up. Astra is part of it now."

"You don't know what she can do." Tytli's tone grew hard. "You don't know the power she wields, the pain she can bring, the terror just below the surface. You saw her anger. One tip. One fall. I have to stop it."

"We have," Rottgor whispered. "We've already stopped it. Isobel . . . she's dead. She's been dead a long time. Astra is not the woman who clawed out your eye out of jealousy for your beauty. That woman is gone and so is her lover. They are dirt in the ground and long-since dinner for the worms they praised so much. Look at the King, his bones have been salted and used as a chair, his skull a lantern. They can't hurt us anymore."

"They *can*," Tytli growled, her single eye narrowing to a slitted pupil. "As long as a drop of their blood lives on, a breath of their life, I will not give up."

"You've done enough, Lili."

Tytli lost her remaining cool. "It will never be enough, Rott."

She charged at him. The golden blade whistled by him, almost lashing across his chest. He narrowly missed the after spray, the stinging liquid inches from his toes. Rottgor stepped away. His mind knew her speed; his body, however, was far too slow. He lumbered backward, the blade missing once more, splitting a tree behind him in half. Splinters soared across his vision, a simple distraction, but effective. Tytli wouldn't need such simple tricks. *You're treating me as a fellow Death Knight.* But he wasn't one. Not anymore. He had no more spells, none of the undead strength or resistance to pain. Rottgor wasn't the Famine Blade any longer; he was a chef and she was still a seasoned warrior.

"You've gotten slow," she said, stopping suddenly. The blade was at his neck, inches from his throat. Beheading wasn't a memory he wished to experience once more. *This time, at least, I wouldn't be alive afterward.* "Put down the cauldron and the little box," she growled. "I want you at your best. You deserve that."

Rottgor did as instructed, then lifted his hands up. "I'm not a warrior anymore."

"But you are a fighter. Fight! Show me that she's worth fighting for. Show me that I'm wrong."

She's right. Astra is worth fighting for. He had no choice, it seemed. Rottgor reached his hand out, vile energy pooling at his fingertips. A small rift of magic opened, tearing through the air as a scar of green on the evening breeze. Rottgor caught Malferioel, the Contagion, the blade he had wielded for centuries, and it ate at his palm. It was far worse than before. The poison ran up his forearm, through his bicep, and up his shoulder. His veins swelled underneath his skin. Rottgor howled. Malferioel radiated a sickly green light. Chasms split the blade, spilling out aether as the metal shattered into fragments. A voice sighed on the wind: *"You are not him. You are no longer my master."* And in the second it took for the sword to explode, the world darkened.

Rottgor had never woken to a quiet room before. The stillness of it unsettled him. The buzzing of flies, the swarm of cicadas and locusts, they were his normalcy. There was an emptiness to the room—one in the air and one in his heart.

The silence caught him off guard. He sat upright in his bed, startled. Salve-dipped bandages wrapped his chest, stomach, thighs, and hands, their thick, herbaceous scent lingering under his nose. He wiggled his fingers and toes and blinked his eyes. *Good. Everything's there.* He felt gratitude—being dismembered wasn't a fun experience either. He gave himself time. All he remembered was the explosion: the bright light and green flames, the smell of the dead, and the brief look of fear and desperation in Tytli's eye. She'd screamed out to him, but everything was happening too fast. Then, nothingness. Nothingness, and then here, in his bed. He stretched, bones popping. *She was right. I'm not who I was.*

Malferioel was gone. Rottgor saw the thick, bloodied shards of the greatsword resting across from him on the mantel above his hearth. Whoever had saved him must've plucked the debris from his body. It was Malferioel's last act of disobedience. Oddly, he held no malice toward his once-loyal weapon's betrayal. The greatsword was built for blood and war and spreading its decay. A life of peace wasn't what it craved. *You're no longer my master.* Without it, was he the Famine Blade? Had he been the Famine Blade since leaving the Ruinous Guard? *Why do I hold on to things that aren't there? Is Rottgor truly dying?*

The thought gave him a chill.

Change.

The Afterlife had been the beginning of Rottgor's transformation. The shattering of Malferioel was its conclusion. What was left? He unwrapped his burnt hands. *I'm not Rottgor anymore.* He had grown so much in such a small time, yet he still hung on to his past. Watching Tytli stuck in her past as well, thriving only on her insatiable revenge, frightened him. He didn't want to be that. He didn't want to be stuck. He had been, all this time paused as a fossil left frozen within resin. His life at the Ruinous Guard, his days among the Six Shadows, the wars and the servitude... All that had happened in the past remained behind him. He kicked the sheets off him and swung his legs off the bed. The floor shook from his weight.

A knock sounded at the door, as he put on his white linen shirt and brown pants.

"Who's there?" he asked. Hearing his booming voice felt nice. He instantly regretted shouting when the person responded.

"I'm coming in." Lady Cleo stormed into his room, blood-orange eyes aflame. Her hot stare caught him. Rottgor couldn't tell if the look on her face was disappointment or indignation. He shrank back slightly. Two masked Slicksters slipped into the room with her, the door closing behind them, while two more stood guard outside. "You and Tytli are maybe the stupidest people I know, and I know a *lot* of stupid people."

"Good morning to you," Rottgor said carefully.

"It's afternoon. You've been out for a couple of days, healing. We had to remove the shards from your body and heart. By all accounts, you should be dead. Or more dead. *Permanently* dead." She paced around the room, her red dress flowing behind her. "Malferioel rejected you and the Soul Backlash almost leveled an entire part of the city. If not for the miracle of your rune and Tytli's intervention, we would've had a real emergency on our hands." Rottgor began to speak, but the red-orange eyes of the heiress darkened, and he shut his mouth. "*You are an idiot.* She is an idiot. You didn't think the royal family *knew* a member of the Aseimon-Denholm line survived? The Crown *knew.* We were the ones who made sure she survived. We were going to teach her when she got older. That. Was. The. Plan. We've done enough judging on her family's past."

Rottgor bit his lower lip. "Did you order the killing of her father?"

"I didn't. My grandfather didn't either. It was the Crown, the King and the Princesses at the capital. I heard they even gave Astra's father a chance. You learn not to question the Princesses or what they wish. All we were responsible for was making sure she found a loving place, a good education, and perhaps a better family. We saw more in that girl—more than just the magical prowess she inherited from the Denholms and the Aseimons. Something of her own. No bloodline is perfect." Lady Cleo crossed her arms. "I would've preferred she stay with a family, but that has proven . . . difficult."

"She told me." That feeling choked him once more.

"Never mind that. What matters is that Tytli is being Tytli and *you are being you*." Lady Cleo came right up to his face, stopping only inches from stepping on his toes. Her words, he reckoned, would do enough of that. She gave him a small shove. "You clung to that sword. That." She pointed at the broken blade. "You believed it was you. And we allowed it and I shouldn't have. You aren't that blade anymore. You haven't been for years. You told me your name when I was five. *Five.*" An angry tear ran down her face. Lady Cleo clenched her teeth. "And I remembered thinking, King Aseimon named you like a pet. He didn't do that to any of the other people he forced to become his Commanders. Only you. You were the guard dog. Rottgor. A funny little name he made for his rabid animal. And I was sad, perhaps for the first time truly in my entire life." She bit her lip, her frustration rising by the second. The Slicksters never looked more uncomfortable.

"You know," she continued, "the earlier books about you said you couldn't speak. That you were all growls and roars. When you spoke to me that day, I was startled. Up until that point, you'd only listened, but I heard your voice and I was happy. You changed me. You gave me a friend, and I knew that releasing you would be my present to you, no matter what."

"Then you asked me what my real name was," Rottgor said. He was thrown back to that day. They'd been in the garden for the first time. He remembered squirming under her curious young eyes, questions bubbling from her lips. She sat by the pond, skipping rocks and picking flowers by its bay. She wore a pair of overalls, too mischievous and curious for the dress of a noble lady. Smaller, but as fierce as the lady she was now. She'd looked up at him, barely as tall as his bone-exposed legs. "You want to know something? I didn't know it until you asked. No one had ever asked, and time and magic had withered my name away. But when you asked, looked at me so expectantly, I remembered. Razgaif the Younger. Razgaif the Champion of the Onyx-Ax. The orc who'd died for his family and become—"

"No 'and.'" Lady Cleo gathered her strength. "You *are* Razgaif, the Champion now. The Champion, and much more. So many things were stolen from you, out of one man's greed."

"I don't feel—"

"You never feel worthy of happiness," Lady Cleo snapped, "but now you don't have an excuse." She took to the mantel, grabbing the lifeless shards of Malferioel and stuffing them into a leather sack. "I should've taken this when you left the castle." A deep stitch of loneliness struck him. *Like watching an old friend's funeral,* he thought. *No—Malferioel was more a colleague, an acquaintance whose path diverged from mine long ago.* Cleo had told him to let go a long time ago, but he'd chosen to hold on. Funny that the sword was the one to break away.

"I have one request," he told her, watching her stow the last of his legacy within her simple bag. "Make sure it goes to a worthy knight. No more pestilence. Treat it like you treated Grim's Hemorg the Bloodcrest." The Deathblade Hemorg had been remade into two swords, its hardened blood becoming Nightvein and False Life, both carried by members of the Ruinous Guard. To see Malferioel treated the same way would ease the guilt and confusion rising within his soul.

Lady Cleo nodded. "Meet me downstairs. Are you well enough to cook?"

He flexed his fingers. "A *siefu*—an orc war chef—is expected to cook, even after battle, unless the wounds are fatal. It's for our honor and our clan. It will give my idle hands some purpose."

"Good, good. Ask for help, if you must. I believe I deserve a meal after saving your life." He knew the real reason. She hid her face, clearly annoyed by her own emotions. Her own responsibilities as the next Duchess were mounting. Her little excursions would no longer be possible soon enough, and she knew that. The Slicksters aided her sudden departure, ushering her out the door. The guards outside quickly understood, folding in behind them, protecting the scattered remains of Cleo's pride.

Rottgor—or what was left of him—stood alone in his quiet room once more. He welcomed the silence this time, his thoughts clear and concise. Cleo had put his world into perspective. No more was he the slobbering beast, poison leaking from the corners of his lips, growls and roars escaping his jaws . . . mind trapped. He walked over to the full-length mirror and peered at its surface. The orc that stared back wasn't a Death Knight anymore. He knew it from his size, the restored flesh and hair, and the return of his Onyx-Ax accent. He'd never truly let it all sink in. He touched his hair, rubbed his beard, and took a deep breath. Then there were his eyes. The sewer green and its glow were gone, replaced by blue sky and gold wheat. *One more meal as him,* the living orc decided, *one last walk as the Death Knight.* A funeral of some sort.

Sunlight was warm on his skin through the windows, and he smelled Flynn cooking lunch downstairs. His senses burned, his mind clearer than before. The bareness of his living quarters still seemed odd, not quite lived in. While the restaurant showed a bit of himself, the upper area did not. He ran his fingers along the spines of the leather books. There was one he hadn't seen before, a gift no doubt from the soon-to-be Duchess. It was a book of the ancient writings of his clan: *Roots of the Obsidian and Its Glory* by Ivagan III. Ivagan. There was no way. *It has to be . . . Did . . . someone survive?* He leafed through the book and saw it. The very same recipe for his elderberry-and-cloudberry-crumble pudding. One of his nephews had lived and carried on his family's legacy. A new kind of joy struck him. *Ivagan lived.* His sister's son, and then he had sons. Maybe they did, too. His family, a single thread like the Aseimon-Denholms, lived. A single note was written in the margins by Lady Cleo.

Remember who you are.

Their faces, his family, became clearer now. All of them.

He took the book, nestling the green-leathered tome under his arm. The Champion in him smiled. There weren't many of them left, but his blood survived. He had to meet his kin one day. *But not before I finish what I have to do here.* He went downstairs.

The Lady and her Slicksters sat in the corner of the Afterlife, the regulars giving them a wide berth. To his surprise, the Slicksters had removed their masks and hoods, revealing their painted faces. What was even more surprising were their smiles. They were no different from the other customers, laughing and joking. Cleo remained herself, though, arms folded, awkward in her formality.

Flynn waved his boss over. "I don't serve royalty," he said bluntly. "Nothing against 'em, but I don't do fancy. That was part of me taking this job and—"

"No worries. I have this." Flynn arched an eyebrow at Rottgor, noticing the change in his boss's demeanor.

"You sure, boss? You almost took the permanent trip over and—"

Rib-Digger waddled over and put his hand on Flynn. "Trust."

Flynn sighed. "Trust."

Clyth, Bao Su, and Waldruk all nodded as well.

Flynn bowed, leaving the head chef to his work. *Simple,* he decided. *They've had enough of the castle's food.* The Onyx-Ax cookbook lay on the counter. Page after page was filled with memories he'd forgotten. He looked at Lady Cleo, who hid a laugh. He wondered how long he'd had the cookbook, hidden among all the other books she'd given him from the royal library.

He considered the cookbook, but stuck with his initial decision—nothing special. He prepared slices of roasted mammoth seasoned with rosemary, left over from the lunch rush; chopped red-beet-and-blood-cabbage soup; and a sweet-potato bread slathered with butter and cinnamon. He worked on each bowl and plate himself, deciding on a cheese sauce for the mammoth flank for the final touch. *Something quick.* He whisked together a few seasonings, threw in herbs to complement the rosemary, and combined a bit of butter, cheese, and cream to make a silky sauce. A delightful smell filled the room as he heated the sauce and poured it over the steaks. Flynn's face twitched, lips trembling.

"You're going to serve the future Duchess this. It's so—all right, don't panic."

"You said that you weren't going to serve royalty, right? And you don't like fancy food, remember? This is as simple as it gets."

Flynn opened his mouth, then closed it. "I hate that everyone here uses my words against me."

Waldruk lowered his head. "Wouldn't happen if you didn't make it so easy."

"Shut up, pretty boy. Bao, you shut up, too." Flynn pointed at the fae fox.

Bao waved her fan, releasing a burst of magical wind. Flynn tumbled back. "I haven't *said* anything."

"You don't have to. Anyway, I trust you, boss. Just don't get the restaurant closed. I'm starting to like it here."

"Don't worry about that." The confidence in his voice shocked him. The meal was simple, one often fed to the orcs of his clan after a hunt or a harvest. He remembered making it for his brothers and sister, their lovers, and their children almost every week. *Siefu mak*—the feeling of gifting a full belly—already filled his beating heart. He imagined serving his little girl, his daughter . . . Astra. The thought no longer frightened him.

With plates of the Hunter's Feed resting on his forearms, he approached the table. The Slicksters cheered for the food. Lady Cleo laughed at them, and Bao Su poured them fresh drinks of their choosing. The Slicksters quieted once they were all served and allowed their Lady the first bite. Cleo began with the soup, dipping her spoon into the red liquid and bringing it to her lips. The Duchess of Death—Cleotraeli Crowsilk, heiress to the Carnation Throne, and Magus of the Unspoken World—disappeared. In her place, he saw the girl with oversize overalls, dirt on her knees, pond water dripping from her hands. She smiled at him.

"This is delicious," she said quietly.

Razgaif the Younger smiled back. "Thank you, Cleo."

TWELVE

Embers of Memories

Razgaif the Younger—Champion of the Onyx-Ax, *siefu*, and proprietor of the Afterlife Crisis—stood by the window, thinking about the people he cared for.

First and foremost, he had ensured Astra's safety. Calfe's "boys"—whomever they were, and he didn't want to know—kept an eye on both Astra and Tytli. To help, Razgaif spent some time using his ears to pick up information, breaking his usual habit of filtering out the world around him.

It turned out that Bao's little friends—the Concord, as she called them—caught some interesting pieces as well. Not unlike their owner, he supposed. Between Bao, Waldruk, and Clyth, the gossip flowed almost as much as did coin. They often huddled together for the gossip. Razgaif now knew much more about the lords, ladies, and common folk than he cared to. Then, there was the man of the hour, the bigmouth himself, Calfe, who visited more frequently, at about the same time every day. Today, he sauntered in, smiling, carrying the catch of the day, oxtails, and a batch of starchy yellow fruits called platyos, all from his wife's homeland. He set the sack down, then sat and began swinging his legs.

"All right, all right," Razgaif said, kneading the dough of a sweet-potato-and-rosemary bread he'd been trying with no success. "Tell me what's happening."

"I thought you'd never ask," Calfe said. "I'm practically bursting at the seams."

"Do tell," Clyth said, sliding into the conversation and lacing his fingers together.

"Tytli—well, she's been staying from place to place within the city, recovering from the explosion. There's been some activity around the Living Vine, but not by who you think. Vom's been moving around, causing trouble." Calfe rubbed the bridge of his nose. "I'm going to kill him."

"You might have to take a number." Razgaif placed the ball of dough to the side and covered it with a towel. He brushed his hands against his apron.

"He's always been a fool about the undead and the summoned being citizens of the city." Calfe leaned back, eyes dark. "The reason that his family—the Brasscrowns—moved down from the Cloud Pinnacle was to amass their riches here on cheap labor, specifically from the undead. They took any shortcut they could to amass wealth, a habit not lost on Vom. Four generations in, and they're only high merchants, if barely. They've lived with that bitterness for a long time. Decency robbed his family of the riches they had."

"Seems rather"—Razgaif reached for the word—"petty?"

"The petty ones are the most dangerous, in my experience. Those who don't have a reason for their cruelty." Calfe rose from his chair. "Well, I guess I should be going."

"Is that all you have today?" Clyth cocked his head. "I thought you were going to bring us better treats."

"Boring!" Bao shouted from the other side of the room.

"I'll bring some more tantalizing gossip next time. I still need to confirm that one story about Lady Arborel and the olive-oil tradesman."

Clyth snorted. "You *need* to get on that."

Razgaif nodded, letting Calfe go.

Clyth helped Bao take the sack Calfe had brought into the kitchen. Bao then turned, a question on her lips.

"So, Raz," she said carefully, getting used to his actual name, "what are you going to do when Tytli comes for you again? She's convinced you'll come to your friend's aid no matter where you are. I believe that, too. You'd do that for any of us." She paused, her tails fluttering, spraying fairy dust everywhere. "Tytli's a legend in the Fae Realm. A martyr queen who gave her life protecting her people. We didn't even know she had been raised to serve her murderer's army until much later. Please . . . don't blame her for her anger."

"I don't. Her anger is justified . . . to the person who wronged her." One problem remained: If he and the Honeycombed Woman crossed blades once more, he would surely lose. His undead strength and Death Knight magic were gone, and now his Deathblade was behind him. He had only his wits and his rusty skills. No true weapon of worth. "I don't know if I can face her." Clyth said nothing, quiet and thoughtful. A cool feeling ran through Razgaif's mind, soft fingers prodding a memory forward. It shook Razgaif's tender heart when he spoke: "Tremorwalker."

He hadn't thought of the name in years. His palm remembered the smoothness of the well-worn redwood, the shine of the black stone ax mined from a great meteor of the valley. More than ever, the longing for that ax rushed through him. He remembered the bravery, the pride, of having such a glorious weapon. It had never controlled him. It was a part of him.

How did I ever forget? The ax—an ax of a true Champion—could match a Deathblade. It had nearly done so once before. This time, he wouldn't fail. "I miss my great ax."

Clyth nodded. "Waldruk will know how to find enough Black Relic Meteorites. Quite a few have been passed down from your existing clan members. Perhaps seeing the last Champion of their clan might compel them to gather the pieces together to reforge Tremorwalker. With your own hands of course. You are the only person who will remember it clearly."

"Of course." Razgaif's body tingled. Using his hands for the rebirth of his lost weapon? Becoming again the protector of the Onyx Caverns upon the coast? He could think of no better honor than to become the guardian of his people once more. "I can try. I'll ask Waldruk when he gets in."

As though spoken into existence, Waldruk entered, hooded and clearly trying his best to act like the mysterious vampire fledgling everyone knew he wasn't. He hurried behind the counter, silent. An odd thing for him.

Flynn, a long pipe dangling from his lips, slunk over to Waldruk. He peered down, pulling the pipe from his lips, green smoke dancing under his breath. "Boy, what happened to your eye?" Flynn asked, loud enough for the rest of the employees to hear. Razgaif stopped stirring the butternut-squash soup he was working on and focused on the young vampire. Clyth turned sharply.

"It's nothing," Waldruk muttered.

"Who. Hurt. You?" Flynn demanded, fingers clutching the bend of his pipe.

Clyth strode over, flames billowing around his brow in a crown of fire. He flung the hood off of Waldruk's head. There it was, his eye, blackened as night and bleeding. The handsome, young half orc turned away, wiping a bit of blood from his freshly trimmed mustache.

"It's nothing, I promise, Clyth. Just a few of the Chosen," Waldruk muttered. "I scared them away."

"Who. Hurt. You?" Flynn repeated. "Give me specifics. I will handle it." Flynn's eyes shone fiercely underneath the shag of his hair.

"No, *I* will handle it. *I will handle all of it.*" Clyth's voice lost its normal smooth edge, replaced by a deep pitch of brimstone and flames. The resident of the Burnt Rooms cupped Waldruk's face with his palm. "I told you to be careful going alone. I'll burn them alive."

Waldruk bit his busted lip and winced in pain. "You can't always be there. I'm a lordling. We have pride, Clyth. But I know you care."

The demon's voice cooled. "More than you know."

It appears they have grown closer than I realized. Razgaif lowered the heat of the stovetop, allowing the already-tender squash to simmer. He approached the young man and pushed his bangs from his forehead. Waldruk's right eye was plump, purple, and bloodied, oozing black from the bottom lashes. Waldruk tried turning away, but Razgaif's meaty fingers around his jaw forced the young man to look him in the eye. He was hurt pretty bad. Razgaif nodded, removing his fingers from his jaw.

"Sit down," Razgaif told him. "I'm not asking."

Defeated, Waldruk took a seat. A live animal's blood was valuable to a young vampire, the life force giving their magic more energy. The Nightswallows, however, had good control over their hemalurgy—the blood magic that gave vampires their strength. *Raw meat will give him what he needs.* Razgaif pulled a slab of beef from the freezer and gently warmed it to melt the ice away. He flavored it lightly, with a few sprinkles of salt and pepper. Nothing too overpowering. Most older orcs knew the taste well enough, though eating it fresh was not as common a practice anymore. He cut a piece off for himself and tasted it. *Not as good as if it were fresh. What if . . .* Razgaif focused once more on the taste of the uncooked slab on the roof of his mouth. He focused on that flavor, remembering the coppery flavor and the ligaments. *Enough, not too much.* He took a deep breath and hoped the simple meal was enough.

Waldruk looked the worse for wear in the brief time Razgaif had gone to search for the meal, swaying where he sat. Razgaif placed the plate beside him and then helped the fledgling up in his seat. A new fury rose in his chest. Though they looked different from the living, it was a common misconception that vampires were undead. They weren't. *Nightswallows wouldn't take this sitting down, and neither would we.*

"Eat up," said Razgaif. Waldruk did as he was told without complaint, and that was when Razgaif knew he was hurting badly. Waldruk took his first bite, his fellow employees surrounding him. Razgaif watched, gripping the counter. After a few more bites, they all saw his strength return.

A bit of blood dribbled from the side of his mouth, which he dabbed away quickly. The bruising below his eye had already lightened, his lips were less plump, and his skin had regained a little color—though not much, as he was still pale as a ghost. Waldruk pulled himself to standing, wiping his tears from his eyes, gold magic from Razgaif's rune still lingering around his lips. Admitting that he, a nobleman of the city, had been scared was below his pride. "That was . . ." He swallowed. "I guess I can tell you what happened," he said.

Lord Waldruk Nightswallow went through his tale. It had

been a simple outing. He was going to the Afterlife after visiting his orcish mother when the Chosen came upon him and tried to beat him to death. Waldruk fought them off to the best of his ability, but he was getting clobbered by their clubs and sticks. His blood magic failed him. Eventually, he managed to break free and run, making it to the main roads where the guards were stationed. The thugs didn't dare a pursuit after that.

"That's it," he said, drinking a blended mixture of mulberry and spinach that Bao had brought over in the middle of his story. He sipped at it, suppressing his soured face. "Can I go back to work now?" he asked. "And please, don't tell my parents. They're . . . a bit overprotective."

"I know." Having a vampire coven and an orc tribe as his family? They would tear down half of Necropolis for their boy.

Razgaif knew embellishment when he heard it, but chose not to ruin the vision of how the fledgling nobleman saw himself. So, he gave the young man what he needed most: a hug. "Do you need the day off?"

"No." Waldruk shook his head. "I'm fine. A young Lord needs to hold his head high in defeat."

"It wasn't defeat," Clyth whispered. "Cowards don't earn wins." He held Waldruk's hands. "Razgaif has a question—if you're up for it."

"Of course."

Razgaif looked down. "It seems rather inappropriate now."

"No," Waldruk said. "The least I can do is help. What do you need, Razgaif the Younger, our Martyr Champion?"

"Do you remember my legendary weapon, Tremorwalker? I . . . wish to forge something similar. But I need some Black Relic Meteorites."

Waldruk nodded. "On my noble blood as a Nightswallow

and on my honor as an Onyx-Ax, consider it done. If Black Relic Meteorites are what you need, then they are what you will get."

Razgaif's mind drifted back to Astra. He wished her safety. The only way to do that was to handle the problems they faced: Tytli and Vom. He couldn't do this alone. *Tytli. Maybe. Back where we started.* One thing was for sure: Rottgor or Razgaif, he had to protect the people he held close.

Waldruk returned, hauling a wagon of black stone and a massive orangewood handle. Though pleased, Razgaif was sure the lordling hadn't eaten or drunk all day, his fervor taking over his judgment. *Quite the change from him. A good one, though.* Outside, Razgaif brought him the finest mug of ale he had, as well as the rest of the beef and the butternut-squash soup he'd made for lunch. Waldruk collapsed on the road, taking his dinner exactly where he sat.

"My. Hard work isn't as glorious as it seems. My legs feel like jelly. Thank you, Champion," he said, downing the ale. It filled itself back to the brim. "Oh . . ." He stared into the cup, then looked up at Razgaif. "Again . . . I'm sorry. If I had known you were the Lost Champion, I would've used any resource for you. . . . I should've respected you more and—"

"It's behind us, Wal, don't worry about it." Razgaif put his hand on Waldruk's. A memory of his brother Ganzon surfaced—prideful yet earnest, insecure yet certain in his ways. "You didn't need to get all of this."

"When I told them that the Lost Champion had returned, they didn't believe me at first. But Grandma Kao stood up for me. She said that she made you a *haogu* and recognized who you were through the cloak of death you wore. Almost everyone listens to her. She only had two requests: Bring some food to the feast, and forge the new weapon at the Midnight Forge in our village."

This was the first time he was hearing of an organized Onyx-Ax community. *My people.* What could they teach him? What could he remind them of? Anticipation built in his chest. His heart longed for one thing, one other person he wanted to be there—Astra. The thought was foolish and selfish.... To take her there would endanger her, pull her from the safety and protection of the Living Vine. But she was young and she deserved her freedom. *If she consents to come, I'll protect her.* Razgaif clenched his fist as though holding on to his new life.

"I'll see what I can do," he told Waldruk, gathering the threads of his fraying courage. "Get some rest, friend. You deserve it." Razgaif slipped him a sizable tip, enough to buy the bow he'd been talking about. Razgaif left him before the protest could begin.

The rest of the day went by in a flash. The dinner crowd came and went, and soon the Afterlife was serving its last customers of the night. Razgaif closed down the shop, flipping the sign outside, then sat at one of the tables, surrounded now only by the memories of the night's boisterous guests. The lingering smells of those final meals hung in the air. He stood and took some leftovers to the chair by the window, the same one he had sat in alongside Astra when this whole predicament with Tytli all started. Sipping on the thyme-and-mammoth-bone soup, he wrote his letter to Astra, inviting her to the forging of his weapon. If his memory served him correctly, it would be a glorious event.

Typically, new orc Champions forged their weapon in the black flame, under the boiling sun and with the burning calluses of their working hands. The Champion designed their companion, gave it life from start to finish, and like any parent, it ended in a name. Tremorwalker had been his, and he mourned the simple black stone ax with its enchanted persimmon-wood handle. A simple weapon. Effective. It had been nothing like Malferioel, which had left a rotten void within his palm, its hilt resonating hunger and thirst at his fingers. His new weapon would be something different, nothing like either blade. Tremorwalker was no more, broken at the hands of the Worm King's crushing army. Malferioel was in pieces. It was time for something new.

He remembered the old weapon and saw another in his mind. One wouldn't expect one child to replace another. Razgaif sipped the rest of his soup and chewed on the last piece of meat. His fingers found his parchment and pencils once more. The form came first, and the rest came soon after. The taste of his childhood bloomed on his tongue, oranges and grilled fish fresh from the rivers. The memories guided his hand as it slid across the parchment, giving way to a final burst of life. He brought his sketch up to the moonlight. *The Great Traveler.* He hoped his rusty skill with the pencil matched the vision living in his head.

Razgaif placed the sketch aside, bringing forward another piece of parchment. He switched from pencils to his finest ink, which scared him worse than forging or meeting his people. He wrote the letter a dozen times, ink drying on his fingertips at every attempt. Nothing sounded right. Why would Thess take him at his word, trust him with Astra's safety? Again, the foolishness of the idea mounted in his mind. He was reclaiming who he was, taking back the things he'd lost over time. Still. He missed one thing: family. All the blood he had known were long since buried. Perhaps he still had a bloodline or two left . . . but Astra was here. Now. He crumpled another letter attempt, tossing it to the pile growing on the floor. Groaning, he dived in once more.

The ending result sounded more like a pitiful plea than a request. Razgaif put down the pen and stretched his cramped fingers. "Why?" he asked himself aloud. *Why do I want this so bad?* Tytli was sure he was under some spell. Maybe he was, in a sense. He stared out the window into the starlit sky. How far had he come in just a few months? Not all the wounds were healed. Rottgor had lived a long life, but Razgaif hadn't. *Serve. Bend. Break.* Those words wanted that space, clawed at his newly sprouting happiness. *Happiness.* He deserved it; Astra deserved it. They all did.

Midnight came over the Afterlife Crisis. The runelight grew dim and the candles burned low. His letter lay unfinished on the table. He brought over the swordfish Calfe had brought that morning, laying the behemoth over his lap. The scent of the pungent fish brought a memory so sharp it almost hurt. He saw his father sitting by the grassy lakeshore, pants rolled to his knees and shirt wet from spearfishing, a pastime he'd enjoyed more toward the end of his life, when sicknesses and age had begun claiming him. *He would've loved this.* Razgaif remembered him, the only one of his siblings who could now.

He shared much with his father: his features, his name, his height, the slump of his shoulders, his eyes, the way he wore his hair, and the way he braided his beard. And somehow, centuries later, his mind, his body, and his tattered soul remembered his father and still learned from him. His father's kind voice and wise words were clear over the scraping of Razgaif's knife against the fish scales and over the embers of the memory. *"I hope one day you'll know the joy of loving someone as much as I love you, son. When you do, and I know you will, hold on to them. Remember the love I gave you and give it to someone else. Let it grow forever. Let that be a legacy. We leave too much hate in this world when all it takes is one person to remember your love and that they love you."* Razgaif tilted his head back, letting a tear fall.

"I do want this," he said to the memory of his father, long crossed over to his resting place. "I want to be a father like you."

THIRTEEN

The Great Traveler

"I didn't think I'd get this far," Razgaif admitted.

"Well, we're here now, big boy. The interesting thing about confidence, I've learned, is that it's usually faked. We pretend that we have complete certainty when there's always a little doubt everywhere. That little doubt is healthy—it humbles us and encourages us to learn. You didn't have to try to reach out to Astra, but you did, despite all the fear telling you otherwise. So, it's time to believe in that flawed logic and dive in, even if you fall face first."

Calfe's counsel was a drink of cold water on a hot day. He hadn't batted an eye when Razgaif had told him his true name. Razgaif's unlikely friend never saw him as a Death Knight and wasn't attached to the legend of Rottgor the Famine Blade. For him, the name didn't matter—the person did. Razgaif appreciated that.

"Thanks, Calfe," he said.

The elf-dwarf snorted.

"Can you please?" Razgaif snapped. "I'm trying to be serious."

"I know, that's why I'm laughing." Calfe waved him off. "But if you wanna be all *feelsy*, I respect you and think you'll protect Astra just fine as a parent."

"How do you do it? The parenting thing?"

"It's a play-by-ear type of situation. You'll know what's right after you get it all wrong a few times." Calfe patted him on the shoulder. "Perhaps don't do what I do, though. I'm torturing my kid with my existence. Sometimes, that's how I work." Calfe shrugged. Razgaif groaned at the thought of being raised by that ball of chaos manifested as a man. "You have another question. I see it on your ugly face."

Razgaif gave him a push and Calfe laughed. "You've been keeping Vom away, haven't you? That's why you've been showing up bloody and beaten. You need any help with him?"

Calfe's face went dark, the jovial and cunning expression replaced by something cold. Razgaif had seen that look before in only one type of people: assassins. It lined up. After some research, he'd found that the Metcoats were rich and powerful property owners, yet their money seemed a little off for that line of work alone. They worked in the shadows, moved assets between places, and kept their ears close to the streets. Calfe always smelled of old blood and a tinge of poison under his light cologne. They weren't professional assassins, Razgaif was sure, more of a criminal underground than blades in the night. *Well, Metcoats does sound a lot like "meat coats."* Razgaif gave a grim chuckle. "I didn't want you involved," Calfe finally said. "I offered you this property, so it's not your concern."

Razgaif cocked his head. "Are you in a gang war?"

Calfe considered, then shrugged. "Hm. I guess."

"You guess?" Razgaif rubbed his temples.

"If I hadn't told you, you'd still be in the dark." Calfe squinted at him. "You see, neither of us can act directly. He would already *be* floating face up in the river if it were up to me. But, it's not. Necropolis isn't like the other cities. We have to play by a certain set of rules. The Duke and the Lady value the city's safety beyond anything, and I do, too. I respect the leaders of our city, and I'm not here to undermine them. Vom is. The Light of the Chosen—what a pretentious name for a lot of fool half-wits—will do anything to stir the undead into action. And what's a bigger symbol of the city and its justice than you and Tytli? And now Astra?" Calfe inhaled from his dwarvish box, blowing peppermint smoke from his lips. "Again, all of this shouldn't be your concern, and I'm sorry. I tend to mess things up."

"Thanks for being honest, Calfe. I appreciate it." Razgaif knew the Afterlife had a cost beyond the price tag. Nothing in their world was free. And he supposed Calfe knew that well enough himself, risking his life, fortune, and opportunity on a man he'd merely happened upon. "If they come for us, we'll be ready. I won't waste my breath on the willfully ignorant." *That was what the blade of an ax was for.*

His heart lurched at a sudden knock at the door, the nerves in his stomach popping as he opened it. Astra's familiar face met him, her hands clasped behind her back and body swaying on the heels of her little boots. She waved, and all Razgaif's anticipation eased. Wordlessly, she grabbed his legs into a tight hug.

"I thought I was losing my mind," she said. "I've been stuck in the house for weeks. I can only read and study so much." Razgaif heard the tears gathering thick at the back of her throat. "I can't stand it. You know how hard it is for me to stay still. It's *torture*."

"I'm sorry, little one. It's my fault." Razgaif held her tight. "You wouldn't be—"

"Be quiet," she said, interrupting him. "I'm happy I get to come with you to this ceremony."

They broke away, leaving Razgaif with a warm feeling in his heart. Apart from her puffy eyes, Astra looked happy. He'd sent the orphanage funds to buy her any clothes she wanted for the journey, and they'd gone to good use. She wore a simple traveler's dress, black leggings, and tall brown boots that hit her knees. A big red bow tied her hair into a large puff on her head, while a few strands of hair dangled onto her forehead. She did a little twirl, and the whole restaurant gave the young lady an applause. Astra giggled and grinned. She finally entered the building proper.

Zennexus, quiet and unseen until that point, suddenly decided that he, too, wanted to partake. He abandoned his elvish form, assuming the full glory of his gargoyle nature. He wouldn't have made it in if the doorway hadn't been meant for an orc. A spell the gargoyle had cast lightened his weight upon entering so as not to ruin the wooden floor. He nodded. "Hello, again—Mr. Razgaif, was it? Strange that fleshies are also willing to change their names upon whims."

"Changed back," Razgaif corrected him. "And it happens from time to time. We get bored, too."

A rumble of a laugh quaked from the gargoyle's chest. He slapped his tail on a nearby table, toppling it over. Zennexus scratched his head. "My apologies, I'm a bit clumsy. Things are rarely the size I think they should be."

"Very few things are giant orc sized, so I understand, but thank you, too, for coming." Razgaif shook the gargoyle's warm hand, which felt like a smooth stone that had bathed in the sun. "You're coming with us, I assume?"

"It was Ms. Thess's condition for this endeavor." Zennexus shook his giant head. "I do not mind. Astra is sweet and understanding. Some children are not."

"That's the truth." Razgaif closed the door behind him. "Come, we still have a bit of time before we leave."

Razgaif followed Astra to the counter, where she, Rib-Digger, and Calfe were carrying on a brief debate. Soon all the staff, and even a few regulars, were chiming in. Bao Su—animated, passionate, and blunt—made poignant points, frequently countered by Waldruk's heated comments. Clyth and Flynn remained quiet, smiling as they observed the little girl at the center of it all. *My family,* Razgaif thought as he saw Rib-Digger fix the bow on Astra's head, his giant fingers moving inch by inch until he'd achieved perfection. *My family.* His heart quickened. *Mine.* The thought excited him, frightened him. When will the war horn sound?

What are they even talking about? Razgaif wondered, snapping himself back to the present. "Cheesecake is not a *cake!*" Astra shouted. *Ah, the important questions.*

Razgaif focused on the food for the feast instead, refusing to join the debate. His nerves eased, replaced by his excitement for the Forging. He remembered his first, barely. He'd been a thirteen-summer orc, chosen as Champion for his size and strength, wit and kindness. It was a lifelong title, earned and passed down by his father. Counting his second life, he supposed he was the longest-reigning Champion of all orckind. But misfortune after misfortune had struck his clan until little was left. He wished for nothing more than to revitalize his clan. *Am I enough?* A little hope, the same hope he had been given, was what they needed now. *Unapologetically celebrate what you have,* Duke Jamis once said. *You never know when you won't have the chance anymore.*

Simple words.

Effective.

Razgaif knew there was no better opportunity than the present. He pulled the marinating swordfish from the barrels he had them resting in, placed them on little hooks, and slung them over his broad shoulders. He looked a bit like a tree, bearing random pieces of meat, root vegetables, and fresh fruit. He brought his cauldron as well, which he called the *Kopsug*, the Cupbearer. One day, it would reach the hands of generations beyond himself. *Plenty. A better legacy than pestilence.* This time, the beverage of choice was a soft juice made of a large orcish grape the size of a fist called the *scopgorg*. A sweet but thick-skinned apple or pear would make a perfect pair for the grilled meats and vegetables on the menu, but alas, he had neither. Fully prepared, he regrouped with his party.

"I'm as ready . . . as I'm going to be," he said.

"I could help carry that," Zennexus offered. "It will be no issue for me."

"No. The Champion bears the gifts for their people as thanks for choosing them—and to bring humbleness upon their person. Or at least they used to. Some Champions have lost their way, caught in the ego of the title." Their clan currently had no Champion. From what he understood through word of mouth, their Chieftain was a child of six, one of the last of his line. There hadn't been a Champion chosen among them in centuries—his spot never claimed aside from brief and unworthy prospects long dead.

"Sounds like a lot to put on one person, literally," Calfe mentioned.

"It is a great honor. I hope to see the Mammoth-Tusk Table once more." How much had changed? *Is it standing still?* Years had slipped away from him, leaving him a rusted feature, no different from a memorial of older times. *I'll change that.* He was awake now. It was time to explore the world he'd left behind. "We should leave. Can't be late for this."

The staff waved them off.

"Open," Rib-Digger said to Astra, making a cupping gesture. "Hand."

Astra followed suit. Rib-Digger pulled a small box from the front pocket of his dirt-stained shirt and plopped it in her hand. Astra squealed.

"Open. Now. Please. Excited."

She did as she was told. In the little box lay a fine silver necklace ending at a heart-shaped spinel gemstone. Astra gasped. "You got this? For me?"

Rib-Digger nodded.

"But—it looks so expensive."

"No. Need. Money. Work. For. Fun. Work. For. Family." Rib-Digger gave a huge smile of blackened, empty gums and few rotten teeth. The friendliest smile Razgaif had ever seen.

"Thank you so much." Astra combated her tears and lost. She put on the necklace and clutched it. "Thank you, Ribby." Rib-Digger gave a happy grunt.

The night air whispered on Razgaif's skin as the afternoon spun toward evening. A bonfire on the cusp of twilight sounded wonderful. Together, they went down the path of Famine back to Blood, with food on his back and the wagon of black-onyx stone behind him. It was no secret that large gatherings of Onyx-Axes weren't much of an occurrence anymore. Few of the Onyx-Axes were left after the Worm King's invasion. Where they did gather was a small area tucked off the edge of the farms of Famine and the busy business streets of Blood. They went on their way, through the winding roads and the shadows of towering stone buildings. The tall runelight lampposts slowly transitioned to homemade lanterns, and the surrounding buildings became cozy wooden structures woven into trees.

The entire settlement within the city held that warm light, emitting from the ground itself. Luminous mushrooms blinked on their path. Root vegetables sprawled along the cobblestone. Well-worn stairs led to houses and curled upward toward the center of the district. A bonfire burned, its blaze a beacon among the black spears and arrowheads. Tree stumps served as seats around the fire, empty now but not for long. This was the setup for the Forging; the only thing missing was the Forger. Razgaif parked the wagon around the side of the bonfire.

Razgaif began working, taking off the skewers of the giant fish and the vegetables from his shoulders and placing them within the fire. He arranged the rest of the food upon the stumps, preparing the dishes as well as he could, using the weapons and tools around the fire. A comfort came over him as he performed the warrior rites once more. Age brought gratitude, it seemed. He flipped the blackening fish and the bigger tubers until they crisped. The smell lured his fellow orcs out of their homes.

One by one, doors opened around him. Whether Waldruk or his grandmother had said anything to their clan about the Forging, Razgaif didn't know. A low chanting started. The rumblings of the tribe's words and the pounding of drums echoed through the hollowing land. More orcs emerged from their homes. Soon, they all stood circled around the bonfire, old and young alike. Silkmaster Kao stepped from the largest building, Waldruk at her side. Behind them, a few orcs carried a magical smelter and its anvil. To see a Black Flame Forger again gave his heart a stutter. The old orcish woman approached him and touched his broad shoulders.

"I knew there was a grace about you," Silkmaster Kao said.

"One that I couldn't ignore. The Lost Champion, the Martyr. Our weakness failed you in your time of need."

Razgaif shook his head. "No more of that," he said, stoking the fire. "Our clan has seen enough regrets. I . . . have enough regrets." He saw Astra smiling out of the corner of his eye. It made it all worth it. "Let us feast, be merry, and witness the birth of the Great Traveler." He straightened his back and extended his hands. The flames erupted, catching wind from his burst of aether, and blazed gold. His visions of their homeland moved through the smoke, the warm caves, the long stretches of rivers and plains, their hunting forest, everything he kept within himself, the memories the youngest there had never imagined. Astra gasped at the beauty of it all.

The images faded and the food finished cooking. Almost fifty Onyx-Axes had arrived for the feast, but Razgaif had made plenty. The Big Sail Swordfish itself was the size of a few men, and he had brought three, enough to cut into plenty of fillets. It would be sufficient, along with the other vegetables and fruits. But he wished for more; they deserved more. Not that the clan was bad off—the Duke and the Lady knew the importance of preserving cultures—but nor were they the proud warriors, hunters, shamans, and druids of their past. Workers and shadows—that was what they had been reduced to. Hope was what they needed. *One day, we will see the caves of our homes and stand in the Tusken Ring once more.*

He thought of his regrets, though he had promised himself not to give them words.

Once everyone was served, the Champion took his place at the Forger. Champions did not join the feast, fasting until their weapons were made. Not all Champions were weaponsmiths, nor were they expected to be. Razgaif, however, knew the craft. His fingers remembered creating weapons like Tremorwalker from the teachings of his father, Razgaif the Older. At least this time, the mining had already been done for him. He began to labor over his weapon, forming what would be the two heads of the ax. The obsidian ore, from which the Onyx-Axes got their name, was malleable under the right temperatures. He worked it as easily as butter, using the tools his people provided him.

Astra watched over his shoulders, her curiosity driving his work. He shaped and chiseled the stone. A weapon needed not be perfect. Practicality and strength were the qualities of a true orcish weapon. Moonlight caressed his sweat-coated shoulders as he attached the ax-heads to the handle. Razgaif raised the Great Traveler toward the sky. The ax's handle curved perfectly within his palms. His fingers flexed around the smooth wood, the twin-headed ax's hue the color of the night behind it. The Great Traveler, the successor of Tremorwalker, lay in his hand—a crude weapon, but his. Astra smiled and clapped, then placed her hand on his knuckles. And . . . he felt it, a course of power through him.

Svadagd reacted. A warmth cut through the coolness of the night and his pools of now-frigid sweat. He tasted fish this time, grilled and seasoned in butter, not unlike what he had prepared for the orcs that night. There was a newer feeling, too, darker but pleasant as a glint of twilight rounding off a fine day. This other aether pouring into his was rose-petal soft, holding a sweet smell of hard candy and taffy. Innocent, yet with a bit of darkness toward its edges, the way death coexisted with the living, this was Astra's aether, and nothing like Isobel's or the Worm King's. No malice. No threatening of control. Only happiness for him and a pride of her own. *Svadagd* reached out with its new comrade and rose to meet the Great Traveler.

Like his enchanted cauldron, his weapon changed. Thick vines ran down its handle, sprouting a variety of fruits and vegetables. At the top of the largest vine near the head blossomed a single velvet rose and the feathers of an owl. Razgaif grasped the Great Traveler with both hands.

"What a weapon," he whispered in awe. He exchanged a glance with Astra, or tried to. She was too busy looking at her hand, mouth agape. "Astra," he said. She shook her head and looked up. The purest type of excitement, one from a child, spilled over her face. It reached him soon enough, stretching the corners of his mouth and filling him with a joy he didn't know he had anymore.

"You did it," Astra said, lightly from exhaustion. Her words made it worth it. His mother and his siblings had been there for the forging of Tremorwalker. To have another family see this moment was a blessing not many had.

"I did." The tiredness came over him in a wave. That was the only thing he missed from his undead life—no sleep. Razgaif took a deep breath, legs wobbling and arms shaking from the weight of the Great Traveler. He plopped onto the ground, all energy leaving him. Cheers rose from all around him. The Onyx-Axes all went to him, serving their Champion drinks and plates of his own food. He tore into the crispy fish, the meal a vital part of the tradition of the Forging. By the time he finished, the early-evening bells were ringing. It was getting late, and he knew it was time to get Astra home and share what he'd been holding on to all night. *Just a little longer, little one,* he thought, patting her on her drooping head. *I'm sorry.*

Silkmaster Kao took her position as the acting Chief of their little clan. Her arms were tucked within her sleeves, which waved under the brisk breeze. "Razgaif the Younger, ancient son of Razgaif the Older and his partner Vera, the Huntress of the Midnight Gale, has returned to us. Lost under the thrall of the Worm King, he became Rottgor the Famine Blade and stayed with that name as the centuries passed, grappling under what he was forced to do and what redemption he thought he deserved. But in the end, fate brought him back to us. There's only one thing to do. Is there anyone among us willing to challenge our Champion to a bout?"

Razgaif knew this was the final step—the Exhibition. Stomach full, Razgaif grabbed his weapon once more. Its energy pulsed. The heart of his clan ran through it, beating among the war drums now sounding around them. He gathered himself, removing his shirt and placing it near the fire. Whether or not he had a challenge, he wanted to look the part. He rolled his shoulders.

"I, Razgaif the Younger, ask of you—do I have any challengers for the Champion of the Onyx-Ax? On the pride of the Chieftains, both future and past, is there anyone among you who will challenge the Great Traveler and me?"

The crowd cheered. No challenge, not right away. Razgaif roared. It shook the land and air. The cheering exploded. No one dared meet his challenge, respecting him enough as their Champion. He hadn't remembered the last time he felt this confident, this strong, this ready to take on his own life. A powerful laugh escaped his throat. He remembered who he was. The Worm, his Queen, and his mistresses broke him so much that he thought nothing was left of this man. *They stole my voice.* He lowered his shoulders and his weapon.

"There are no challengers," he said, making a show of it. He heard Calfe chuckling in the back. "Then welcome your Champion—"

"You don't mind if I interrupt, friend?"

The voice drove a knife into his budding confidence.

The crowd turned as the woman in the golden robe and silvered veil stepped forward, drawing every eye toward her. The lights of the lanterns and the bonfire outlined her silhouette, large wings furling over her shoulders. The honeycombed sword slid from its sheath, bending around her body before slashing into the road. The orcs gave her a wide berth, opening a path toward their appointed Champion. Tytli removed her veil with one hand, holding Soshadyel in the other. "I'm not here to challenge you for your title. That is not my place. I can say, however, that we have unfinished business." She turned her attention to the now awake and terrified Astra. Calfe and Zennexus moved to stand between them. There was clearly doubt warring against the resolve the Fallen Queen had made long ago. "What do you see in the little wormling?" She closed her eyes. "Perhaps I am a relic of the past, a rusting sword or a book with faded pages. Or perhaps you're blinded by what you think will help you escape from the pain of your lives. Have you put aside who you are, Rottgor? Can you live knowing what they did to us, what they rewrote us into?" Her one eye found Astra's. "Are you okay with that?"

Where Tytli's resolve faltered, Razgaif's grew. He stepped between Tytli and his friends, his weapon tight in his hands.

"She is not them, nor any of their other descendants. When does the revenge stop, Tytli? When do you live the rest of your life? After Astra, then what? You'll search the world, finding yet another faint strain of a dead legacy of a dynasty that never made it off the ground. He's *dead*. Gone. And that girl." Razgaif pointed to Astra. "She taught me happiness."

For a moment, Tytli's sadness and confusion hung in the air, but then anger bubbled up, burning away her uncertainty. "I see.

Then we're at an impasse, Rottgor. No, not Rottgor. You're not him anymore. I guess in that way, the last one who understood has died. Razgaif the Younger, Champion of the Onyx-Ax, allow me this request." She stepped forward. "Show me what it means to live before you die." The emptiness in her voice pained him. At least in the city, he had people around him. She had no one. Her revenge was rooted so deep it poisoned her thoughts. *I see that now.*

Razgaif took the Great Traveler in both hands. Little fruits and vegetables sprouted and bloomed down the hilt—persimmon, cherry tomatoes, grapes, crab apples, sunroots, and onions—spiraling down the pearwood handle and ending at the mysterious red-black rose. He raised the weapon back up, taking his battle stance once more. The orcs of the settlement erupted at their Champion's resolve. While he was grateful, his eyes flicked to the scared Astra, hiding behind Calfe and Zennexus. *For her,* he vowed, *and the future I once refused to look at.*

"Then come forward, Fallen Fae Queen Tytli Bhihadra, one of my dearest friends!" he bellowed. "Witness the full might of the Onyx-Ax!"

FOURTEEN

A Bee Dancing in the Midnight Dew

Razgaif the Champion knew his opponent this time around. The Fallen Fae Queen, his friend and now opponent, came for him—the only thing standing between her and true vengeance. As fast as a stroke of lightning, she closed the gap between them, her long whiplike blade swinging toward him. He saw her attacks now and struck them away, the enchanted stone of the ax unbroken by the metal of her Deathblade. Razgaif gave a hearty laugh, a sharp contrast against the dragon woman's snarls.

"You're much less quiet than you were before," Tytli said as they exchanged fierce blows. He watched her carefully.

"It is easier to be quiet when you have no voice."

They danced under the light of the moon, his ax a starless night sky and hers the light of day. Razgaif swerved and parried her lightning-fast attacks. Close range and long range—she was a master at both. He rushed forward, within his swinging range, the great ax his measuring stick. He swerved, and Tytli's sword-whip whistled over his head. Using the handle of his ax, he smacked the whip away—earning the Great Traveler its first scars. He laughed, he cried, he roared. *More.* His muscles tightened, vision sharpened. He wanted more.

The serpentine blade caught him on the cheek. Pain. He felt blood drip down his cheek and onto his knuckles. It was not quite the vibrant red of the true living, more a black, but it was still warm. The tempting descent into rage was so close it intoxicated him. Tytli's fatigue started to build, eating away at her speed. She swung her blade once more, narrowly missing Razgaif's torso, then turned at the last second, whipping it across his face. More blood splashed against his nose. The slash hadn't torn his nose from his face, but it had been close. He laughed and rushed forward.

The sudden and bold attack caught her off guard. Rottgor was cold and calculating; Razgaif was aggressive in his fury. He pushed through the swirling whips, knocking them aside with brute strength. He smashed his way through the hundreds of cuts and slammed his ax into her chest. A blow like that wouldn't kill her, not the Lili he knew. And lo and behold, despite the massive blow, she had sustained only a scratch on her plated shoulder and chest. She frowned at him. "I do not know this orc, but he seems to know me." A glitter of life flashed in the suppressed grin, twitching up the corner of her mouth.

Without warning, Tytli flung herself into the air, propelled upward by her wings. The Honeycombed Woman soared at him, the sword whipping at his side. He dodged the first blow barely, his big feet nimble and light. Surprised by his speed, she increased hers, changing her direction in midair and slashing him in the chest—more blood. Someone in the crowd screamed. Little did they know that the pain felt good in his heart, each scar like a step toward healing, both for his body and his soul.

He remembered his mother saying that, and now he understood. *You have to hurt to heal.*

And you've hurt far too long, Lili.

The sword-whip cracked near the side of his face, and the Great Traveler parried it once more. A crude weapon like his ax shouldn't have stood a chance against the weapon of a Death Knight. Yet it did. Enchanted with his aether and Astra's, it held his hopes and dreams for the future. He pushed forward, ignoring the cuts on his knuckles and slamming the ax up as Tytli fell upon him from the sky. She blocked him at the last second with a shield made of her scales. She pushed the ax-head aside, twisted, and landed on her feet, skidding across the ground. She brushed a droplet of blood from her lip. "I never thought I'd face you like this. Perhaps I did expect to have to subdue you one day, but to face you with such clarity . . . It's sublime."

Orcs believed there were two ways to the heart: through the stomach and through battle. A *siefu* like Razgaif knew the recipes for both hunger and violence, which showed clearly as their blades clashed once more and they danced around one another over and over, knowing the steps. The crowd around them cheered, louder and louder. The fight between their Champion and his challenger was a sight, a beauty, a spectacle. But Razgaif knew it wasn't enough—he had to win. She had been hurt, and like he had been, she was stuck that way. Preserved. She was the bee caught in amber, forever locked away from the flowers she deserved. *Not anymore.*

"One more," he cried out, slamming his ax into her twisting sword. She recoiled from the impact.

"I don't see it," she said, a weak laugh escaping her lips. "You're so happy. I don't . . ." The words choked, stopped on her lips. "I want to understand. I want to *believe* so much that we can move on. Galelin found his peace—in the end, he was satisfied, happy, fulfilled. I can't . . . I can't move on."

"Who says? We're still here. We don't have to be unhappy."

"Then what is left of us? Rot—" She pursed her lips. "Raz. Do you believe in her? Do you believe that she's different?"

Razgaif nodded, stealing a glance at Astra. She clutched the hem of her little dress. "I do."

"Why? Why do you have such a heart to believe that?" Tytli, too, stole a glance.

"Can't answer that. I believe it and I feel it, too—it is as simple as that."

"Faith is dangerous."

"And sometimes warranted."

Her eye went dull. She rushed at him, but this time the blade disintegrated into a swarm of insects midswing. The wave of insects struck him on the arm, their stinging intense. The swelling left by the insects' bites and stings made it hard to hold the great ax, and the small movements of his muscles were accompanied by a flame of irritation. He pushed through all the same, keeping on his feet and avoiding the controlled swarm of her weapon. He danced around the bonfire, losing the chasing hive through the flame's bellow before circling back toward Tytli. This time, he leaped into the air, the trunks of his giant legs propelling him higher than he'd imagined possible. Razgaif came crashing down upon her, ax-head shearing through the wind. She re-formed Soshadyel at the last second, bringing it up to meet Razgaif's ax, keeping her from being completely overwhelmed. He bounced off her blade, pushing himself backward and away. Somehow, that got a laugh from her, a sweet sound he had never heard escape her lips.

"What are we doing?" she said as she caught her breath. "This is ridiculous!"

"I'm having fun, you?" Razgaif took a small persimmon from his handle, still miraculously intact despite the fighting, and popped it into his mouth. A burst of energy came over him, and the stinging on his forearms eased. He knew his food held some magical properties thanks to *Svadagd*. The fruits on his ax, however, were cultured for *him*. *Svadagd*, abundant and plentiful, rushed through him. He squared his shoulders. "Well, are you having fun, Lili?" The anger she was so desperate to hang on to didn't mix well with what he knew stirred in her heart. "Let out your anger. Not on her. Let it out on me and let it all go."

"I don't . . ." Tytli clenched her knuckles around her hilt. "'I could watch you break a thousand times and still be enamored by your shards.' Do you remember when Isobel Denholm said that to me? You were there. You had no choice but to watch the door as she ripped out my eye and smashed the last remaining eggs of me, my husband, Anjay, and my wife, Umma. The Worms had plans for them, but in Isobel's jealousy, she murdered my children and left me watching with one less eye. I promised her the same fate through the haze of my pain."

Razgaif remembered watching her remaining eye scream, her mouth forced closed. He remembered reaching out in his mind's eye, begging Isobel for mercy. But Mistress Isobel knew nothing of clemency. "I do remember. I was just as helpless as you were." He saw her anger flare once more. She lunged at him. Black honey ran down from one eye, and petals rained from the missing one. Her sword came down hard. It was his turn to block at the last second.

"And then I saw her," Tytli snarled. "*Her*, a spitting image, and she had you. She has a smile! I promised never to see a Denholm smile again."

"Look at her," Razgaif said. He quickly yanked his blade from under her sword, interlocking her sword-whip around his ax and pulling her around to face the crowd. Over his shoulder, he saw Astra. She was smiling through her worry. Neither Isobel Denholm nor the Worm King ever held a smile of such purity. "You said all it takes is one bad day. I don't think that's true. Evil isn't created in a day. It's built little by little. Resentment here. A sprinkle of hatred there. A bit of a grudge and a lot of bad directions. But joy and goodness are built in the same way, bit by bit. Your revenge is that little girl's smile."

Those words brought the opening he needed. Her stance softened a little too much. Razgaif pulled her forward, using all his strength and more, and heaved her up from her stance. He swung her and his ax toward the ground, crashing her onto her back. She landed with a thud. Razgaif yanked the Great Traveler loose and put one ax blade to her throat. She looked up, her hair sprawled across the cobbled ground like a web of black. At the center wasn't a spider. It was a queen bee who had lost her hive, a dragon who had never lived.

"You win this round, Razgaif the Younger, Champion of the Onyx-Ax," Tytli said, her voice soft. Razgaif drew back his ax. "It seems Rottgor is no more. Go on," she told the crowd, "cheer for your hero. He deserves it."

The throng of orcs and friends joined in a single cheer, war drums sounding around them. They welcomed their Champion. Strength meant nothing if not tempered by kindness, and Razgaif had both. He helped Tytli up. Her sword dispersed and with it her resolve. Truly, he wouldn't have stood a chance if she had been serious, what with the death and fae magic she possessed and the nature of her weapon.

She examined him. "You've changed. It's . . . nice." She put her hand on his shoulder. "It fits you." She paused. "Let me see the child."

The crowd eased and split off, the festivities ending. Silkmaster Kao gave a low bow and returned to her cabin. Razgaif had had enough, too. Battered and bruised, he limped toward Calfe, Astra, and Zennexus and stepped between them. His eyes weighed heavily, his breathing rough and ragged, but he had to see this through. He forced his back straight through the constant aches and pain running up his spine. *Gotta remember I'm centuries old still.*

"Astra. I want to introduce you to someone. You've met her before, and she tried to kill you."

"I remember," Astra said matter-of-factly. "It wasn't that long ago."

"It feels like it," Razgaif said, slumping. "Well, this is my friend Fae-Levia Queen Tytli Bhihadra of the Glimmer Glade Veil."

"Former Fae Queen," she said sadly. "And I suppose I owe you an apology, Astra."

"I understand. I do." Astra shuffled her feet. "You were scared. You *are* scared. You're afraid that in the future, I'll be another . . ." She couldn't bring herself to say it. *Another Isobel. Another Worm King.* "But I'm not. I want to be me."

Tytli understood everything in that moment. "I—" The Fallen Fae Queen looked down, a tear caught in her eyes. "You must forgive us adults, child. We make assumptions and think ourselves wiser because of them. Raz was right. I could've been your one bad day, and you don't deserve any of those. My hatred isn't yours to bear, and I was foolish to have you shoulder it." Tytli kneeled. A hard gasp caught in Razgaif's chest. She had vowed on the Last Day of Darkness, when the Six Shadows and their allies had routed the remaining death throes of the Worm King's army, that her knees would never bow for anyone ever again. "Could you find forgiveness in your young heart?"

Astra frowned. "I know you didn't mean it," she said. Children had an ease with forgiveness that adults lost somewhere along the way. "I wish . . . oh, it's silly . . . I wish I could change . . . something." She touched Tytli on the face. A soft surge of aether rippled through the wind, smelling of rose and baked bread. The wilted black lotus on Tytli's face gained color, a beautiful pink, before falling away into petals. Underneath, an eye the color of that lotus shone. Tytli blinked in confusion. So did Astra. Everyone did. "I—I'm sorry. . . . I didn't mean to. I—"

Tytli brought her hands to her face, moving her fingers across her once-tainted side. A shocked silence came over them. What *could* they say? Astra shook a little from embarrassment.

"I—" A single tear slipped down Tytli's sharp cheeks, those black vines nestled underneath her skin gone as well. "I've only given you hate, and you gave me a gift. It appears I still have things in this world to learn." She rose. "I'm truly sorry once more, and your—" Tytli paused, looking to Razgaif. "How about I let him speak?"

Razgaif felt his heart drop from his lungs down to his stomach. *This is it.* Astra looked at him expectantly. Calfe, too. The words were almost there, just beyond the tip of his tongue. In that fragile moment, he didn't see the obvious danger. He didn't see the cloaked men in the stilled shadows or the woman holding a crossbow atop one of the cabins. He didn't see the men coming from behind them, didn't notice their soft boots fall under the crackling fire. "Astra, I want to be your d—"

By the time they heard the sharp, shattering sound, chaos had ensued.

Zennexus fell face first on the ground, dull and unmoving, the shattered gem nestled in his beard now shards on the ground. Three other men, all in cloaks of purple and gold, acted as one. The first moved quickly, sending a lightning bolt toward Astra before she knew to react. The young girl shrilled, then fell unconscious before being tossed over another man's shoulders. All in seconds.

"Astra!" Razgaif, Calfe, and Tytli all called out, reacting too slowly as the lantern lights and bonfire went out all at once from a cold blast of icy wind. The three men were already halfway up the road. A bubbling fury and a maddening panic made thinking impossible. Razgaif rushed after them, but his body resisted, his adrenaline leaving him. The wear and tear of the day was too much. Still, he pushed and followed, his skin cold from sweat. More men jumped from the shadows. He cut them down, foam curling at the edges of his mouth. He was getting no closer.

"Perfect *timing*, boys," came a voice from the shadows, amplified by one of the dwarves' magic horns. "Didn't I tell you I would get my revenge? I've been watching you, Rottgor. Or is it Razgaif now? A new coat of paint on a broken-down house." Vom's voice circled them, taunting. "Calfe always stopped me, y'know, watching like the little guard puppy he has always been."

"How about you bloody shut up and say that to my face," Calfe said.

The darkness was on Vom's side, keeping him hidden as he jeered at them from afar. "And fight on *your* level? No. I think not. Tonight is my night. I knew your guard would be down. I have a prize now. This little girl. Remember when I said the undead are meant to *serve*? Well. Here's the key. This girl is the perfect investment for all of that. And all I have to do to control her is hang you over her head." Vom gave a piglike laugh, snorting between his words. "I *win*. I *bloody* win."

The orcs of the Onyx-Ax came to their Champion's aid, but it was already too late. The cloaked men slipped through their ranks, guided by the shifting tricks of shades, controlled by shadow runes. Tytli and Calfe followed the best they could. They waded through the cloaked figures, swords and daggers flying. Razgaif pushed on. *No, no, no, no.* They were too far; the shades were slowing them down. Distractions, all of them. He was a rampaging bull and all he saw was red. The Great Traveler swung over and over. Nothing. Nothing mattered but *her* safety. A flash of hot pain struck him. One of the shades had buried a sword in Razgaif's shoulder. He roared and crushed the shadowy figure into dust.

"Enough!" he shouted. "Give me back my *daughter*."

But they were gone.

Gone into the deep of night.

A cold numbness blanketed his emotions. He shook and roared until he couldn't anymore. Among the sea of dead bodies, an orc who had wished to become a father that night wept for a girl he couldn't ask.

"It's my fault," Razgaif heard for the thousandth time from his friends.

He didn't know who said it this time. Voices melded together and became noise on the other side. They had searched the settlement and all surrounding areas before retiring back to the Afterlife Crisis. She was gone, as though she had slipped through a crack in the city no one could see. They ended their search as the sun rose, beams of orange light cresting over the surface. The news was spreading. Necropolis, the city of the dead, was the safest city in all of Dargath, and a child had been kidnapped on the city guard's watch. *Not only their watch,* Razgaif thought grimly. He hadn't felt so helpless since he'd been trapped in his mind, under the Worm King's control. *At least then I was too dulled.* Though the restaurant itself was closed, he let in anyone who had heard the news of Astra's kidnapping.

Razgaif skulked to his big chair in the corner. The previous night's hearth fire was long since cold, and there was a nip in the air where warmth and hospitality should've been. He rested his forehead against trembling knuckles. The comfort of his chair normally gave him the space he needed to think—clear his head. The fog didn't subside that day. It stayed, hanging over all his thoughts.

"Razgaif!" Calfe shouted. The sudden sound stirred him awake. He must have drifted off in his exhaustion. Drool dribbled down his beard, and Razgaif quickly readjusted in his seat. Someone had relit the hearth and thrown a blanket over him. His brain throbbed against his skull. "You dozed off. We let you rest for a while, but we need you."

"Need me," he repeated. "Need me." His tongue slipped over the *bridge* language. He hadn't spoken *orken* in centuries. But *bridge* sounded weak, too small for his feelings. He strung the savage pieces of himself back together. He had to keep calm. They wouldn't do anything to her. No one was held hostage without reason. "What would Vom want from her? She hasn't lifted a finger to this man."

"I have, and that would've been enough on its own. But his main motivation is and always will be money. It's always money with him." Calfe gave a low groan from the back of his throat.

"More than likely, he sees the success of the Afterlife as a slight of some sort, a piece of a pie that he missed out on. This was his property, and until now, no one has done well with it. And success by the undead . . . he hates sharing his air with people like you."

Tytli approached the hearth, holding her hands over the warmth of the fire. "That still doesn't explain why he stole Astra. No doubt he knows that she's special to Raz, but I feel like there's more. What has the Light of the Chosen been trying to push? What's their goal?"

"The living and their native superiority for the most part," said Calfe. "They believe the dead and summoned have no place here, that they are here only to serve. At least that's what the Chosen are working toward, but for Vom, it's all about profit. It's . . . it's about profit." Calfe's shoulders tensed. "A necromancer outside of the College . . . He's been looking for one for decades. The Crown and the College of Boneskies watch for any potential necromancer within the city for proper training and ethics, but Vom wants one for his own use. Of course, any *adult* would ask for a cut of the riches, so he couldn't have that. But a child he can threaten. A child he can scare."

The room quieted at the sickening thought. All this. For what, free labor? Could a man be that greedy? Perhaps so. Sky dwarves' lives depended on their wealth, their families losing and gaining power by the Rule of Coin. Stronger families ruled the Pinnacle, and weaker families left.

"I hate him," Calfe said flatly. "Alas he's already left and emptied his home of all evidence. I made sure my boys checked there first. The coward slipped through his secret tunnels. I'm going to stab him in the face."

"Rightfully so," Razgaif said. *He deserves worse.* "I hope they can repair Zennexus."

"He will be fine," Tytli said, "as long as a piece of their core stays intact, gargoyles from the Realm of Stillness and Stone can be returned. No worries about that." She sat at the bar, eyes scanning the myriad of labels. It had been a long evening. "We shouldn't dally. It's only a matter of time before they move her out of the city. The Black Dread will not tolerate child abduction here and will string them up on the walls if they stay. It's pleasant seeing Oron's Black Dread remain so vigilant. Some things don't change."

"Others do," Razgaif said solemnly. His nerves had calmed. She was right. They didn't have a lot of time. They had to act. He pondered the idea of asking Lady Cleo or his former comrades in the Ruinous Guard. But time was passing quickly, and the thought of Astra being harmed in the slightest while court held him up . . . No, he'd handle it himself.

Not alone, he thought.

The door of the Afterlife opened. Clyth sauntered in, sharp in his fine black vest and dark pants. He stood looking confused in the doorway, seeing the three of them by the roaring hearth and the restaurant emptied. It appeared he hadn't received the message from the sending stones.

"What in the far blazes is happening here?" he asked, wiping a monocle clean. "Lady Tytli, I swore you were at odds with my employer and Mr. Metcoat. You look like you want to kill someone this fine morning, but it doesn't appear to be either of them. Can anyone explain the situation?"

"The Light of the Chosen took Astra," Calfe said.

Clyth blinked. "Excuse me." He carefully removed his gloves, and a fireball formed from his skin, pure fire leaking from his pores. "No, no, no. This will surely not do. I would like to help retrieve our little lady if possible. My father and sister were slated to come by today, so I will inform them that a problem has arisen."

"Sister and father?" A pit grew in Razgaif's stomach as realization dawned on him.

Clyth tilted his head. "Yes, my sister. Baroness Yavari. Surely you're not surprised."

Razgaif opened his mouth. "What is a Baron of the Burnt Rooms doing working at *my* restaurant?"

"Everyone has their hobbies, Mr. Razgaif. Do not judge me for mine." Clyth shrugged. "Also, I'm the fourteenth in line, I'm barely a Baron."

"That's a lot of children," Calfe said, groaning.

"Fourteenth out of thirty-two children." The whole room gave a small prayer to his mother. "Never mind that. We need to act. I'm telling everyone else. More than likely, they have some sort of base they're operating from. We need to find it. However, all three of you look dreadful and are in no condition for a lengthy search. Allow me to do what I do best: pull strings. Get some rest. I'll handle the heavy lifting."

Clyth didn't give any of them a chance for rebuttal. He ushered Tytli and Calfe into a side room, returning to help Razgaif out of his chair. His bones popped and his limbs screamed in protest. He pulled himself together and headed upstairs, Clyth following behind him. The upper area was colder than normal, the empty hall void of all sounds but their footsteps. He had never felt the loneliness of his home as deeply as he did now. His heart wished for more. The room across from his stayed empty. If Clyth saw his despair, he didn't say anything. He just opened the door and led him into his room.

"I will be here all day," he announced, "making my inquiries. But promise me you'll sleep. A little rest can change a situation." He gave a reassuring wink. A small part of Razgaif believed then that it would be all right. Another part doubted.

Clyth left him to his devices. The room was somehow quieter than the hall. Razgaif paced the room, thunderous in his worry. The memory played over and over. It lived with him. As Rottgor, he had seen terrible things, and he'd tried putting those to rest when he'd abandoned the name. *This* was a whole new pain for a whole new man. His rage built. *We'll find her,* he told himself, but hope scared him. Truly, it did. *I'm always one step away from breaking. Serve. Bend. Break.*

He heard that cry, the crackle of stunning lightning, and the scream of a young child when he closed his eyes. The Great Traveler found its way into his hand. Fury came upon him. Everything around him was washed in red. He heard her screams once more, clearer than before. More anger, a smell of blood, blood that he didn't have. *A young girl. Hurt. For greed.* Razgaif the Younger lost his temper and broke everything in his room, including his last remaining thread of calmness. Finally, Razgaif's rage and exhaustion pulled him into unconsciousness upon his broken bed.

FIFTEEN

A Banquet of the Just

Tytli woke him, stepping over the wreckage of what was once his room.

"She's out there," Tytli told him. "Somewhere dark, underground. There are catacombs aplenty underneath the city. I suppose she will be there."

Razgaif arose, his body protesting, but the need to act pushed him forward. Like Tytli, he had seen Astra in his dreams. She was in a dark, deep-underground room where bones lined the walls and weathered statues loomed in alcoves. Sightless stone eyes looked down upon her, a single flameless torch shining bright in a single corner. Those purple-silk-robed men surrounded her, tall spears made of bones and strips of rotten, undead flesh tight within their grasp. Astra held back tears of anger and fear. They glinted in her eyes, threatening to fall every second. If Razgaif could catch her every tear, he would. That was the motivation he needed.

"Have you heard anything?" he asked, keeping that broiling anger at bay.

"Come downstairs and see." Tytli turned and walked back

out into the hallway as he gathered himself. That day, he chose the garb of a warrior, and a Champion and a Chief's son would wear attire made of fur, hide, and leather. He emerged from his den wearing his bear-fur vest, an orcish leather kilt known as a *kiret*, and leather-banded sandals that reached his lower shins. He had adorned himself in mammoth and tiger bones, a symbol of protection and grace for the day ahead. The Great Traveler and the Cupbearer remained downstairs after the prior night's debacle. One was for giving, the other for taking. He knew which he would pick that day. *Stay strong, Astra. I'll be there soon.*

He exited his room and saw Tytli reclining against the wood walls, reading one of his books. Her newly restored sight and the kindness from the person who'd restored it had changed her. She seemed to see him differently, took in details she hadn't before, as though the world itself had opened up. The anger, though it would forever scar her, had eased, and a small seed of a smile bloomed. Her shoulders dropped with the weight of shame, and she stared at the pages before her, seeming to look beyond the parchment and ink. She closed the book. "If I hadn't challenged you, Astra wouldn't be in danger."

"I don't hate you," Razgaif said.

Those words only deepened the shame on Tytli's face. "But hate is all I've done. It's a part of me."

Razgaif went to her side. "You're not made of hate. You were hurt."

"I suppose I cannot tell the difference anymore."

For Razgaif, the centuries had been marked by inaction, the constant state of doing nothing but serving. For her, it had been hurt and pain. She'd held on to it for so long that underneath the scar tissue, she had forgotten there was flesh. The rest of the Six Shadows were similar—three of them had gone on to the beyond still holding that regret. Now given this chance, Razgaif refused to squander it.

"Lili, we deserve life. We've lived long enough in the shadows of our former lives."

"I—" Tytli tossed her hair, flustered. "I suppose you're right." She brought down her veil once more, preparing for the company she wasn't as close to. While he stomped around, her footsteps barely made a sound, each one measured and calm. *A ghost. She lives her life like a ghost.* Never seen. Never touching the living world unless bringing retribution.

"This will be my penance, and then I will leave you once more," she told him.

"No."

"What do you mean *no*?" Tytli spat. The queen frowned. A blatant refusal? Unheard of.

"I said no," Razgaif repeated. "You're staying."

Tytli cocked her head. "I like to think that I have a say in where I go after I make amends."

"You do." Razgaif shrugged. "But you already know that running away only leads to dead ends."

Tytli folded her arms. "When did you become so wise, Razgaif the Younger?"

"I've watched the world long enough." Razgaif allowed himself a laugh. "I hope I've picked up some wise words by now."

Razgaif took her by the arm, a commonplace gesture for escorting royalty. He had done so a million times for Lady Cleo and hundreds of other nobles, leading them down to feasts and banquets. They descended the creaking staircase. The warmth of the hearth and the smoke from a cooking meal hit him first. Confusion struck him. They'd closed the restaurant's doors, accepting no customers until Astra was safe and sound, but the restaurant buzzed with life. His employees and the community had turned it into a command center, their determination palpable. *What's happening?* Razgaif's throat dry, they made it to the restaurant floor and greeted a small gathering of people.

All his employees, members of the Black Dread, regulars of the Afterlife, and general members of the Famine Street community were all there, invested in Astra's safe return. They crowded the area, leaning over what appeared to be a map of the entire city. Clyth stood on a chair while the rest brought together all the tables in their makeshift war station. Seeing Rib-Digger carrying more chairs and moving more tables meant still more had yet to arrive.

Rib-Digger waved at them. "Come. Sit. No. More. Worrying." The big patchwork pulled up the straps of his blue overalls. "Almost done."

"Almost done?" But Rib-Digger had wandered off for more chairs.

Razgaif escorted Tytli to her seat before taking his own, as was customary. There were more people than should fit in the small space. Above them all was the confident smile of Clyth the Forever. Funny. Everyone seemed confident in what came next, wearing the same smile as Clyth. Bao Su bowed to her former queen. "Lady Tytli, it's an honor."

"A Summersweet? Here?" Tytli frowned. "Why are you so far away from home, little gem?"

Bao shrugged as though the politics of her homeland meant nothing. "The Court got boring. Stopped going. Father had loud opinions; I had louder ones. I chose to ignore his. I got tired of his voice. Lost a few of my tails as a result."

"Zeion Summersweet is known for his . . . intolerance of his sons and daughters leaving the Glimmer Glade Veil and traveling into the mortal world of Dargath. I sometimes wonder how my own father is doing." An annoyed expression came over the former Fae-Levia Queen's face. Her father was born of that court; her mother was born of Dargath. *All had been torn away from her by a single man.* From her furrowed brow and deepening frown, it seemed she didn't really care to find out. To the Court, hundreds of years meant nothing, and they *did nothing* involving this world. *Not even to save one of their own.* The bitterness of her father's inaction forever remained on her tongue. "I understand your position all too well."

Bao Su brought over two cups. She poured her boss and former queen a beverage that smelled like honeyed ale. Razgaif took his without question; Tytli hesitated. He took a sip and looked around. The room didn't seem frantic—the opposite, truly. Hope and comradery permeated the space, and belief swelled in his heart. *We can do this,* he prayed to whatever god was willing to lend their ear. *I have to.*

"I believe I promised a plan," Clyth said. Razgaif's attention finally turned his way. "And I may have succeeded. But first, you need to eat something." He placed down food, sliced turkey, stuffing slathered in the Afterlife's signature mushroom gravy, and a mix of vinegared greens and honeyed carrots. Razgaif's appetite hadn't surfaced until now, buried under his worry. Seeing the plate before him caused the beast to rumble. He began eating, his fork finding the slabs of turkey first. "Yes"—Clyth bowed—"I hope you enjoy the little feast we put together before we get to our main event: my glorious plan." He turned his head to Tytli, remaining within his deep bow. "Would you like anything, Your Majesty?"

Tytli eyed Clyth. "I do not need nourishment—" Her stomach growled. She stared, blinked, and bit her lower lip. She sighed, her pride clearly taking a savage blow. *Astra restored more than her sight.* Razgaif laughed. "Maybe just a small bite . . ."

Razgaif grinned. "She'll have what I'm having, and bring her the tea, the best we have."

Calfe returned the smile. "Of course, at once."

He was there and back within the span of Razgaif finishing his side of stuffing. Tytli sipped her tea and took a bite of the pastries.

"I can taste it," she said softly. "Before, all food and drink tasted of ash and dirt. This." She held her emotions at bay, locked behind the softest smile. "Fine black tea from my mother's homeland, spiced by sugar, cinnamon, and cardamom. Did you decide this for me, Raz?"

"You always spoke of how you missed your mother's tea. I guess I hoped you would taste it again one day." Razgaif took another bite from his meal.

"You knew I would come, and . . . you thought of me." She paused, taking small bites of her meal now. A childlike glow came over her. Tytli Bhihadra had lost her true smile long ago; his restaurant's food brought it back.

"You have the same kindness, y'know. You and her." Tytli pushed her empty plate aside. Her bites weren't that small after all. She laced her fingers together. "It's the unmistakable kindness that less worthy people envy and vile people cannot understand. In the Veil just outside the Glimmer Glade, we call adopting a child who possesses a similar soul to yours *aalea*. Choosing an abandoned child is a rare practice among the childless fae."

"So the rumors of fae abducting children in their sleep are true?" Razgaif grinned at her.

Tytli opened her mouth and closed it. "It's not . . . untrue?

I wouldn't say they're abducted. Some unfortunate children are taken to the Veil for a better life. The fae are selfish creatures, but when they see a similar soul to theirs in distress, they choose to help. You chose to help out of your kindness, and I can say, without a doubt, you already have a lead on my father. Trust yourself. You'll make a fine father."

Razgaif wished he believed that. Astra's kidnapping shook his confidence to its core. *Trust yourself,* Razgaif the Older's voice echoed from his grave beneath the persimmon trees. *If you can't trust yourself, who can you trust?*

"It appears you both are done regaining your strength. You will need it."

Clyth explained the plan. They had narrowed it down to the catacombs known as the Halls of Dust, Salt, and Grafted Bones with the aid of Tytli's dream. With the city on high alert, Vom and his crew had no choice but to stay underground until it lowered, and would then have to escape through the north gate. That was how they would catch him. They would set up on both ends while Rottgor and the rest dived into the catacombs. A simple plan but effective. "I think it's a great—"

The door swung open.

Thess rushed in, cloak billowing behind her. She slammed the door closed and stomped to the middle of the room. "In all my days as the caretaker for those children, I have *not ever* had a missing child before the two of you." The rims of her eyes were just as black as her irises. She tossed her hair back, then unsheathed her sword, the blade green and covered with moss and small lily pads. A dozen yellow slitted eyes opened on its surface and the bottom of her hilt yawned a row of crocodile teeth. She pointed the Morass Blade at them. "You had one job. *One.* Bring Astra home safely." The words seethed from between her teeth, venom touching letter after letter. "I do not see her here *safely*! I should cut you both down where you stand."

Tytli straightened her back and Razgaif followed suit.

"I do not expect your forgiveness," Tytli said. "It was not his neglect. It was mine. I distracted him."

"You don't have to take the blame alone, Tytli."

Razgaif fell to his knees on the warm wooden floor. He laid his forehead on the ground and outstretched his hands. "I will ask for your forgiveness. Astra means as much to me as she does you, and I want her safety more than you realize. She has been a light in my dark days, and nothing around here would have been possible without her. Please allow me to find her and make amends."

Thess paused, her fury radiating above him. Razgaif couldn't see her face, the one blessing in his begging. A Champion of an orc tribe on their knees meant the truest sincerity, not just from himself but from his clan. Honor wasn't restricted to glory. Sometimes it was the opposite. It meant accepting yourself at your lowest. *I was at the top of the world and fell down the mountain's side.*

"Please forgive me," he said, the most earnest he had ever been.

All Thess managed was a sigh. The door opened once more, this time softer. Another familiar voice interrupted the caretaker's anger. "It is all right. We will find her." Two sets of thunderous footsteps rang through the restaurant. Razgaif brought his head up. Zennexus stood behind his brother Gosladau, towering in their massive gargoyle glory. They squeezed through the door, quickly readjusting their height and size as they passed.

"Zennexus! You're okay!" Razgaif shouted.

"Simple fix. Shattered my form. Put me to sleep." He smiled.

"That's the worst that you mortals can do to us when you bind us from the Stillness. We are forever. We are the Quietness. Now, if you want an apology, Lady Thess, you should also expect one of me. I was remiss in my vigilance, and do not have the excuse of fatigue."

Calfe threw his hands up. "Enough with this blaming crap. You can blame her, or him, or him. It doesn't matter! What matters is that our little girl gets home safe. We have a plan, and if you want to *contribute* instead of lashing out, that would be swell. The rest of us have heroics on our calendar."

The Afterlife went quiet, all the patrons exchanging awkward glances with one another. It was Razgaif who broke the silence. He got to his feet and laughed. It was a true one, one he felt in his gut. *Trust yourself,* he heard his father say, whose voice was clearer than it had ever been. Where the words of a broken thrall once burned his head, his father now stood, picking up the broken pieces of his son and pushing him toward the light.

"You're right," he said. "We have some heroics to do."

The strike teams—consisting of Calfe, Tytli, Thess, and Razgaif and then Clyth, Rib-Digger, Flynn, and Bao Su—set out as the noon sun dipped toward the horizon, the two groups covering the ends of the large catacombs. Waiting for nightfall was too risky; the enemy might have already moved. The Great Traveler, Razgaif's glorious new weapon, rested firmly in his grip, its pearwood handle fitting his hand like a familiar friend. He had truly forgotten what it meant to hold a weapon without guilt or shame. Astra's gift—a velvet rose—was nestled among the crystalized fruit. He touched it briefly before plucking a sunroot.

The crystals fell away, exposing the root vegetable underneath. He hadn't realized it would happen when he'd plucked the persimmon during his battle with Tytli, but a new one had started regrowing in its spot. He walked, examining the sunroot he'd just plucked. It appeared normal enough. Shrugging, he tried the tuber. Sunroots had never been his favorite—somewhere between a potato and an onion, they were meant to be eaten raw. That one, however, was the most delicious he'd ever tasted, sweet and starchy like the finest sweet potato with the crisp bite of an onion. Perfect in every way.

A newfound strength surged through his core soon after. His body felt lighter, his armor and weapons like feathers. The people around him were walking too slowly. *That can't be the case.* With the flavor still rustling in the back of his mouth, the remaining fatigue left from his weak nap melted away, and his quickening and worried heart slowed its pace. He stared down at the Great Traveler and realized a simple fact: These fruits and vegetables were also magical. Astra's rune and his had made a superfood, its restorative properties beyond compare. He flexed his fingers.

When he got his hands on Vom . . .

They made it to the entrance of the cemetery that lay in the territory between the two orc clans, the Duskgrave and Onyx-Ax. Headstones there were little stone effigies, memorializing the departed with reminders of what they'd brought to the clan. Some were put in caskets made of stone and earth, while others remained in mud patches where the earth had reclaimed their bones. They walked among the simple men and women, not warriors as other orc clans might still be, but common folk of Necropolis. Razgaif paid his respects with a whisper. One day, his resting spot would be there, but that day wasn't going to be today.

The catacombs began at a single grave to the north of the cemetery. The faint red glow of the late afternoon gave the entrance an eerie haze. The cooler air of the graveyard tingled his forearms as he walked closer. He had no reason to be afraid. Death was a part of life, and those who had a good life feared nothing in the end. What bothered him was the simple act of not belonging there. A resting place was for the dead and their families. The Light of the Chosen had trampled upon it, holding no regard for the sleepers. *More reasons to have my hands around his throat.* He carried that anger alongside him as they descended into the Hall of Dust.

An odd feeling of familiarity struck him the moment his feet hit the cold ground of the catacombs. They left the door open, planning to use it as their escape, and waded through the dark path, following the dim purple lights of the torches. Bones lined the walls—the Worm King had decorated them with the bodies of his slain enemies, unfit for being raised. He imagined the necromancer king walking through these halls, proud of his accomplishments. Funny that the remainder of his bones was used for a chair and a lamp. Sometimes Razgaif wondered how the dead king squirmed in his afterlife. But it wasn't his memories that drew him to this place. It was her. His legacy and his only redemption from a world that he had once only poisoned.

They moved on. The air fell cold. Turn after turn, the catacomb's icy clutches choked him. Aether built up around them—Astra's aether—making the already-trapped air more like sludge than anything breathable, thick with her panic. Astra was scared. She was scared, and he hated it. He quickened his pace, snaking through the constant sharp-angled turns and bending corridors. He swore he heard her cries around each corner. *Help me. Help me.* His legs moved faster. *A little longer, Astra, just a little longer.*

Razgaif heard the briefest of noises, the sound of a bowstring, and his years of training returned in a moment. He caught the arrow by the shaft. They met a fork in the tunnel, three arched paths leading up toward different tombs. The man who'd shot the arrow stood flabbergasted in front of Razgaif, the hood of his cloak doing nothing to hide the fear in his eyes. Razgaif crushed the arrow by its shaft, the two halves falling at his feet. A smile, one forged by anger and bloodlust, spread across his face as he approached, not saying a word. His speed was blinding, his fury precise. One large lunge, one that quaked the earth and rattled the bones, and his hand was around the man's throat. He held the Great Traveler in one hand, a show of power and ability.

"Consider this a message." Nothing more, nothing less. He cut the man in two.

SIXTEEN

Saving a Home

The first strike team attacked, the two former Death Knights leading the charge, their styles of precision and strength complementing each other. The high-elf noblewoman fell in behind, swinging a jagged crocodile sword—the Morass Blade. Calfe took the rear, his footsteps echoing softly through the corridor. They cut a bloody path, following the scent of aether through the Halls. Astra's voice became clearer in Razgaif's head. She was reaching out, her words muddled. The Great Traveler dragged behind Razgaif, streaking a line of blood behind him. A monster. He always was a monster. Death Knight or not, that part of him remained, though he was now a new type of monster protecting his kin. *I'll take on everyone if I have to.*

They battled their way through the Halls, the once-twisted corridors leading to gulfs of white sands and salt and half-buried columns. The waves of skeletons, mages, and mercenaries fell to their blades until they finally made it to the largest of the three Halls, the Grafted Bones. No doubt, it was almost night. Razgaif could see the walls closing around Vom. *We're coming for you.* They dived through the last of the three catacombs, regaining their strength through the determination of nearing their goal.

Astra's aether shot through the darkness of the Hall of Grafted Bones. Tytli's eyes glittered in the light of the torches that lined the walls. Astra's aether was softer and lathered in uncertainty, but it belonged to the Aseimon-Denholm line all the same, and Tytli clearly struggled as she felt it. He saw the anger creeping back in her eyes and feared their blades would cross again.

She stopped. "Astra doesn't deserve this," she said. Razgaif exhaled with relief. "If only—"

"Don't think about it. We keep moving." Razgaif pushed forward. The gold aether of *Svadagd* rose from his shoulders and caressed up his back and through his neck. Honeysuckles, fresh-cooked fish, and citrus rested on the roof of his mouth. "We can't change what happened," he muttered, "but we can change the future. She's scared. I feel it. She won't be scared anymore. We're coming."

They made it to the treasure room. Tumbled statues lay against the walls. Once, they had immortalized the Worm King, his Queen, and his paramours, with space for all their children. Yet nothing was left of their dynasty now, a pretty wineglass empty of juice. Behind the broken marble face of Isobel Denholm and her dead, irrelevant sons was another passage. The hallway had little of the gold sheen from the rest of the catacombs, undoubtedly a getaway that led somewhere within the old castle. Astra's aether grew stronger there. She was close. Razgaif's quaking steps thundered through the Hall, shaking the ground like a giant's march.

The hidden passage stretched on for what felt like a millennium. Razgaif's fingers ached now. He licked his lips and pushed down the fatigue, which melted once he heard a cry for help. His footsteps quickened, his heartbeat rose.

"Mr. Razgaif's gonna stomp you into the ground!" *Astra!*

"Shut up, girl, he's not here!"

I have you now. This was the plan, to stay within the secret passage, wait for anyone to go by, and then creep back toward the entrance from where they'd come. One problem—there was only one entrance, it seemed. Isobel Denholm had never had a chance to finish the secret passage, confident in their victories. Surely she had wished for it when Tytli came for her that deadly night. *Another deadly night; another hunt.* Razgaif followed the sounds of Astra's muffled cries and the scent of roses.

The trail led them to the last chamber of the secret hallway. It was an expansive room, the walls lined with countless gold-dipped skeletons, fastened so deep into the floor that lifting them up proved impossible without damage. Tomb raiders had taken the gems from the eyes—no more rubies, emeralds, topazes, and sapphires staring across the room. A large chair and a few smaller ones were tucked into the north of the room, made of more bones of enemies Mistress Isobel had deemed worthy of her seat. The bone-claw cupholder on the arm of the chair held a goblet. The chair also held an occupant, lying across the side from arm to arm, snuggled perfectly in the low grasp of the two humeri. Vom craned his head, staring at them across the room. He laughed, weak and annoyed, as though this were all a game.

"You're not the type to come at me like this, Calfe. I thought I had you." Vom cleaned his nails, scraping the dirt from them using the tip of an expensive dagger. "You've always been cautious when it came to me, waiting for my plans. But you didn't catch this one, did you? It's funny. I've never seen a dead man so hurt before as when I saw your friend panic. And then there was your *helplessness.* Oh my, I'd pay to see that expression again." He sat upright. "But that's not why we're here, are we?"

Razgaif stepped forward. "You know why."

"Ah, no more steps." Vom clapped his hands, the sound echoing through the hall. Two men emerged from behind the throne, one holding Astra by the back with a knife at her throat, the other man pointing a staff at the door. "You're *not in control*. This is *my* city. *I* deserve a place here. And yet, my family could get nowhere in this broken society. That's not a life. I see mockeries everywhere." Vom's breathing swelled, his eyes wild. The room was quiet, all but for him. He gestured at Razgaif and Tytli. "Look at you, rotting balls of flesh. I hoped you would kill each other. But no . . ." He scanned Razgaif. "You may look more normal now, but that doesn't change anything. I know what you are underneath. Worms." He cocked his head back, then shook it. "This was supposed to be easy. Simple—*don't move!*" he shouted once more. The knife moved closer to Astra's skin. She yelped. Razgaif clutched his weapon. "You've embarrassed me enough already."

The madness in Vom's voice rose. He jumped from the chair, walked over to the soldier holding Astra, and licked his dry lips, pressing his finger against the edge of the soldier's dagger. "It's *simple*. What does an undead creature need with any of this? I'm living. I'm breathing. I deserve more than rotting flesh does." Spittle stuck to the dwarf's now-messy beard. "Why should they succeed when I have to work? Why do they deserve happiness when I have to claw up? They don't belong. They aren't natural, yet, yet . . . hmmm . . ." Vom laughed, though nothing he said had an ounce of humor. He circled Astra. "Yet they are *honored. Praised.* And this girl, is she supposed to play house with this abomination? I'm saving her. I'm helping her realize she can make the living stay above the dead like we always *have been. Either serve or stay in the ground.*"

Calfe took a careful step forward, squaring his shoulders. "This is over your fragile pride, Vom?" he began. "Your pride?

Pride that makes you believe that if you fail and other people succeed, their success becomes a burden? There's not enough space in the world for their happiness and yours? Don't make me laugh. You're not that important." Calfe drew his knives, but he hadn't moved. They were sheathed one second, and out the next. Razgaif gulped. A hostage situation wasn't anything new for a Death Knight Commander, but all the other times he'd been far removed. He didn't want to risk Astra's life. *What are you doing, Calfe?* One move, one slice, and Astra's young life would be over. In the City of the Undead, life was still life. Raising wasn't a replacement for the first life. "When will you accept that your failure is up to you alone?"

The murderous look in Vom's eyes turned venomous. "And what do you know about failure, Calfe—or success, for that matter?"

"More than you, apparently. Kidnapping a little girl, for what? Profits? What do you think you can do to scare her into submission?" Calfe shook his head.

"When you have someone they care about, scaring someone becomes easy. Right, Razgaif? That *is* your name, right?" Bloodlust shot across Vom's eyes. "She is willing to do anything for me as long as I leave you and the Afterlife Crisis alone. You know I have people ready to tear your little home to pieces as we speak. You didn't think I knew you were going to come running? I'm not as dumb as Calfe allowed you to believe. I didn't get this far by playing a game I don't know the rules of. Hedge your bets, and you'll learn to never lose." Vom tapped his fingers together and smiled. "So, either you step away and let us go, or the little home you've been building won't be there when you get back. That will break our friend's heart to pieces, won't it? I don't think she will ever recover from it."

That smile.

Razgaif hated it.

The Afterlife didn't matter; she did. He knew that. Astra, a child, wouldn't understand. She saw it as his dream, and in some ways, it was. It had brought him back together and mended the stray pieces of the orc inside. It helped him remember who he was. But . . . so did she. He gripped the Great Traveler, all anxiety gone. Saving her meant everything. He went to make a move, to the Depths with everything else.

But Tytli and Calfe took it into their own hands.

Calfe exhaled and breathed a cloud of smoke. Soshadyel, in turn, whipped from its sheath in an instant, extending further than it ever had before, hitting the man holding Astra on his elbow. He cried out, blood spilling from his arm, but his scream didn't last long. The bladelike whip curled back around, and he was dead before his body hit the ground. Astra didn't waste a second—she was away the moment she was free, dashing across the room. The other men tried grabbing her, but her little legs were too quick. Razgaif swooped in, madness giving him the strength he needed. She ran toward him, but one guard stood in his way. Razgaif roared, smashing through him with the entire weight of the Great Traveler. He swept Astra behind him with one arm and put himself between her and Vom and the rest of the Light of the Chosen.

Astra grabbed his leg and let out a frustrated cry. She was still wearing the dress from the ceremony the night before. The bow was gone, and her dress was torn and bloody, obviously from a fight. Other than that, she appeared unharmed, not a scar or a bruise on her. She clung to her spinel necklace. Razgaif patted her on the back. The hug would have to wait.

"Thess," he asked, as gently as he could, "take her from this room. Don't let anyone else get in the way."

Thess understood. She nodded, taking Astra by the hand. "She is safe, you have my word."

"Mr. Raz! I'm sorry, I didn't—" Astra frowned. "I'm sorry."

"You don't have to apologize." He gave her the bravest of smiles, one she returned. Razgaif slowly tilted his attention back toward Vom and the Lights. "You, all of you, will spend the rest of your short lives begging for forgiveness."

"*Get them!*" Vom shrieked.

Seeing all his work fall away, Vom dashed off toward the door. *No. Not this time.* Razgaif went for the kill, chasing after the snake of a sky dwarf, whose arms and legs flailed in fear as he ran. The third man, the same one from the kidnapping, appeared, conjuring again those pesky shades, which collapsed on Razgaif and met the Great Traveler. But Vom had escaped through the only path behind them. The shadow mage, now face-to-face with an angry orc, widened his eyes.

"Reinforcements! We need—"

Dead.

The shadow mage got his dying wish, however. More men rushed in, covering their boss's retreat. There was nowhere to run. A sickening feeling rumbled against the ribs of his chest. The Afterlife Crisis might not be there when he got back. He knew there was little he could do. They'd been stuck down here. Bile rose from his gut. He made his choice and would make it over and over again if need be. The sorrow remained, though. Razgaif prepared his mind for the worst, gathering what little energy he had left.

Mercenaries kept flowing in, group by group. So much time was wasted as he, Calfe, and Tytli fought. Razgaif grunted, holding his bloodied great ax. The war horn of that grim day blared in his ears. *I failed once, and that was one time too many.* Razgaif swung his ax, cutting down two men in a single swing. Another went for him. Slow. Too slow. Fatigue clung to him, his strength failing. The longsword struck across his chest and he thought, for a second, it was over.

Until Rib-Digger appeared out of nowhere.

The patchwork abomination pulled Razgaif's attacker away and threw him across the Hall. Razgaif never knew the horridness of the Fleshmeisters and their creations. Rib-Digger swung his large hook, known as the Patchwork's Meatflayer, twirled the chain, and launched the hook square through the man's ribs. His accuracy was fearsome. *Ah. That's how he got his name.*

"Protect! Family!" His roar echoed through the catacombs as he rampaged through the treasure room. Wave after wave of men fell at the massive blows of the patchwork and his cyclone of death. "Protect!"

Flynn, Clyth, and Bao Su rushed in behind him. Razgaif hadn't known their skills outside the restaurant, but he watched as Clyth burned men to cinders, Flynn cut them down with the practiced ease of an ex-soldier, and Bao Su waved her fan, enchanted wind tearing through her enemies, the sounds of wind chimes ringing after every spell cast. They quickly ran to Razgaif's side—aside from Rib-Digger, who still rampaged. Another wave fell. One patchwork served as an army, as the saying went. *I'm sorry your hook found blood once more, Rib.*

"We got this," Flynn said. "Rib-Digger ran off in this direction, and his heart was glowing." *Astra's necklace. He had it enchanted. That genius.* "Let us handle it here. You go back!"

"How?" Razgaif growled, frustration high. *We're going to be too late to save the restaurant.*

"Don't give up yet," Tytli told him. "I might have a way out."

Calfe froze. "I don't think there's any faster way to get out.

Except . . ." He looked up. "Except . . . ," he repeated, a smile growing on his face. "Do you think . . . ?" He craned his head up. "Where are we now?"

"In a tomb underground," Razgaif said. The blank stare Calfe gave him was worth it.

"You know full well what I meant," he snapped after a moment.

Tytli rubbed her temples. "I'm assuming under the Detritus given this was a secret passage for the King and his consorts."

The Detritus was a ruin left within the city where the old Castle Vem had stood. The people of Necropolis knew the history and the death that had plagued the land—history wasn't taught by forgetting. Castle Vem was once one of the largest spectacles in all the land. Built on the backs of the undead army, it spiraled toward the sky in hopes of touching the heavens the Worm King dreamed of conquering. History and time chewed away the Worm King's once-great home, leaving a meatless bone of debris above. The once-endless halls, massive towers, wide keeps, and miles upon miles of battlement were all gone. Only bricks dug into blackened soil remained of the great Castle Vem.

"And do you think that . . . ?" Calfe peeked at the ceiling and then to Tytli.

"Huh," she said quietly. "I believe that I can."

Tytli shot out her hand. Dozens upon dozens of butterflies and bees rose from her skin and danced around the room. The stale air dissolved beneath a soft, refreshing breeze, as though a window had been opened to springtime itself. A sparkle came upon the space around them, twisting and turning through various colors and shapes. Pink and red flowers and mushrooms emerged from the cracks in the ground, and vines bearing small red grapes coiled around the pillars. Soon the vines claimed all the floor and all the ceiling. Small will-o'-the-wisps swayed across Razgaif's face. He touched one, a warm feeling catching in his chest, so soft and inviting that his limbs weakened and his vision whirled. The butterflies, bees, and wisps dispersed in different directions, seeping through the walls and flying up toward the city above.

Tytli stood there for a moment, eyes glowing. She hadn't touched the Glimmer Glade Veil in centuries, in fear that her corruption would taint the magical realms outside theirs. To have that back was a greater gift than her other eye. Razgaif never realized how thin the barrier was between their physical world of Dargath and places like the Fae Realm, the Stillness, and the Burnt Rooms. There she was, touching the other side, like putting a hand through water in a lake. Her swarm returned, blending back within her skin. Tytli pulled herself away, one single tear rolling down her face.

"I never thought I'd see it again," she said softly, "yet here, I . . ." She swallowed her thought. "Never mind that. Above us is clear. Prepare."

Nothing could have prepared him.

Queen Tytli Bhihadra, the Queen of Fae, Lady Lotus, and the Mother Who Never Was, awoke. Aether rose from her feet, coating her in webs and combs. The cocoon swelled, conquering the space around it, and the room crumbled under her growing form. Before long, the cocoon filled over half the room. Razgaif and Calfe pressed themselves against the walls. The cocoon shook, breaking and cracking. Her wings emerged first, torn and enveloped in black ivy, unlike the weak ones she'd had before. These were strong wings that took the form of both a butterfly wing and a dragon's, shadowing the room and waving in the same way the Veil itself did when it broke around her. Her massive draconic body smashed through the cocoon's hide next. Her slick scales were the infinite colors of a bismuth gem, slipping from one hue to the next in the torchlight. Though large and muscular, her body held sharp angles and hard spikes, which hung around her joints and face. She took a deep breath, and a chill ran through Razgaif's body. *Effortless power and majesty.* Isobel's envy was warranted.

Tytli craned her long neck and folded her wings. Her large eyes followed them across the room. "It's been a long time since I've assumed my true self. I won't let him live my life for me." She spoke from all directions, an enchanting song, alluring to them by its simple existence. "I was a mount and a weapon, unable to act outside his will. No one will ever treat me the same way. I . . ." She pondered her next words. "I do not take this lightly. I vowed no one would ride my back like a common beast, but . . . there is no other way. I won't allow your dream to falter on my deeds. Razgaif the Younger. Calfe Metcoat. Consider this my gift: a voyage to the skies."

Razgaif took some cautious steps forward, strapping his weapon to his back. *Gods, she can swallow me in a single bite.* His throat went tight. *Do I just . . . climb on? A little rude,* he thought. He did it all the same, climbing up the side of one of her spikes, moving toward her back between her soft wings. Calfe followed suit, his stout legs somehow making it. He exhaled loudly.

"Have you ever done this before?" Calfe asked nervously.

Tytli snorted. "Can't say that I have." A churning feeling bubbled up in Razgaif, who gripped at the root of his friend's delicate wing.

"It doesn't hurt, does it?"

"Truly, if you fell from my back and tumbled to your death, I wouldn't notice until I landed." Tytli shrugged. The men gave a weak laugh. "Don't worry. I'll make sure you both stay alive."

Tytli gave a long stretch, forelegs forward and hindlegs up. She shook, tufts of moss and lotus raining down from her side, and gathered her height. And then . . . she jumped. Along with her swarm and the roots and vines under her command, she tore through the ground and the ceiling, rupturing through the earth like a wound. The hidden sanctum of Isobel Denholm broke away as they ascended, the catacombs crashing all around them. Razgaif caught a glimpse of Rib-Digger gathering up the rest, shielding them from the debris as they escaped through the chaos of the now-closing entrance. He sighed in relief. *All of you are getting a raise.*

Tytli dug her way upward, her claws ripping through stone and metal and clay, assisted by the vines and her swarm. Not minutes later, they were tunneling through the land itself. The catacombs soon disappeared out of sight.

The ancient dragon proved her mettle. She furled her wings for a last push. Razgaif and Calfe lowered themselves as close to her back as possible. They soon realized it was for the best. Tytli corkscrewed, drilling through the last layer of earth, scales ripping through the crust of the land. The world cracked against her as they emerged through the black stones of the Detritus, spinning up and up toward the sunrise sky. It was almost early morning. The sun reached over the horizon, and the cool open air slapped against their faces. They were above it all, the streets, the castles, the ruins, and the people.

Gazing down at their shambled, hodgepodge cloak of a city, the orc pup that slept within Razgaif cried out in joy. From up there, everything looked so bewitching, so tranquil. He had spent so many years protecting the city, never truly living within it. Necropolis was gorgeous in its grimness. *I helped make this,*

Razgaif thought. His life, suddenly, seemed far more than its wreckage. Tytli stretched out her wings farther than Razgaif thought possible. She scoped the city and gathered her bearings. And then... she flew faster than before.

Joy and determination melded together among them. They flew over the city, moving freely, like birds who'd found their wings. She made a beeline for the Afterlife, the city's painted bricks leading her from above. Razgaif saw the commotion. Scores of Vom's men were already upon his restaurant. Tytli dropped farther down, lowering her speed for the descent but keeping a hurried pace. The street was too narrow for her. *I would rather not cause millions of gold in property damage.* Razgaif groaned.

"How are we—" he shouted.

"Do you trust me?" Tytli asked simply.

"I don't like that question. It usually means something *foolish* is about to happen," Calfe put in, groaning.

Tytli took a deep breath. "Yes or no, say it now."

"We do," Razgaif said.

They were on the back of a dragon, soaring through the sky, and then just like that, they weren't. The weight underneath them disappeared, leaving them hanging in the air. Tytli popped back to her preferred levia form, free-falling like the rest of them. Razgaif kicked and screamed, the air choking him, the ground closing in on them. He tried not to look down, holding on to his ax for dear life. How was this going so fast yet so slow? *Trust. Trust. Trust.* It became harder the farther they plummeted. His heart caught in his throat. The green-painted road was going to have a bit more red. Razgaif closed one eye. One more second and—

Millions of butterflies and bees caught them by the shoulders, wrapping under his arms and around his waist and easing him down. Razgaif shook off his now burnt nerves. His head spun, his throat so dry it hurt. The sweat was the worst. Living, admittedly, was still quite gross in that regard. He calmed his nerves. Calfe was none the better, hurling the contents of his stomach onto the side of the road. Tytli tossed her head back, unperturbed. "Please get it together, you two. I wouldn't have let you die." She waved it off. "You were never in danger."

"Could've fooled me," Calfe muttered, wiping spittle from his mouth. "But you're right." He took a shaking step, eyes blinking wide. "All right. We can do this."

Razgaif agreed. He put aside his fatigue. Famine Street was crowded, with shouts and crashing. The sickening feeling from the fall was nothing now, replaced by a new urgency. He rushed down the street, Tytli and Calfe at his back, pushing through the crowd of spectators and wading through the sea of people. The crashing grew louder. Men and women shouted louder as well. "Someone please do something!" an old woman shrilled.

Razgaif pushed through the final part of the crowd. A group of men and women in normal clothes stood across from the Afterlife Crisis, gripping large gray stones, standing shoulder to shoulder.

Astra stood her ground, flanked by both Zennexus and Thess. Skeletal men stood beside her, held together by sheer force of will. The side of her forehead was a little bruised, blood dripping from where one of the rocks had hit her. Razgaif held his weapon, all too ready to unleash his brand of violence. Tytli stopped him.

"They aren't soldiers or hired swords. They're people. Frustrated people, but people nevertheless. Vom wants us to do this. Show that we're monsters. Don't fall for it."

Razgaif stiffened. "I can't just sit by. They're—"

Someone in the crowd threw another rock at Astra. Thess slapped it away, the flat of the Morass Blade sending it flying back toward the crowd. "You throw one more rock at a child, and I will abandon all hope of peace. She begged me not to kill you after you threw the first. A child's forgiveness is far greater than my own. Now, you must be foolish to slap away the hand that's holding your lifeline, so I'm willing to ignore it once more. Only once. Do not test me further. Her forgiveness is on a different scale than my mercy."

Razgaif, Calfe, and Tytli slipped a little closer. It took the willpower of all his ancestors not to end it all right now. Razgaif prayed for his self-control. He focused on Astra instead. She looked braver, a confidence unseen before. She had no business being there. She had been kidnapped by men like these, scared beyond comparison. But she'd come anyway, rushing through the catacombs and beating them back after their battle was done. All to protect his dream. He gripped the Great Traveler. *If they touch her.* The thought of another rock sailing and striking her down in cold blood made his stomach roil. The building didn't matter. She did. She always mattered. Astra cleared her throat.

"I don't know what made you all so angry," she began, "but this isn't going to make you feel better. Tearing down what people worked for isn't going to leave a space open for you. Dead, brought to this world by magic, or living, we made this city together. This is our—" She closed her mouth, face scrunched, fists tight. "No, I'm going to say it. This is our dream. He wanted this place; I want this place. He's been nothing but good to me, and I'm going to protect it." The skeletons bulked up, spikes protruding from their shoulders. Roses blossomed on their chests, black armor coating their arms, legs, and skulls. The two skeletal lords formed golden spears and rose shields. *Bone Templars, Isobel's favorites.* But . . . they weren't hers. These stood prouder, armor glistening, eyes soft and diligent. Astra didn't force their assistance. She'd asked for it.

The man up front, thin and yellow-toothed, wiped his hand across his dingy white shirt and overalls. Poverty was minimal and lessened every day, but it remained. People wished for things they didn't have and resented those who had them. Razgaif understood. The man straightened his back.

"We ain't going to ever feel safe, little one. These dead ones will one day be controlled by another like the Worm King, and then they'll tear us all to pieces. It's bound to happen. Why should they have another chance at life and have it be better than ours? Why do we suffer when rotting flesh get to have the world? They had their chance."

"Why?" Astra snapped. "What have they done? They didn't even choose this, and you're blaming *them*? Have you talked to them? Have you sat down? Have you talked?"

The man recoiled. The entire group did. "You don't know the real world, kid."

"Really? Me? An orphan. I can't understand, I couldn't." She blinked. They recoiled again. "Maybe I don't. Maybe I don't get this 'real world.' Somehow, that's me being gullible. But maybe *you* don't get it. People deserve a place to be happy—you and everyone else. This is our home and this is our dream. So please, *leave!*"

The crowd lost its voice. One by one, its will dropped. Whether it was the words or the snapping sword of the Morass Blade, Razgaif couldn't tell. The magiian man up front tossed down his rock.

"It ain't fair," he spat. "I want to believe you, but it makes me so mad that I ain't getting anywhere while dead folks are."

"It's not their fault," Astra repeated, this time calmer. "You can't see their lives. You can only use the chances you have. I like to think that everyone can protect their dream. It's a little silly, I know, but I don't want to lose that."

Razgaif, too, lost his anger. He stowed the Great Traveler away. *No more blood today.* Lowering his shoulders and his center, Razgaif walked over. He stood between them, making himself smaller than he was.

"What are your names?" he asked, forcing the malice out of his tongue, biting it in the back of his throat. The believers of the Light winced a little. They noticed. They always did. No matter what the shaping did or the new life his rune and Astra's created, he was still a bit dead. "I'll go first. My name is Razgaif the Younger, but you may have known me as Rottgor the Famine Blade." The surrounding townsfolk looked on in apparent awe. "And there has been a rift. I didn't notice it much when I was in the castle. My duty was to the royal family and nothing more. But living away from that, I see we're on opposite sides of a raging river. The Three Whispers at the castle can try to build a bridge, but they aren't here. So, I'm offering. Anytime you need to, come to this restaurant and I'll feed you. The only thing I'm going to charge is your time. We're going to learn together."

The Lights of the Chosen froze, embers cooling in their hearts. The leader of the mob spat, a black glob landing near his hole-ridden boots. The malice was gone, or at least suppressed under a wall of shame and regret.

"Sorry 'bout that." He pointed to his head, where he'd hit Astra. "I guess I'll fall for anything. I'm just . . ."

"Tired," Razgaif finished for him. "Come back tomorrow. I'll make sure all your stomachs are full, and we'll talk like sensible folk."

"Y'all can eat? Not like living brains and stuff?" the man

asked. The rest of the crowd muttered weirder questions under their breaths.

"Real food. Good food. I'll explain more when we talk. Now please, step away."

The once-angry mob split away, unable to hide their shame from Astra's cutting words and feats of bravery. The rest of the townsfolk gave them a horrid glance, but a shame came over them as well. *Easier to watch than to step up,* Razgaif thought. He knew that from experience. He turned to Astra. Her skeletons had returned to dust, all energy leaving her in a single moment. Razgaif caught her as she fell to the ground, holding her to his chest. She was still breathing. *Breathing is good.* The day had withered her adrenaline. Razgaif cradled her in his arms, wiping the blood from her purpling bruise. As long as she was okay, he was. *A simple thing, love is.* He vowed that if she would allow it, he would be the best father she could ever have.

Much to Razgaif's surprise, Thess allowed him to carry Astra into the broken Afterlife, and he shoved through the shattered doorway. Shards of glass lay on the floor, crunching underfoot. A few tables and chairs were torn apart, and cow blood and manure were smeared all over the walls. A faint smell of oil hung in the air. Apparently, they'd planned a more sinister end for the day and had not gotten their wish. *We can clean this. You shouldn't have risked your life for a simple building.* But was it a simple building for her? Or . . . was it home to her, too?

The thought took a back seat for now. Razgaif carried her up to the living quarters, to the door where he hoped she would stay. She awoke a bit in his arms.

"I'm sorry," she muttered. "I'm a little tired."

"Stop apologizing, you did great. How's your head? I'll fetch a doctor."

She made an annoyed sound. "I hate doctors."

"I have to make sure you're okay. I—"

"You care." She smiled.

"I care," he repeated. "All you need to do is rest. I'll make some food when you wake up. I'll check on you every half hour."

"I heard your shout when they took me. It . . . gave me strength. I knew that I had to see you again. You were about to ask me something before." Her little childlike smile brought him the courage he needed. "You wanted to ask—"

"Can I adopt you?" Razgaif blurted out. He froze, unsure if he'd said too much, but the words were already out. "What I am asking is—can I be your dad?"

Astra looked up. Relief so pure—so clear—spread across her features. She laughed.

"Okay, they must've hit me harder than I thought. I already started to think of you as my pa," she admitted. "I kept seeing you and me, making those pies. I kept thinking about living at the restaurant and waking up to everyone here. I knew it was something I wanted but didn't want to assume. I—" Her delighted giggle soon opened the floodgates for her tears. "I'm not a good kid. I'm not great. I get angry and I'm bad at studying and I wander off without permission and I—I—"

"No, you're perfect as you are," Razgaif said at once. "I've been telling myself that I wasn't ready, worthy, or capable. But I couldn't get it out of my head. Even when you were miles away, I knew. My heart . . . my heart *knew*. That's how I knew you weren't controlling me. My heart always remained. My heart was something I could trust. I didn't think . . . I didn't think I could feel so strong."

"But you're the kindest person I've ever met." She lowered her voice to a whisper, soft as petals or moonlight. "I never felt more

myself than around you. Lady Thess is nice, but she's not you."
"And I didn't know who I was before you. This restaurant is my passion, but you made it all clear. And . . . you deserve a place. You deserve this home. It's already yours. Would you want that? I can't promise I won't make mistakes. I've never been a father before." His vision blurred, voice cracking. "I'm probably going to do so bad. You're allowed to say no. Thess and Lady Cleo can find you a proper home and proper parents—"

"Shut up!" Astra shouted. "Shut up, shut up! I don't wanna *live* with anyone else. I wanna eat here and sleep here." She pounded her fist against his chest. Razgaif feigned pain at the heavy blows. "I want *you* to be my pa."

"So . . . we're going to be a family?" The beating in his heart quickened.

"Yep." Her voice cracked. The tears began anew as they held each other. Razgaif never felt so much joy in his long life. His tears overflowed. They burned and poured, vision swimming, salt on his lips. An ugly kind of beautiful, he reckoned. He held her close, big arms cradling his daughter. *My brave little champion. My pride. My joy.*

"I'll protect you. I promise." Razgaif had made a lot of vows. Some forced, others out of duty or purpose. This was for him; this was for her. He opened the door to her room, which was nearly empty. The last light of the day came through the simple window. The room never looked better. Exhaustion swayed the young girl back to sleep. Razgaif's fatherly instincts already stirred, he placed her on the bed, checking her breathing, temperature, and the small head wound. Nothing else mattered anymore. There was only one thing to do now: protect her at all costs. He sat by her bed all night.

SEVENTEEN

Consequences, Coronation, and Community

Thess acquiesced to the adoption after hearing hours of meticulous arguments.

Morning light poured in from the reopened Afterlife. They had restored the building to much of its former glory, thanks to the community. Mohek and his boys, still sitting at the counter and enjoying their second breakfast, had brought all the furnishings from Astra's room at the Living Vine and more, anything to impress Guardian Thess, who was sitting across from Razgaif at that very moment. They quietly munched on the iced blueberry-and-orange scones and sipped on the honeyed lemon tea, the intensity of her dark-black-and-yellow, frog-like eyes unyielding. She had said yes, but how she stared at him gave him the creeping feeling that she would tear it all away if she had to. She took another long sip of her tea.

"I hate to admit it," she began, "but you might be the only

person who *can* parent her. Both of your strong wills make my head hurt." Thess straightened her back. "But I have some stipulations."

"I suspected you would," Razgaif said. His foot nervously tapped against the floor beneath him. The entire building of the Afterlife Crisis trembled at his fidgeting. Astra held in a groan.

"She'll finish schooling at the Living Vine, then move on to specialized training in weapons and rune mastery with my chosen mentors. You and Tytli should suffice as tutors there, given your status as former Six Shadows, and I'm sure Calfe will take her to the university for any rune training. When she comes of age, she should have a proper grasp of skills as both a warrior and an upstanding necromancer in our society. You will then and now use any connection you have to facilitate her dream profession and *any* hobby she wants to pursue. Do not spoil her—"

"When have I ever—"

"Astra," Razgaif warned.

She shrank in her chair. "Sorry."

"Studying is important, and it's hard work, and so is being a father. I will not accept anything less than the terms I've laid out."

Razgaif tried to open his mouth, but a cold stare met him. He kept it shut.

"Lastly, give her a loving home. Feed her properly, and make sure she has a *refined* palate. She may never be a Lady Cleo, but she will be *the* best version of herself. You never know where she will land. She needs to handle all situations . . . but . . . first and foremost, she needs to be a child. Treat her with love by showing her respect and giving her the safety she deserves. Be there for her and she will be there for you." A long quiet snaked its way between them. Thess continued staring, blinking slowly now. "You can speak," she said, after sipping her tea.

"Oh. Uh." Razgaif thumbed the side of his cup. "It all seems reasonable. But if she objects to any of it or it seems like we're controlling her, I want us to listen. After all, it's her life—not everyone's lucky enough to get a second chance like me. Do you object to any of this, Astra?"

Brief flashes of thought came across Astra's face, her lips trembling and eyes wandering. She wasn't one to struggle with words, but when she did, they built within her until she couldn't hold it in anymore. Breathing through her nose, she settled on her thoughts, looking toward Razgaif and nodding.

"I *really* didn't want to keep studying. But if I *have to* . . ."

"It'll be good for you."

She rolled her eyes. "That's what every adult says."

Thess nodded. "Of course. Plans change, and so do children when they become adults. But I do not worry about that future. She deserves to forge her destiny. All we can do as guardians, teachers, and now parents is to make it as bright as possible."

She finally brought out the documents for signing. There were stacks upon stacks of them, requiring signatures for the finalization of the adoption. His hand cramped and his eyes burned by the end. He looked at the last page. Orcs typically didn't have a surname, taking the name of their clan. Alas, surnames were the important bloodline of a magiian. She deserved to have one. He pondered the thought for a while.

"Onyxus. Astra Melu Onyxus, how does that sound?"

Astra's eyes shone. "Onyxus. Oh . . . that sounds wonderful." Her smile grew bigger. Aseimon. Denholm. No, *never*. She was a proud Onyxus, daughter of Razgaif the Younger of the Onyx-Ax clan, and her kindness and strength would be her glory—that he knew. He set the pen-quill down, ink staining his already-charcoal skin.

"Well, it's done, then," said Thess. "I suspect you have her accommodations in order here. Normally, I inspect the living quarters, but that isn't needed. I've seen enough of this place already." Thess straightened in her chair, plopping the last scone into her mouth and swallowing it whole. She unceremoniously stood up and dusted the crumbs from her lap. "That is that, then. Miss Onyxus, I will see you at your studies, and tardiness will result in the same punishments as usual." She turned to Razgaif and gave a deep bow. "And congratulations on fatherhood. Also, don't you dare lose sight of her, or I'll be bringing my blade instead of my pen-quill."

Thess collected the contracts and left without another word, closing the door behind her.

Was it done? Razgaif turned, looking at Astra. Her eyes were wide, her lips trembling. She looked back at him.

"She really said yes." Astra's voice cracked. "This is really happening."

"It's really happening," Razgaif said. Wanting it was one thing; having it happen was an entirely different moment. He rubbed the sides of his head, heart throbbing. "I'm a father."

Tears filled Astra's big eyes. "I'm your daughter."

The Afterlife Crisis's patrons looked at one another, smiles spreading by the second. Once everyone was sure that Thess was out of earshot, the place exploded with cheers. Employees and regulars alike roared. His friends surrounded him, patting him on the shoulders. Bao Su brought him a giant mug of beer and Astra another batch of cookies. Razgaif reclined, his body settling down. He drank his mug.

There was only one worry now that stayed on his mind, spoiling his celebration. Vom was still out there, slipping away through the cracks of the confusion. He'd never surfaced at either entrance, taking another way they didn't know of. It had worried him since. *Positive. Don't let it ruin our day.* He guzzled his beer, wiping the foam from his mouth. *I won't let him near my home.*

"Let's check those wounds," Razgaif said to his daughter.

"I'm *fine*." Astra pouted. *"Fine."*

Razgaif and Astra retreated to the living quarters upstairs. The thin, gray Duskgrave orcish doctor had prescribed Astra only sleep, food, and an energy tonic of aetheroot and monkfruit for a full recovery. He followed his daughter in.

Not yet a day in, Astra's room already looked more lived in than his own. Tons of new and old books were stacked in piles on the floor. Maps of Dargath lined the walls, alongside the watercolor paintings of places she wished to see. The floor had a rug made of plush purple fabric, and the windows were cleaned and curtained with light-purple silk. Stuffed animals, rabbits, bears, and a particularly worn-out tiger sat on the bed, where she sat. Astra looked at home. She was back to who he knew her to be, happily within comfortable sleeping clothes, poofy hair fixed, and bathed. A small bandage on her forehead was the single reminder that anything had happened. Astra's face softened.

"I can't believe it." She swallowed hard. "I was . . . I thought Thess would never say yes."

"Me, too." The brighter the light, the more you felt lost when darkness fell. *Today, the darkness won't win.* Razgaif sat beside her. "But we are here." He hardly believed it himself. "This is your home now and will forever be, Astra Melu Onyxus." Tears blossomed in her big eyes. Astra flung herself at him—her father—and grabbed him around his big chest with arms far too small. More of those ugly, joyous tears ran down her face. He patted her on the head, keeping his own tears at bay this time. "You need your strength. Get some rest. If you want to come back downstairs, I'll be there."

Astra nodded, pulling away and wiping the tears from her eyes. He let her be, closing the door behind him.

"It suits you," a voice said from the hallway. "Fatherhood, I mean."

Tytli leaned against the wall, her dress gold and her face veiled by a thin layer of white. She lowered her gaze a bit.

"I'm a little jealous. No fault of yours. That's on me. I'm . . . hurt. And like you say, hurt people hurt other people. I can't help but think about what-ifs—of the lives I would've nurtured. But perhaps . . . perhaps I wouldn't have been a good mother anyway."

"Don't say that, you don't know." Razgaif stood beside her, leaning against the wall as well. "I didn't even want a kid. My brothers and sister are roaring in the afterlife right now."

Tytli laughed. "And raising a descendant of your greatest enemy as well. There must be a riot over there."

"But I don't regret it, not one bit. It's not always going to be easy, but . . . I want the best for her. Always." Razgaif put his hand on Tytli's shoulder. "Please promise that you'll stop roaming now. Find a place to put down your roots. You've been in the wind far too long."

"That's a hard request, Rott—Raz." She straightened her back. Her regality returned. "Are you sure it's okay for me to help with tutoring her? Thess . . . didn't give me the clearest answer. I have plenty to atone for."

Razgaif hugged her, much to her surprise. "Stop atoning, start there. There's always more to atone for. And one day, you'll see. Life is more than just fixing your past mistakes."

Astra put her hands on her hips, standing between her father and Tytli. "We're here to see the Lady," she said to the guards.

"That we are!" Razgaif nodded back.

Razgaif led the way, despite Tytli also knowing the castle as well as he did. They beelined to the throne room, heading through the familiar halls he had walked a thousand times. His feet remembered their patrols, itching to return to the barracks. A few of the Ruinous Guard greeted him here and there, shouting his old name. A bittersweetness came upon him. He was no longer that man—no longer holding the great and powerful swords made of magic and crafted of souls. One recruit caught his eye. A younger orc-levia revenant—torn from his life too soon and raised at his own request—wore a sword made of glowing green steel that made the air taste of garlic and fermented vegetables. A slight buzzing rang in Razgaif's ear, not of the constant corpse flies but of singing crickets and soothing cicadas. He would recognize its voice anywhere.

"Your name, son, and what's the sword's?"

The recruit flushed as much as a dead man could. "Uh, my name's Nerr Witherweep, and this," the Ruinous Guardsman said, past heroics shining in his soul-flared eyes, "and this is . . . I guess it can be translated from levia as 'the Lasting.' It's formed from the shards of the blade of a great Death Knight, I've been told."

"Really?" Razgaif said, pushing Rottgor's smile down. It was Malferioel, his old friend in its new life. "Well, I hope the best for you. And remember your vows, save the dead, protect the living."

"Will do, ser!" Nerr snapped a clean salute.

Razgaif ushered Astra ahead before she blurted out the truth. The guard would find out where his sword came from sometime in his afterlife, and *who* it once belonged to. Right now, ignorance was fine. The small tinge of happiness remained, however. Seeing the reforged blade felt like reuniting with an old comrade—familiar, but bittersweet. They had gone their separate ways, and no longer spoke or contacted one another, but the fondness remained. From the sounds of its humming, it was for the best. *Goodbye, old comrade. Serve him well, and spill no innocent blood in this life.* He swore he heard its buzzing at his back, as though satisfied with its new lot in life and ready for what lay ahead.

After passing through the castle's security, they stepped into the throne room, where Lady Cleo sat on the Carnation Throne. The comforting rain's thrum against the black stone of the castle filled the room. The mulberry-purple and crimson curtains appeared beautiful, and vibrated in the dimness of the lightly showering afternoon. The skulls and bones of the evil necromancers glowed slightly from their salts, and the runelight torches burned enough for a clear sight of the entire area. The long carpet led up the stairs. He hadn't truly walked up the stairs before, not as a guest, always stationed beside the throne made of the Worm King's bones. The new Lord Commander knew his stuff, however, and the room was guarded by the Slicksters and the Ruinous Guard alike. Razgaif had left them in good hands.

Lady Cleo smoothed out her purple dress and readjusted her crown. It was a simple band of silver over her thin eyebrows and underneath her freshly shaven head. Her hands rested on her lap, and her staff was firm in her grip. The twisted elderwood staff topped with a simple amethyst orb appeared so powerful within the grasp of such a serious woman. The intimidation remained, even as one of her closest friends. Her cultivated coldness, an icy wind on a soft winter morning, washed over the room. This was the Duchess of Death, and she was taking her throne. He wondered how long the transition had been happening.

"Very prompt," she said from the Carnation Throne. "You look well, Raz. And Tytli, you as well. It appears a lot has happened since I last saw you at the restaurant."

All three of them fell to their knees.

"And this must be the amazing Astra that changed them both. Please stand. A friend of theirs is a friend of mine." Astra stood but kept her head low. "Come on, don't be shy."

She walked up, her courage shaking. She walked up those steps all the same. Seeing her ascend toward the throne was surreal. Centuries had passed since her great-grandfather had sat upon the throne, yet she was here, her cruel parentage memorialized by the bones embellishing the halls. A stranger's family now sat in what might've been her birthright in a different life. She didn't have a single thread of jealousy. Awe—that was about as far as it went. Seeing this moment, bringing her there, this was Lady Cleo's last test, and Astra's innocence alone peeled any doubt from the Duchess's eyes. She held Astra by the hand.

"I've never seen a rune like ours feel so warm and inviting. Spirits are linked to yours. No wonder the Death Knights see much in you. With the right training, you have great potential, Astra. If you'll have me, I would like to tutor you as a simple repayment for a close friend."

"You—the Duchess, training me . . ." Astra coughed, suppressing her emotions. "I would like nothing more, Your—uh . . ."

"Grace," Cleo provided.

"Your Grace." Astra nodded along. "I would enjoy that."

"Then it's settled." Cleo reclined on her throne. "After your schooling, our tutoring will begin. Is that okay with your father?"

"We are unworthy—" Razgaif paused, daggers from the Duchess's eyes falling on him from the top of the steps. He readjusted his face, standing to his feet. "Of course, Cleo. We wouldn't want anything less."

Cleo visibly sheathed the daggers from her gaze, taking a more neutral approach once more. "I did not call you only for that. The Lights of the Chosen. They've been quite the stain on our city with their anti-undead and anti-summoned sentiment. Letting them speak their mind was my grandfather's position, not realizing how much hate poisons a city. They are allowed their close-mindedness on their own time, but when it comes to harming people, that's unacceptable. You should've involved me."

"And you know what would have happened," Razgaif said bluntly. Tytli bit her lip at his brashness.

"Yes, my fury would've been swift," Lady Cleo said, unmoved. "I don't see a problem with that."

"I can't ask you to solve all my problems, Your Grace. Not every citizen can walk to your throne room and get an audience." Razgaif knew the simple truth of his words. She could not be there all the time. Yes, she was still his friend, but she needed to trust the system she and her family had created. "I am Razgaif the Younger, Champion of the Onyx-Ax and proprietor of the Afterlife Crisis. This is the life I chose for myself. One you allowed me to choose."

"In a way, I'm glad. You've taken my advice and built something of your own. That I understand. However, I could not stand by. Your friend Mr. Metcoat was an absolute pleasure to work with." The daggers once in her eyes moved to her lips in a smirk. "Tell me about your experience first."

Astra returned to her father's side. They recounted everything they'd experienced so far, down to the smallest detail. Lady Cleo listened all the way through, as intently as a child would during story time. She cocked her head, asked little questions, and listened to the facts as they arose. After they were done, she paused, allowing herself a sip of her strawberry wine and a single bite of a chocolate truffle. Somehow, that made what she presented next that much more ruthless.

"Bring him in."

From the side corridor, Calfe emerged, dragging Vom by the collar of his rags. His face was almost unrecognizable from the bruising and swelling.

"He thought he gave me the slip. *Me*," Calfe whispered. "I'm sorry for the gruesomeness, Astra. Your little heart is forgiving. Please stay that way. But some adults can't let injustice go. This man hurt you, a child, and I hope you can forgive us for such cruelty."

Astra lowered her shoulders, putting her head up high. "My teacher, Thess, always told us: The people that enjoy cruelty on those who mean them no harm deserve what they sow." She turned to Vom. "I don't think I can forgive you." Astra held her father's hand. "Orcs have their laws. I'll allow my father to decide your fate. I'm much too young for this." She smiled, knowing all too well her father's fury.

"Oh?" Calfe asked. He threw the chained Vom to the ground. "What laws are those, Razgaif?"

Razgaif looked down at the beaten Vom, who was crawling toward him. They had done a number on him, beating him from head to toe. Ripe purple and red bruises covered his face, and his lip was split open so wide it looked more like split squash. Calfe or the dungeons—he wasn't sure which one—didn't bother pulling punches. They had cut his hair and beard with a dagger. Vom glared up at him, eyes quivering with self-pity, remembering the mephitic venom dripping from Razgaif's words. Razgaif had imagined millions of ways to hurt him and nurtured that thought during his dreams. Right then, all of that meant nothing. One thing stood above the rest. A simple orcish law, one that all the tribes still in existence recognized.

"The orcish laws are brutal, Your Grace. I'm invoking our law of dishonor."

Lady Cleo pondered. "Oh, *that* law. You know which one, don't you, Vom?"

Fear stretched throughout Vom's entire body, which now radiated a palpable panic. He scooted away. "What? Not—no. I'll—"

"You'll keep your life," Razgaif said, this time lower. "A simple repayment for an orc. When you wrong us or our family and you're not fit for honorable combat, this is an offering." Vom looked around the room and found no allies. His lips quivered. "Actually," Razgaif said finally, after a long time without an answer. "I would normally do this myself, but I do not want to make my daughter ill. So, Lady Cleo, would you do the honors?"

"I will have my people provide that for you by the morning," Lady Cleo said, as though he had merely asked that a crate of apples be sent over. Vom made a soulful scream through his busted lips.

"You can't do this to me, I'm a Brasscrown! My father will know about this."

"Your father, your mother, and your siblings pretend they don't know you. When you're sour and your family is sour, it's all about hedging bets." She waved him off, unamused. "Of course, I'll make sure it's perfectly aligned in the orcish way. Now get this man out of my sight. His screaming is becoming too much for my ears and is ruining my peace." Cleo shooed them away. The Slicksters heaved the crying dwarf, kicking and screaming helplessly against his chain. Once he was out of the room, Cleo turned to Razgaif. "One more question, my friend. Would you mind providing some food for my coronation meal? I did truly enjoy your cooking."

The Duchess kept her promise, and a point was made. Raz left one prize at the castle as a sign of good faith toward the Duchess and her Slicksters, and the other found a place in Calfe's office. A relief swept over him, a grim justice for all the things he had put himself, Astra, and the city through. Astra knew what orcish justice was. However, a young girl of her stature deserved a bit more civility until she got older. *Then*, she could learn more about the orcish law and its payment. Proud of how far he had come, he peered around his reconstructed room.

The paint of his dark redwood-stained walls was dry now. The furs of the rugs and the wall tapestries of various animals surrounded him. Astra had painted little cave drawings on the walls, mimicking those he had told her about. It warmed his heart seeing them. They'd filled the room with more of Mohek's furniture, smaller things such as drawers, chairs, tables, and a writing desk of his own. Of course, above the fireplace was the weapon rack that held the Great Traveler in all its glory, wrapped nicely in leather straps, blades shined to perfection. Beside the fireplace was Cupbearer, gleaming gold, his aether so infused within its metal that it took on its scent, changing into delightful childhood memories. That day, it smelled of honeyed bread cooking over a fresh campfire. *I might just cook that later.*

Alas, he had his work cut out for him. Dressing simply, he prepared for his day. The Duchess's coronation was on the horizon. The announcement of her official ascension and her grandfather's retirement shook Necropolis to its core. Lady Cleo had been slated for the position her entire life, a title her father had refused. She knew of duty, and she also treasured and respected it. Necropolis needed a strong hand in the coming days, Razgaif reckoned, and hers was made of steel and bone. *Seeing the city from the streets is different from seeing it from the castle,* he mused. He wondered what he'd hear at the restaurant that morning. He left his room, threw his apron over his white shirt, and headed to work.

He noted quickly that Astra's door was already open, the room clean and tidy and the bed fixed. She was an early riser like him. As far as he could tell, a few of her books and her pen set were missing. She was more than likely working downstairs among the early patrons. She enjoyed the sounds and the company. She wouldn't start traveling back to the Living Vine for studies until next week, allowing her to adjust and recover, but that didn't stop her from her studies. Driven, his little girl was. He respected that. Razgaif took himself downstairs.

The restaurant was opening. The smell of the early-breakfast meat and freshly brewed coffees from the San Isthmus filled the air. The regulars poured in, including the men from the mob. They kept their promise but gave Astra a wide berth, ensuring they were far away from any potential mix-up. They flinched a bit when he came down the stairs, no doubt hearing the fate Vom had earned through his cruelty. *Perhaps you'll learn.* Ignorance wouldn't be tolerated under the new rule of the city. That much was certain. Razgaif ignored them for now, heading to his daughter, who was sitting at the table he'd set up for them right by the window. She looked up at him. "Pa!"

"Hey, little champ, how's your morning?" He leaned over her shoulder. She was drawing, as usual, this time quick sketches of their clients. It had to be dozens by now, all within little spaces on long sheets of parchment. *Pencils,* Razgaif decided, *this girl is going to need a lot of pencils.* She was in the middle of a sketch of a skeleton man sitting alongside a close friend. She'd caught their expressions flawlessly. "You're amazing," Razgaif told her. She made an embarrassed noise that landed somewhere between a nervous laugh and a happy squeal.

"I think I'm doing okay," she said finally. "Pastry?" She offered him a large raspberry-filled pastry, top crossed by layers of icing. He took it without question, sitting down beside her. "Flynn said, and I quote: 'He better get to cooking this fancy food for the coronation 'cause I ain't gonna do it. I cook for actual people.'" The impression was near-perfect, down to the grumble and the huff at the end. Flynn narrowed his eyes from across the restaurant. Wal snorted and got bonked by a ladle on the back of the head.

"I don't have to cook for the whole castle, Flynn," Razgaif shouted from his table. "Just a few things for the Duchess and her circle. So stop worrying."

"Then you can help me with breakfast before you rush off, ya big oaf!" Flynn shouted back.

"By the Depths, let me have my breakfast, boy, and I'll get to the kitchen." Razgaif gave the loudest sip of coffee that he could, staring Flynn directly in the eye. The undead sky dwarf smirked from underneath his shaggy hair and mustache. Astra got quite the laugh out of it. Razgaif took another pastry—this one filled with cloudberries—and devoured it whole. A blur of nostalgia mingled with the fresh memory. He held both tight to his heart.

They had their breakfast together, talking and listening to one another. Excitement still hung between them. They were a family now. The Afterlife buzzed around them. People came in and out, their orders coming and going. The morning energy brought all his emotions back, not only for himself but for his people and his daughter. The world that had once been bleak held color, form, and music. He rose from his seat.

"Continue your studies. I'd hate Thess to come by and tell us what a poor job *both* of us are doing."

Astra groaned. "Tell me about it."

He kissed her on the forehead. "Time for work."

"Good luck!" Astra kissed him back on his forehead. The warm feeling of love washed over him.

Razgaif took the head of the kitchen from Flynn, who smoked his long pipe, enjoying his break from the crowd. Bao Su, Waldruk, and Clyth worked the floor that day, on cleaning duty. Rib-Digger, though scheduled to be off, came in anyway. He helped Astra on math and history, but no subject seemed too far from the patchwork's field. *He should probably be her tutor.* He made a mental note of it for Thess. *Her reaction will be glorious.*

He focused on his art—his cooking. The simple trance of work quickly took him. Weaving the dishes for the coronation feast and his guests became easy after a time. He wasn't expected to bring the main courses for the catering. The castle's cooks were sensitive, so for their sake, he kept it simple. He'd bring a few of the sweet and savory pies, a large vat of spiced mammoth-and-carrot stew, and a board of cheeses, fruits, honeys, and bread. Nothing too fancy. Flynn winced at the idea of serving such simple foods to nobles.

"It'll be quaint for a lot of them and a breath of fresh air for the others," Razgaif reassured. Flynn made a noise from his nose.

Before he knew it, the day was half spent. The lull between lunch and dinner gave him a little time to himself. His fingers and wrist ached from the chopping, dicing, and kneading, and his legs burned from standing. The door opened. Tytli walked in, a little different than she'd been the day before. Her hair was down, falling over the shoulder of her collarless gold tunic and down to her white pants in a single long braid. She wore no jewelry, and the veil she normally wore was replaced by a thin layer of silver cloth around her chin. She sat at the bar, ordering food and a drink. Razgaif served her tea himself, steeping a fresh cup and adding the milk, sugar, cinnamon, and cardamom as she preferred. She took a long sip.

"I took a job at the Living Vine," she said.

Razgaif folded his arms. "Excuse me?"

"I did, I took a job at the Living Vine."

"That would mean..."

"That I had to be interviewed by Thess. Yes. That's exactly what happened."

Razgaif had a hard time wrapping his head around the idea of them speaking. Thess didn't trust anyone, but practicality was valued. The children always needed caregivers and protectors. Who would keep them safer than a soul that had once protected Dukes and had slayed an evil King and one of his mistresses?

"I'm not envious of anyone in that room, Lili," he said. She laughed.

"You asked me to stay, and I will do just that. But there is one thing that also swayed my intention to stay."

"What is it?" Razgaif brought her the rest of the mushroom-and-chickpea curry he had been working on for those who ate little to no meat. He placed a plate of rice and a steaming hot slice of bread before her. She scooped up the perfect amount on a single spoonful, the first bite bringing a light to her eyes. He knew it struck home somewhere deep inside. "Hey," Razgaif said. Her attention snapped back. "What is it?"

"There may be one of them... still..."

"One of what?" Razgaif said, cocking his head.

"One of . . ." She took another bite and sipped at her tea. Emotions gripped her, and she could no longer keep her normal cool demeanor. "One of my eggs." Razgaif felt his heart drop from his chest to his stomach. Hope, again, was a dangerous thing. "There was always a rumor that Isobel Denholm had kept one of my eggs for herself as a trophy. She couldn't hatch it, so she kept it like a giant gemstone. I—didn't believe it. I always thought that she'd destroyed all of them in her fit. But she might have kept it as a hostage. Or a potential card to use against her enemies. And . . . I have to see it through. There may be another sanctum within the city and it's my duty as . . ." She shook, dropping her spoon. Razgaif helped her pick it back up, easing it into her hands. "As this child's mother and now as the protector of all the children of the Living Vine, I must see this through."

"And Astra and I will be here. Don't be afraid to ask for anything." Razgaif took a pastry from the glass dish in the back corner. He offered the cherry one to her, and she took it gracefully. "Keep us informed and . . . thank you, Lili. You've always cared."

"Same to you, friend. I have to do this. I have to see where this leads."

"Correct me if I'm wrong," another voice said, "but I think that's another job for me."

Calfe appeared at the bar, no sign heralding his presence beforehand. He plopped down on a stool, smoking his odd dwarvish box. He looked . . . happier? That wasn't quite the word. Calfe's brand of happiness was satisfaction, a warm content glued together by the love of the people closest to him. He also ordered food. Razgaif noticed he wasn't big on food, eating perhaps once a day. From the weariness in his eyes, Razgaif could tell he needed it that day. The war chef served a simple hearty meal of meat and potatoes left from the lunch rush, as well as some apple cider. Calfe began scarfing it down.

"I'll look into it, Tytli," he told her, wiping some of the gravy from his chin. "It probably hasn't left the city—if it did, they don't know what they have. Kept that long, away from its parents or a magical source, it has probably gone dormant by now, right?"

"Yes . . . ," she said, finishing her meal. "How do you know that?'"

"Research."

"Novel . . . research," Razgaif added, grinning. Calfe shot him a glare.

"You write novels?" Tytli asked.

Calfe coughed. "Never mind that. But yes, dormant. If we can find it, we can restore it, correct?"

"I believe so. . . . It has been done before. I just . . . I don't . . ." Tytli gripped her mug of hot tea.

"Don't think about what could go wrong," Razgaif told her. "It will work out."

"It will," Calfe assured her. He reclined. "Well," he said, "looks like we're all new parents." Razgaif blinked at him. That. *That* was different. The tiredness that Calfe's eyes held was from a sleepless night alongside a birthing wife. An uncertainty seemed to grip him. Was anyone truly certain about becoming a parent? How could they? This was a child, and their future was in your hands. "His name's Kerein. He's already a handful."

"Like his dad," Razgaif and Tytli said at the same time.

"Gods, I hope not. Don't wish that on that child. His mother is stubborn as a horse."

Razgaif gave a laugh—a dad's laugh. "So that's going to be the most hardheaded child in existence."

Together they ate the rest of their dinner in quiet contemplation. Razgaif found himself watching Astra as the preparation for the coronation dinner began. She helped pack the food onto the carts, tucking them within little dwarvish devices similar to the larger one that Razgaif had to keep his food cool. These, however, could warm the food as well. Once they were done packing, Astra wandered over, a bit of sweat gleaming on her forehead.

"Are you ready to go?" she asked, rocking back and forth on her heels.

"*You* want to go to the castle so you can eat desserts." Razgaif wiped her brow clean. She gave a sheepish smile.

"I want to see everyone in pretty clothes, too," she explained. "But yeah . . . you're right."

Razgaif gave one more look around the Afterlife. The dinner crowd was a bit thinner than usual thanks to the upcoming coronation of Duchess Cleo, his more reserved patrons holing up in the corners of the establishment. Flynn and the rest could handle it until he got back to close. He found his *haogu*, pulling his arms through the silk jacket's sleeves. He quickly checked himself, freshening up the best he could. As a caterer, the etiquette wasn't nearly as high for him as if he were a guest, staying along the edges of the fanciful life without committing. He liked it that way and Cleo knew that.

They returned to the Afterlife Crisis at the crest of night after the coronation. A beautiful type of quiet fell over the building, and the last patrons left for their homes. Razgaif held Astra, her sleeping head on his shoulder. *So much drool for a young girl.* He didn't mind it, considering his drool leaked out of the corners of his mouth when he slept, too. He slouched through the door, the now familiar creak of the hinges and the ding of the bell greeting them. They were home. He held her tighter with one arm, dragging the rest of the equipment behind him. The Afterlife Crisis was empty, or close to it. Flynn and the rest of his people were closing up shop. They waved good night. Razgaif gave a farewell.

He abandoned the wagon of stuff for his future self to find, now coddling the sleeping Astra. He carried her up to their little loft above the restaurant. The corridor was a warm relief from the cooling night, his lumbering footsteps and her quiet snoring the two things breaking the beautiful night's silence. His battle with sleepiness was reaching its conclusion, and he was losing quite handily. *Gotta see her to bed. Gotta see her to bed.* That gave him enough strength to make it to her door. He opened it using his foot, grateful she hadn't closed it tight on her way out.

Razgaif slowed, careful not to wake her. He placed her on her bed. She stirred a bit. "Pa," she called out. He smiled at that.

"Yes, little one," he responded.

"I love you." Then she turned over and fell back to sleep.

Razgaif reveled in the happiness pouring into his chest. She filled that part of himself he hadn't known was empty. He brought over her stuffed bear—Mr. Skelly—and her star-woven blanket, layering them both over her sleeping form. "I love you, too, Astra Melu Onyxus." She carried the blood of his greatest enemy, yet she gave his life roots it had never known. He left her to her dreams, closing the door behind him gently so it wouldn't squeal.

The silence of sleep soon reached his bed, and this time he welcomed it.

EPILOGUE

A little under a year had passed, and they wouldn't change a moment.

Razgaif the Younger awoke, tired but pleased from another late night. The buzz of the morning crowd rustled underneath his floorboards, the sounds of his crew already on breakfast duty. After centuries of being a shambling corpse, filled with rancor and rotting, his treasures were now hot baths, fine soaps, and oils. Once he completed his relaxing morning routine, he searched the room and grabbed his apron and uniform from over the hearth. One step at time, he enjoyed the simple pleasure of wearing comfy clothes, forgetting he once knew only plate armor.

The Great Traveler and the Cupbearer lay at the head and foot of his bed. He smiled at them, pulling his long hair back into a ponytail and wrapping his belly-length beard into a thick knot. "Another day," he told himself, taking a deep breath and opening one of the windows. The morning air filled his old lungs, his large chest expanding outward like a rooster about to crow. Necropolis never looked better.

It was time to head back to work.

He left the comfort of his room, noticing that Astra yet again beat him awake. Having now seen eleven seasons, his daughter was just as proud as the day he adopted her. More than likely, she was already among the rest of his friends and employees.

Razgaif wandered downstairs, his footsteps sounding his arrival. By now, they knew when the *siefu* had arrived. The early-morning patrons lit up as he stepped into the restaurant.

"Welcome," he said to all, his voice a joyous thunder. They barked their morning greetings, cups of coffee held high. Bao Su, Clyth, and the little animal troopers were already serving the breakfast crowd, with the constant clank of plates and cups shuffling. Flynn was in the kitchen, stoking flames and working the grill. Waldruk worked the counter, cleaning up yesterday's specials and writing that day's in a scribble of chalk. And lastly, Rib-Digger sat alongside Astra, moving an abacus with his large fingers. *Math. Someone* had to do it. Luckily, Rib-Digger rivaled even Waldruk on the subject.

"How's it going, little one?" Razgaif asked. She planted her forehead on the table. "That bad, huh?"

"Test. Today. Frustrated," Rib-Digger said.

Astra covered her mouth and screamed a muffled shout. She groaned, grabbing tight to her parchment. *Ah, her greatest enemy.*

"I can do this," she muttered, sounding much like him.

"'Frustrated' is putting it mildly," Bao Su added from the other side of the room.

"She's getting the hang of it." Waldruk counted the coffers, balancing last night's work and jotting it down in the ledgers. "You need to be well rounded in all endeavors."

Clyth smirked. "You're sounding more like your Lord-father by the minute, love. Is that why you picked up sword lessons?"

Waldruk muttered under his breath. "I cannot allow a youth to have better skill over a sword than me. I'm still a noble of the city. It's expected of me."

"You're getting the hang of it." Astra had raised her head at the word "sword." "Why can't I just train today?"

"Test." Rib-Digger crossed his arms. "Test. Important."

"I know. I know."

Razgaif watched her tackle her studies, earnest in all subjects. She had talent using the blade, favoring the classic longsword and shortsword. Magic as well. She aimed for complete control over it, not willing to put anyone she loved in danger. She excelled in history, language (especially *orken*), and literature. Arithmetic was her stumbling block, a beast she hadn't conquered. At least not yet. "Have you had breakfast?"

"Yes."

"No." Rib-Digger gave her a stern glaze. "Pastry. Not. Count."

"All right, I think I do need a bit of rest. I've been at it all morning."

Rib-Digger pulled her chair out. "Good. Job."

"Thank you, Ribby."

Razgaif helped his daughter out of her chair. She wore more casual clothing, her longsword and dagger resting on her hip. He hoped to give her a properly named weapon, but for her age, those were enough. She leaned against his side. "You're doing fine. It'll come to you. Let's make you something to eat. No child of mine is going to leave here with an empty stomach. C'mon, let me fix you something."

They shuffled their way to the kitchen. Flynn worked his magic behind the stove, flames licking over the cooktops. He looked over his shoulder, foot tapping against the footstool and pipe resting on his lips. "Ah, boss, you're ready to lose again. I believe last night I gave you quite the wallop. Four to two dishes in my favor. The Duke Council was quite pleased with my dishes."

"You misremember." Razgaif waved him off. They competed any chance they got, improving their craft in any way possible.

But when it came to Astra, there was no competition. "Now we're making Astra breakfast."

"You can't be biased," Flynn told Astra. "If he loses, he loses."

Razgaif grunted. He rolled his shoulders, cracked his neck, and tightened his apron strings. Flynn whistled. "Oh. I'm serious," said Razgaif. "Not gonna embarrass myself in front of my kid. Bring it."

The *siefu* took to his battleground. The flames stoked and the tools prepped. The two cooks began their battle. They set aside their favored ingredients, staring each other down as they wandered around the kitchen. Flynn ran his mouth, trying to get Razgaif off his game. He got him the first few times, but now Razgaif had learned to ignore the man's banter. Instead, he let his hands do the talking. Razgaif the Younger performed his magic. Not his rune, *Svadagd*, but a simpler type of magic. Astra watched him in wonder as he diced, minced, chopped, and whisked.

"You're going to have to do better than that, old man," Flynn said at his own station. "You're looking kind of slow."

Razgaif's weariness from the late night burned away, his passion eliminating it. Simple excitement came through. Why had he ever doubted this? Times were difficult, and some days the hard work outweighed the love. The Seclusion, the struggle, the resting of Rottgor, he would do it all again if it meant seeing his daughter's face in wonder.

They completed their meals around the same time. Flynn served his signature omelet, topped with cheese, bell peppers, tomatoes, and a hearty steak alongside a stack of hashed-brown potatoes and one of his orange-cranberry muffins. He smirked, puffing a ring of smoke in his confidence. Razgaif stared back at him unblinking.

The orc wasn't below a challenge. Flynn's was a good meal—he knew that from the smell alone. Flynn was talented and knew his customers' palates well. On Razgaif's plate were small egg muffins topped with dwarvish bacon and white elvish cheese, a stack of fluffy orcish banana pancakes, and slices of grilled salmon, seasoned lightly with herbs. Astra bounced up and down, pleased at both of the plates. The two chefs and the entire restaurant watched in anticipation.

She'd almost finished the entire spread by the time she made her decision. Astra let them struggle for a while, pondering back and forth. She nodded and took a deep breath. "Pa wins this time. The pancakes won me over."

Razgaif pumped his arm and shouted. Flynn rolled his eyes. "All right, the pancakes couldn't be that good."

"Try them."

"What?" Flynn crossed his arms.

"Try them," Razgaif said again. "Say they aren't great."

"Fine." Flynn stepped over, holding his hand up. Astra offered him the plate. He stabbed at the pancake as though it had stolen his favorite boots. He plopped it in his mouth, chewing slowly, then he took another bite, the light in his eyes undercutting the scowl on his face. He raised up a single finger and took one last bite. "It's—" he began, shaking his head. He bit his lower lip. Then came the cursing. "It's fine, I guess. It could use more . . ." He scratched his head. "You know what, you're lucky. You're lucky. That's what it is." Razgaif let out a loud roar of laughter. "Don't laugh at me! You—" There was another string of *dwarvish* curses afterward. He stomped away, pulling off his apron and tossing it over his shoulder.

"What did he say?" Astra asked.

Razgaif laughed. "Maybe study your *dwarvish* next." He

glanced up at the clock Calfe had given them. "You better get going. I will *not* have another visit from Thess."

That put her gears into motion. One second, she was at the table. The next, she was gone. Up the stairs and then down with her schooling supplies, his little champion returned. Astra hugged him and then jumped up to kiss him on the cheek. "Gotta go. Gotta go. Gotta go."

"Tell Lili I say hi," he said as she fled toward the door.

"I will. Have a nice day at the restaurant."

The restaurant, staff and patrons alike, waved goodbye as she left to conquer another day. Her willingness, her hardworking nature, her energy—they were infectious. Razgaif knew their time together would pass. She would grow up and become a strong woman. Until that day, he and the rest of the Afterlife Crisis would stand by her side.

Razgaif the Younger, Champion of the Onyx-Ax and proprietor of that fine establishment, prepared for another day.

"Everyone, let's get to work."

ACKNOWLEDGMENTS

To Meg, Cozy Quill, and my amazing community and beta readers—we've made it! It's here. All the hard work and anticipation have led up to this moment. We've weathered the ups and downs together, and we are out to change this world with our book and bring a little light to the darkness. Fight for your dream!

THANK YOU

This book would not have been possible without the support from the Cozy Quill community, with a special thank-you to the Second Breakfast Club members:

Aden Cook	Holly Blakemore
AH	Jem Lainée
Alura Renee Adams	Jennifer Bobo
Alysia Michelle Cruz	Jess Draut
Andi Swagler	Jess Moran
Angie Elder	Jess Pagac
Ann Hawkins	Jessica Pfeiffer
Beth Lynne Gage	Jessica R.G.
Bloosier	Jessica Whitaker
Brandi Dove Black	Jordan Peterson
Brittany Ward	Julia Solaire
Brooke Bauch	Kalena Medina
Carissa C.	Katie Krishnamoorthi
Carolyn Hanson	Kia Borner
Celeste Wasche	Lacey Ridder
Channing Stapley	Laura Gracy
Christine Neal	Laura Miller
Dawn May-Christ	Laura Stanley
Hannah Pluta	Lynn Mullin

Margaret Garland
Mary Morris
Megan K
Melinda Orellano
Mirandia Berthold
Natalia Hernandez
Natasha Pierre-Louis
Ollie Trager
Rachel Emily
Rachel Marie
Rhonda Wallace
Samantha Rush
Sara Cochran
Sara Roswell
Sarah Wade
Savannah Spratt
Steph Pilavin
Stephanie Lines
Stormy Avalos
Tara Tasse
Terri Noftsger
Toni Kintzer
Vasny Camacho Sánchez-Aldana
StacieH
Resamay
MandiG87
Micah
BarakahBooks
booksdogsandcoffee
RainyDaysLibrary
TangledSeaweed
madisonkia
CarrieBear

kmasse331
katieisalion
mickeybooklore
Vixen
Sweetteeth
Shawn
MrsMcKellar
Pageheart
Buffy
Shalet
melkoperwiek
MCreger
Casey
arrowofthequeen
Coleen
Michdenisereads
Theshireshelf
ambmarsh
trapkhaleesi
Anxiouslyandi
GastronomicQuill
Lish
Ben
aimeeroo
Cyndol98
foolofatook13
AthenaKT
EliotWallflower
MollyHannah
JessiRose7

ABOUT THE AUTHOR

DESTON J. MUNDEN is the author of several books, including *Tavern*, also set in Dargath. Born and raised near the Outer Banks, he can be found writing, cooking, playing *World of Warcraft*, and cosplaying in the way-too-hot North Carolina weather.

Cozy Quill is an imprint of Bindery, a book publisher powered by community.

We're inspired by the way book tastemakers have reinvigorated the publishing industry. With strong taste and direct connections with readers, book tastemakers have illuminated self-published, backlisted, and overlooked authors, rocketing many to bestseller lists and the big screen.

This book was chosen by Meg Hood in close collaboration with the Cozy Quill community on Bindery. By inviting tastemakers and their reading communities to participate in publishing, Bindery creates opportunities for deserving authors to reach readers who will love them.

Visit Cozy Quill for a thriving bookish community and bonus content:

cozyquill.binderybooks.com

MEG HOOD is a bookish creator and founder of Meg's Tea Room, an online community of cozy fantasy lovers. Her cozy community loves a magical tale full of found family, inclusive characters, and whimsical worlds. She is known for being one of the first champions of the cozy fantasy genre through her early promotion of *Legends & Lattes* by Travis Baldree.

TIKTOK.COM/@MEGSTEAROOM

INSTAGRAM.COM/MEGS.TEA.ROOM